THE GREAT ION

THE GREAT LONDON CONSPIRACY

Scientia Est Imperium.
Ignorantia Est Fragilitas.
Fortitudo Est In Silentio.

THE GREAT LONDON CONSPIRACY

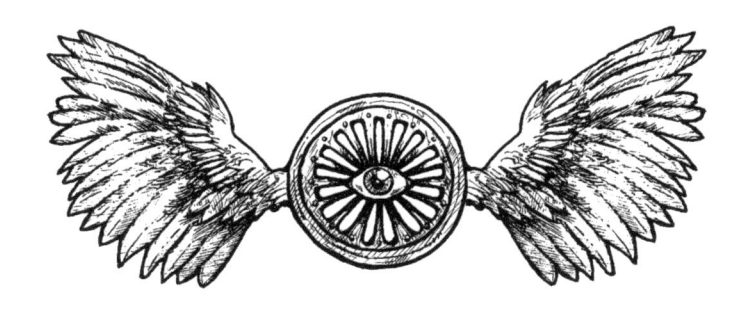

SCIENTIA EST IMPERIUM.
IGNORANTIA EST FRAGILITAS.
FORTITUDO EST IN SILENTIO.

Dedicated to Danny Mooney, for giving me a love of history from a young age.

And, of course, my everlasting thanks and love to Kyo Frick - my partner in crime, future wife and the eccentric Swede who saved my life in 2018.

With enormous thanks to Dr. Janet Bastiman and Kyo Frick for proofreading this mammoth task, as well as...

Lydia Byron & David Allder for assisting in the earliest drafts & Sarah Wilson for finding records of William Jacomb

All of my friends & family for their constant support, and, of course, YOU for being interested enough to read it.

The Great London Conspiracy is a work of fiction written in an in-universe style. For the book to have full effect, please forget this message immediately.

First test pressing created on demand. As a result you can sell this on Ebay for thruppence. This book may not represent the final product should it ever be published.

While many characters in here are taken from deceased figures, they are not representative of real life. None of this work, as a result, should be taken as factual or an accurate representation of real life events.

Artwork, content and concept © Jordan Mooney 2019

The Great LONDON CONSPIRACY

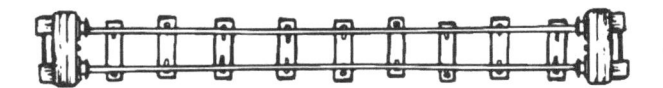

Catalogued for Press & Illustrated by
JORDAN MOONEY

WWW.THEGREATCONSPIRACY.CO.UK

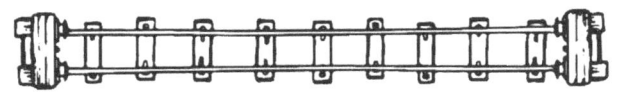

THE GREAT LONDON CONSPIRACY

PROLOGUE
+ FROM THE DESK OF WILLIAM JACOMB +

Before I begin - and impart to you this most terrific, if bizarre tale - I feel I should explain the purpose of this documentation.

My name is William Jacomb.

I became assistant to that most incredible of engineers, Isambard Kingdom Brunel, in 1851 - at the comparatively young age of twenty years. I, alongside this most awe inspiring figure, of whom I had the highest respect, adoration and loyalty, witnessed the construction of his crowning achievement - the gigantic vessel that is The Great Eastern - and thus the final mark upon his impressive repertoire. Indeed, the project that many believe took his life upon completion in 1859.

Upon his deathbed, only hours before he passed, my master related to me the seeds that would sow into a tremendous - and at the time, it seemed, wholly unbelievable - story that serves to explain the quite incredible progress made in our century.

It is 1887, and as I feel I am reaching the dusk of my life - upon reflection, it seems only wise to repeat this tale onto yourselves, no matter which era, generation, or indeed iteration of humanity to which I may be outreaching.

This is the story of the Empire's fantastical striding into this modern era of progress. It is, as far as I can possibly ascertain, a tale of truth, and one corroborated by many of our Kingdom's greatest minds. Gaps have been filled by many learned gentlemen whom also have had access to this doubtless controversial information. Some are inventors, some are scientists, and some are gentlemen - should such a thing exist, which I believe to be wholly untrue - of Parliament.

Before I truly delve into the following, it feels only correct to provide historical basis for my own achievements. Many of you are likely to dismiss me as a foolish theorist, trying to plant a conspiratorial view upon my Government and fellows for my own gain. This could not be further from the truth.

I can prove my qualifications; and will do so in this volume. It is throughout my colourful career following the death of Brunel that I have made my incredible discoveries behind our great empire. I write to you now at my desk as the Chief Resident Engineer of London's South Western Railway, which I have held since 1871. There is a relatively cool air this evening in Waterloo station and, for whatever reason; I now feel it is time to present the truth. It is under considerable opposition that I continue writing - many warnings, threats and even confrontations have taken place in the preceding weeks.

Many men more powerful than myself, and, I dare say, those reading this volume, would rather this piece not be published. I have been asked constantly if I fear for my life in such circumstances; I have been begged by my family - whom are as of yet uninformed as to the true nature of my manuscripts - to relent the creation of this record. In answer to these questions, I say only this.

I do not doubt these gentlemen and their ability to remove me from this plane; but if I am to meet my maker I would far prefer to do so in clear conscience.

I thank you for taking the time to educate yourself, and I hope that, should you find yourself too sceptical to take this literature seriously, you shall find the content titillating.

I shall begin with the words - and circumstances - of the man whom first relayed this story to me. I cast your minds back to 1859, and my master, Isambard Brunel - beginning from the final days leading to the Great Eastern's launch. I am afraid it is not an enormously pleasant tale; nor one that will bring us to an exciting conclusion quickly. Rather, it will plant the first seeds in your understanding, as it did mine.

>Yours truly, and with great sincerity,
>William Jacomb,
>C.R.E of the South Western Railway
>Waterloo Station
>1887

+ THE FINAL DAYS OF BRUNEL +

Isambard Brunel - my master, and the man from whom this great truth would be revealed - was a worn, tired gentleman by the time his ship was due to be fitted to the utmost luxury.

At measurements greater than that of the Ark that saved God's creatures from the terrible floods, it was the final - and most impressive - mark upon the world left by my master. I dub him a gentleman, but I doubt many would agree.

If any men in this tome could be dubbed as truly ingenious - and I stand that most of them should be - my master was perhaps the greatest of them all.

His monolithic structures towered across our mighty empire. His ships were modern, almost futuristic in quality - and his work in bridges and structure remain bowed to, even now, almost thirty years since his passing. He was, however, not popular among his peers.

Known for his rude, confrontational, short tempered and incredibly perfectionist nature. Brunel was often dubbed the Napoleon of our trade; seeking glory rather than financial return, and bankrupting many rich men in his time for the want of his own success, discovery, and spectacle. It is perhaps this natural rebellious streak in the short, powerful man that spurred him to expose the shadowy group he worked both for and alongside. This great moment of rebellion was with some of the last breath he took - and I feel his decision to do so was made with the belief his life was nearing its end.

I stood with him across the bank from the enormous vessel, which sat as still in the water as an iron block would upon the sodden ground beneath us. It looked flawless in shape, despite being unfitted, and looked so powerful in the dark currents it seemed like a natural component of that great, murky, amphibious atmosphere - like a particularly enormous mill in the London skyline.

I looked down at my master, as he took a step closer to the bobbing flow of murky, black liquid - that I hesitate to truly call water - only inches ahead of us, and the vast silhouette against that heavy, smoke-laden air that, to this day, characterises the Isle of Dogs and its shipyards.

The wake of the ship's impact upon the river seemed to still be dissipating towards us. I noticed small splashes of that filthy liquid upon my master's shoes - which were already streaked with mud from the river's equally unkempt banks, almost to the knees of his trouser legs. It was no great distance to travel, at Brunel's mere five feet of height and, even if his clothes had been immaculate for the occasion, he did not look at his most distinguished.

His hairline had receded, and his eyes - already starved of sleep, as ever they had been, for my master demanded only four hours of sleep an evening - had lost that witting, sharp rapier that he had always maintained in the years leading up to this grand moment.

I had spotted tears in his eyes. There was a slightly stronger spring than usual in his now hobbling, unsteady walk. A sharp breath of pride was swelling in his already laboured chest. The man whom I assisted needed more assistance than ever these past few months; and I'm sorry to say that even in this grand moment he looked a shadow of his former self.

I have no doubt, of course, that should he have heard me say such things he would have responded in a line of language I dare not print. Brunel was immensely proud and, as many proud people tend to be, had a particularly fragile attitude towards his height, age, and, perhaps most importantly, his public image. He truly was a short man, which placed him somewhat at odds with his engineering peers and, although in his marriage this was unimportant, it often brought smirks to the faces of ladies when they happened to have seen him walking down the street. It was for this reason that Brunel's top hat, even for what was fashionable, measured up as being unusually tall and slender in shape. It gave the illusion of a man with a far greater stature, and, in his mind, meant a more considerable demand for respect. He never cared for what the investors thought of him; but the general public was his finest source of praise - and he depended, I fear, on the working class man for his ego. It's perhaps this reason the ship had become such a point of obsession and thus such a matter of pride in this sight of it roosting in a natural habitat.

The colossal vessel - 'the Great Babe', as my master had dubbed it in his earlier, happier progress of the enormous undertaking - was finally sitting regally in its nest, just off of the Isle of Dogs, and only a few hundred metres beyond its remarkable slipway. This may seem, to those living in more modern times, as a standard moment in a vessel's life; perhaps you do not understand the true scale of the Eastern. It may be that at your time of reading it is long gone; in which case I need only tell you that at 18,000 tons and nearly 700 feet in length, it was of truly monstrous proportions - so much so, in fact, that it had to be launched sideways to guarantee a fit into the Thames.

This was not the only epic aspect of the Great Eastern - indeed, there was a herculean task for Brunel in creating this substantially sized lady of the sea, which, I am immensely proud to say, I oversaw the construction of personally.

There had been many claims that the ship had laid on itself some sort of absurd curse or hex. Some even voiced it had been infested by the ghosts of workers whom had died over her construction (*and, I am afraid, there were a great many due to the often careless practise of other parties.*) Some even claimed it was God's will against a ship larger than his biblical commands.

In any sense, the trouble for her had begun early on and seemingly continued relentlessly. Brunel had accepted the offer of tender of one Scott Russell; he was, at the time, one of the finest shipbuilders in the country, and one with whom Brunel had worked in the past for his smaller, less well remembered steamships.

Who could blame Brunel for trusting his word?

The working relationship was amiable enough for the first year. Or, at least, just under.

Russell was a traditionalist and had more than enough ego to butt heads with the men he collaborated with. It began early, too, with him insisting the ship was built in a dock - and trying to demand money for a new one's construction. After all, he claimed, no ordinary yard could accommodate 691 feet of ship. Brunel, being the man he was, instead took lease of the dock neighbouring Russell's yard and built a railway line to transfer materials - which came up to a far smaller sum. Russell's ire was instantly risen - he could not profit from such an arrangement.

Next, Russell had tried to interfere with the launch. He had never worked with such a huge scale, and insisted it be 'slipped' in the traditional way, slid along vertically into the great depths - despite the lack of turning circle she would have in such a narrow spot of the Thames, and the requirement that the entire vessel's gigantic frame would have to be raised in the air, purely to ensure the correct angle of approach. Brunel had, out of simple common sense, ignored the experienced shipsmith's advice, and insisted on pioneering the new and unusual.

Russell next blocked the concept of a mechanical launch on the matter of expense. Hindsight is a wonderful thing, as you shall find for yourselves shortly.

Unbeknownst to Brunel and myself, there had been an immense fire in Russell's yard before work had even started and he had only been partially covered by insurance. The debts to his yard were enormous. He had begun selling iron behind our backs at the very impetus of the project, and had continued to do so in efforts to cloud his own immense financial deficits. In 1856, Brunel - in his usual shrewd, inquisitive manner - had taken suspicion, and advised the company to take possession of the ship.

Almost immediately, Scott Russell's yard went into liquidation, his yard was seized and the truth of his colossal debts - a sum of £23,000 over his actual assets - came to light. Over three quarters of the work upon her immense hull was incomplete, and there was a not insubstantial discrepancy of 1,200 tons between Brunel and Russell's sums - the loss, of course, coming clear in Brunel's calculations.

The Great Babe became property of Russell's bank - who agreed to lease the ground, on which she was still standing dry - at a cost of £1,000 per month. They demanded Brunel "Get out and clear up" by the middle of August, and only permitted him to go beyond this date provided they were paid promptly. They took more of his hair, I feel, than any barber - thanks to the immense stress they laid on him.

The ship's size was such that the first, second and third launch - all only weeks apart in 1858 - had failed. This had predictable results, with the farcical mockery of my employer, the ship, the creditors and, more tragically, the death of a shipyard worker as the enormous chains broke under the ship's immense weight, spinning the winches out of control and striking him.

The following two launches had been assisted by hydraulics, which were largely destroyed, in an explosive - but unfortunate - spectacle. Indeed, this was a year of many technological failures across the country – many will note the transatlantic cable had suffered a disastrous loss at very similar time, and was now being discussed as a mere hoax.

The sentiments were not dissimilar.

Our - or rather, Isambard's own - costs were spiralling out of control, and the ship had now become but an enormous joke: a gigantic punch line to the cruel words of the newspapers and the general public. To make matters worse, the company had called her **Leviathan** - a name Brunel found incredibly distasteful.

My master improvised this matter, and had turned to extreme circumstance.

This had consisted of contracting the latest hydraulics in the Kingdom, some from as far North as Dundee. Several of them, forcing the incredible object into the water at a cost of thousands of pounds per inch, against an ingenious - albeit costly - series of rocking cradles, checking gears and chains.

He had taken to sleeping in his office, that neighboured the slipway. This being despite the continuous hammering of those enormous apparatus that tried desperately to shift the ridiculous tonnage of 'The Babe'. The complete process had taken nine months; and nearly a third of the vessel's complete budget.

Now, it lay there, standing in the water - but the celebrations and the look of delight on Brunel's weary face was not to last. Only the next day, creditors arrived to take inventory of his every possession, should he be required to sell anything to cover the ship's enormous overspending. The press - both professional and public in trade - crucified Isambard as creating an enormous folly of continuous mishap, over-confidence and ego.

I stayed with him, and throughout these days, before he left for an essential holiday, he seemed to speak in strange, trawling sentences - a level of, what seemed, from the outside, vacuity, that felt quite unlike his usual character. I recall one lunch time, in which we were sat for a meal of goose and beer, he looked up at me with those tired eyes and made one of his most damning - or so I interpreted - remarks towards me.

'You don't understand half of the work I do, Jacomb.'

I took this for his usual conceited ways - but I must confess it was rare he took my own skills into question. Brunel was not a man to affirm or tear down another's talents unless they had either impeccably impressed him or particularly incensed him, respectively. Despite being his assistant, in truth, I was rarely present - nor did I often take part - in his professional moments. He preferred to draw and write alone; a solitary man who's main source of exercise was pacing his office frantically, puffing thick, grey clouds of cigar smoke into every facet of space in the room. He would call me when finished, and one would have to traverse a great smog to even witness his latest masterpiece of draughtsmanship, lit dimly by the pale yellow glow of his desk lamp. I suppose in many ways I didn't understand Brunel; but his work? Always.

I sat there, quite still - interrupting my silence only to chew the remainder of the poultry in my mouth. My eyes darted, wondering if something had taken place to silence him prematurely. I expected him to finish his statement with a witty jab at my youth, or perhaps a confession of his personal problems. It never came.

We continued our meal in silence, and, when we were finished, I finally felt I needed elaboration.

>'What do you mean?' I finally asked, my voice perhaps betraying the tension I had felt at his comments.

I had not taken into account the fifteen minutes that had passed, obviously lost as I tried to consider his words, and the increasingly evident dulling of my master's mind. The optimist in me insisted this was due to the fourth load of beer only recently drained from his favourite tankard; but I knew better.

Brunel, by this time, had long forgotten his remark, and grunted in response - a questioning sort of grunt. He was too tired to articulate after the short walk to our carriage. His smoking - over forty cigars a day on a particularly productive week - was catching up with him, much as his age seemed to be. I felt the need to add further detail myself, before I should be granted access to his.

>'When you claimed that I don't understand. About your work?'
>'Yes, Jacomb. You don't understand.'

His walking pace quickened, and his eyes darted around the immediate vicinity as he climbed into the carriage. We sat, once again, in silence. I tried to enquire, but he responded with only a shake of his head. I felt like he already regretted his remarks; it was quite unlike the man to ever apologise, so I simply took this as his admission of guilt. The carriage trundled merrily along, bouncing and hammering against the uneven country roads that connected our favourite pub to the bustling - and relatively well paved - city of London.

I found out, not long after, that he was indeed regretting this remark - but it was not in guilt towards my feelings. Rather, it was towards the very safety of my person. He had almost, that very afternoon (*a rare January afternoon of bright sun and warm air*) revealed a most terrible hidden world that, I admit, was far beyond my comprehension at that time.

However, that experience had never left me - even when my master returned from Egypt in a darker tone; not simply due to the capture of the sun upon his person, but in an even greater sense of burly contention towards his hardships.

His intemperance seemed to have only peaked in his absence from work. His wife, by contrast, seemed to have a delightful time. While Brunel had greatly enjoyed his inspection of Egyptian architecture, this will probably infer to you the level of obsession he carried for his professional life of iron, mortar and timber. He felt highly uncomfortable away from his duties.

My master returned only a few days before the fitting was completed, and the maiden voyage growing ever-closer. It would be sailing before the smell of fresh paint had even left those elaborate wooden panels within - but her designer would not be present.

I and my master explored the decks, and deeper within the ship's vast innards. We witnessed the first steaming of the engines, and those enormous crank shafts, like heavy, stiff limbs, creak into motion. She was alive!

Alive, breathing contentedly; and the power - oh, the great power. Reverberating with every beat, the sheer forces the Great Eastern felt like the most heavenly music I have ever experienced. I have never felt such satisfaction since. For Brunel it was simply a moment of relief. That simply indescribable, hefty sound was irreplaceable for either of us - to this day I believe it rings in my ears, and produces goosebumps upon my skin. It was like the first words of a beloved, long-mute child.

We sorted out my master's private cabin - ensuring it was not at the strain of too many stairs - and he expressed his great satisfaction at the fitting of the great babe's interior - despite many of the grander aspects being dispensed of to restrict on our already immense costs. However, even this enthusiasm did not come with his usual lustre. I almost wondered if some terrible event had taken place over his holiday; but, recently, I felt it a dangerous practise to question my master's manner of speaking. It seemed to be an undying development with his advancing age.

It was on the day of the maiden voyage - to the backing of a great brass band - the ship's enormous horn blew its victorious refrain - to the delight of London's populous. Indeed, thousands of people, some to travel, and some simply to witness the incredible spectacle of the ship in full steam, were packed along the river's great length.

The press - despite their earlier, immense criticisms against my master - now fawned upon him once again. He was celebrated - rightfully - as the empire's greatest engineer, and the photographing apparatus surrounded him at every corner. Almost at once, the men with their cameras requested photos of him on the deck of his marvellous boat.

The banging of the camera flashes was the only thing to drown out the roaring from under the ship's decks, where the power of an estimated eight thousand horses was building.

I turned away for but a brief moment, to take in the view of Weymouth below our mighty iron heel, when there was another dull thud. Following were shouts; a great commotion. I turned back to find my master no longer on his feet. He was, instead, on the floor, his stick beside him, his tails spread upon the wooden boards. He was conscious - but unable to stand. His skin was pale, his hat slumped against him in his hand.

My master, on the 5th of September, 1859, nestled upon the breast of the very lady he had brought to our world, had succumbed to a stroke.

Talk began to erupt that he wouldn't last the evening, and the Great Eastern's voyage was delayed by a further day - either out of respect or to clear the press out of the vicinity.

I was quite sure this was my share of calamity, and that this moment would be the end of it. I had no clue what would await me, following on from this terrible event.

Brunel had planned for his misfortune - well in advance.

+ A LETTER ON THE TABLE +

I was quite unsure of my master's condition, or indeed that of the ship's departure, when I finally arrived at his home on Duke Street, Westminster.

The odd person to have caught wind of the story had already collected near his door, and the press were waiting for news. I entered the home sharpishly as they requested comment, and was met almost immediately by his distraught wife.

It always seems curious to consider Brunel as a married man; he almost certainly was - in the rare moments he was home - by all accounts, a marvellous husband, and a loving father.

Mind, even this seemed curious to me; it was quite rare to see any kind of warmth from my employer in any capacity, be it towards children on the work sites, or the elderly on the same.

His love of women was no secret by contrast: it had, until his marriage, always been a powerful vice (*and even now, his flirtation with barmaids and the like often knew no bounds*).

His wife, Mary, was to all - not only my own - views, a very beautiful, intelligent, and confident woman. She was gifted in music and the arts, had a strong social life, and a most endearing smile that could bend even the great engineer's iron will. It had often been commented that they were a business marriage - one of status rather than affection. I saw evidence to the contrary upon this day.

Mary Brunel now stood face to face with me, sobbing with worry at the merest mention of her husband's condition. For the first time, she seemed considerably frantic.

The doctor, a particularly weasely looking man, came down the stairs. He looked upon me quizzically, almost accusingly, his beady eyes peering over the wire frames of his little round pince-nez glasses.

His thin moustache twitched in what seemed like contempt as I strode towards the staircase, and my master's chambers. He reminded me irresistibly of - dare I use such language? - A particularly agitated rat; a rotten, sneering weasel of a character - dressed in brown tweed, with a rather weathered bag in his hands.

'You can't go in there.'

I span upon my heel to meet the doctor, who was now glaring through those little round lens with a renewed anger. He repeated his words in a tone dripping with contention.

I felt I was quite polite in my explanation, identifying myself and the business that I had to attend with the gentleman upstairs, but it seemed to bring no avail to this sudden, unexpected obstacle.

The lean, bitter gentlemen only repeated the same sentence, this time, slower. Practically every word was spat; quite why this confrontation was taking place seemed to be irrelevant.

The doctor's constant reiterations only tried my patience, which had already been worn ragged by the lecherous men from the newspapers. I simply needed, urgently, to ensure that Brunel was well and, had a lady not been stood so close by, I would have delighted in shoving this odious figure out of my way.

It was Mary whom ended it, offering the man a cup of tea and a slice of Shrewsbury cake. She led him away, insisting he leave me and my master be. I was left puzzled; even for an expensive doctor - whom so often, in my experience, tended to brim over with arrogance - he struck me as a particularly vexatious fellow. I decided it best to pay him no heed, and continued on my way.

The luxuries of the household's bedchamber did little to add warmth to the scene as I stepped into the room.

Brunel lay there, ashen faced. He carried a curious complexion. The remains of the sun upon his face from Egypt was now only evident in two drawn, red cheeks on an otherwise cold, grey skin. He appeared, with no exaggeration, a deathly ill. For his comparatively young age he looked horrendous and, I must confess, my heart sank upon the very sight of him: hatless, fragile and without that infectious confidence he once took with his every step.

His eyes opened, struggling to focus to the figure in his doorway. It took a while, but he soon picked up on whom it was. He slowly croaked my name; the result of the many medicines inside his person was a hoarse throat at best and violent sickness at worst. I felt as if he was motioning me to come forward, which I did, planting myself in the seat alongside his bedside table. The silence, excepting the deep ticking of his clock upon every second, was deafening. I had not in all my years found the company of Brunel so difficult to endure.

His wife soon joined us, trying to hold back further tears, and the man's younger children - Marc and Florence - attended at points wherein it was not inconvenient. They were well behaved, but still, by nature, had that natural spice of life, that inquisitive nature of Brunel's. As a result, even with the circumstances, I found myself surprised by their silence. They did not ask a thing, nor even speak a word.

It was as if their father was already dead.

Part of me wondered if he would ever recover from this ordeal even if, by some miracle, he survived it. It seemed to be more of a personal trauma than a stroke that was striking him. The ship was his pride and joy, the final hurrah; his winning achievement - and yet, it was sailing to its home port without him.

Days went past slowly, the mood at the Brunel home never lifting - and yet, down the end of the Thames, the ship had been forced to stop several times over due to crowding of small vessels charging a fee to view the great wonder of the industrial world. Brunel's ship, on a public standpoint, was an enormous success - and I was greatly looking forward to telling him of the public's rather incendiary reception the next day.

Sadly, this was, if anything, a day too late. On the 12th of September, off the coast of Hastings, the celebration of the vessel's completion was cut short. I am unable to voice from personal experience - but, armed with newspapers - which I have kept since - I feel comfortable describing the events as they, from what I can assemble, took place. I am greatly indebted to the ship's captain, William Harrison, who sadly - and, I'm afraid to say, mysteriously - died in 1860 - as he provided much of the details.

The Great Babe's first steps - and the ongoing voyage - had proven her an excellent runner. She operated like a gigantic knife through butter - smooth, powerful and remarkably comfortable. The colossal engines had hammered their worth beautifully, and newspapers were all reporting with great enthusiasm of the ship's incredible capabilities. Lines of people awaited the ship's passage through their parts of London. By all accounts, she was an experience to witness - and quite like no other vessel in the empire.

Russell was on deck for inspections and writing reports, happily taking much of the glory regarding the ship as if he was the genius behind every steel plate.

The vessel's motion had calmed after a period of swaying waters - and those sheltering briefly in the Grand Saloon were now back on their way enjoying the light ocean spray from the incredible paddle wheels' motion as they roamed the ship's decks. I mean not to give the impression that the ship provided a surreal serenity from the outside world - I certainly doubt that would be the case for any mode of transportation - but, regardless, I feel it's fair to say that the atmosphere on board the biggest wonder of the industrial world was at least largely one of calm, leisurely pace.

It is perhaps the hands of a higher power we must thank for the passengers leaving the Grand Saloon's comfortable seating; for if they had been there but a few more minutes, we would have surely had a different tale.

There was a terrible crash from directly under the Grand Saloon, and with the power of thousands of horses and several hundred pounds of searing steam, it was ripped out of existence within the blink of an eye, the massive vessel groaning in pain as her decks were torn out from asunder, blown skywards as if thrown by one of the leviathans for which she was nicknamed. The noise, the smell and the screams were terrible. Some of the gentlemen in the boiler room were so disorientated, blinded, deafened and terrified that the unfortunate souls wandered directly into the belly of the great, fiery beast that had brought about such calamity in such sudden circumstance - to near immediate incineration at the hands of the Great Babe's boilers.

The ship halted as quickly as it was capable, but little could be done - in one single instance, she had claimed five lives, most scalded so terribly that their skin peeled off of their hands as if it was a white, silken glove. One man was so horrified that he jumped overboard, believing the Great Eastern would be lost. He was gone in an instant, swallowed by the ship's enormous paddle wheel, and chewed up by it into a tangle so horrific not a soul could recognise it.

The screaming continued for a while; eventually, when it was clear she would remain afloat, the captain and his crew had to judge the damage and what could be done to steady her in a journey back home. By now, every move was joined by the clatter of wooden frets, floorboards and panels falling down the great chasm that had opened under the vessel's saloon floor. The number one funnel had been launched from the decks as they were torn, flying skywards at such force that it had now disappeared from view, irretrievable for the men on deck.

The tumultuous behaviour of the passengers was finally quelled, although it was not without difficulty, and Russell and his men declared the ship safe to continue - at reduced speed.

Rather unfortunately, it was a catastrophe that would have been prevented should Brunel have been present for the final preparations. The stop cocks in place on the feedwater heater had been left closed; I've no doubt my master would have noticed this issue immediately before the ship's departure and ordered it rectified.

The ship had sullied her reputation, despite being so young, due to negligence on the part of the men who were holding her, just as the same had gone for those whom built her. She drifted for a few miles before being towed back to Portland Harbour by several tugboats, each finding it a terribly laborious task thanks to the ship's immense size. Repair costs were high, and it took several days for the ship and the true extent of her damages to arrive at Portland harbour for repairs.

Testament to Brunel's immense design, the ship was not structurally damaged - indeed, it was found the explosion had been pressured by the ship's heavy bulkheads, which had held their own successfully against this sudden force exulted upon them. Lesser incidents have sunk a great many vessels since.

I tried desperately to keep the news from my master, fearing the stress would be too great for him. Yet, it felt like an incredible disservice to the man. He would no less want to hear bad news as that of a positive nature; and I felt the need to turn to his wife for advice. She was horrified to hear of the Great Ship being laid up in Portland.

> 'Please, *please*, William, I beg you. Do not tell Isambard. He shan't survive the news. He'll be heartbroken!'

I looked deep into her wide, brown, tear-filled eyes, and - for but a moment - felt a flash of my stiff upper lip shaking. She was gripping my shirt sleeve so tightly I was fearful the stitching would be torn. It was a rare loss of grace for Mary, and I felt my heart sink at the sorry sight and situation we were surrounded by. I could not bear to face somebody so struck by emotion - especially when I disagreed with her.

I was Brunel's assistant; I worked with him on his passion, his lifeblood. I was, contractually, purely professional, and it was my profession that demanded the ship's creator be made aware of any news regarding his 'Great Babe'.

I desperately tried to reason with her, trying to explain my stance, but eventually gave in. I felt rather pig-headed, and in retrospect it becomes a particularly awkward part of the tale to recall. I now feel I acted entirely inappropriately for trying to argue a professional standpoint with the man's family. In hindsight, it was perhaps a result of my loyalty towards his business affairs - but it does not calm my regret.

In the end, just as I walked into his chambers to tell him but a day or two later, his wife was sitting by his bedside, clutching a copy of **The Times** that had the disaster splayed across its front page in typically abhorrent, opinionated and trite detail. She had seen my point before I had seen hers.

Brunel's hands shook, his eyes were only half open but full of so much fragility and emotion that they were almost unbearable to witness. His mouth, slightly sunken as a result of his stroke, and no longer carrying that knowing smirk so typical of him, quivered. For the first time, I saw tears rolling down his drawn cheeks in remorse. His ashen skin no longer carried the vaguest hint of his holiday, and seemed paler than I have ever witnessed on a man with a pulse, or indeed, without. His wife kissed his cheek and left the room, casting me only a momentary glance that seemed to answer any questions I could have possibly asked.

She closed the door, and I sat in the chair alongside Brunel's bed in silence as he wrestled, in silence, with his own confusion, frustration, anger, disappointment, concerns... and, of course, his mourning. His ship had taken lives during construction; now she did so in service. I think it was at this moment that I knew Brunel would not last the night.

Brunel's lips finally parted - in great surprise to me, as I assumed he would be mute, or, at least, imparted, thanks to the effects of his stroke. He relayed my name, as if to confirm to his poor senses that it was indeed my person in front of him.

I nodded to him, almost on the verge of tears, and battling to keep them away. I felt that unleashing my own emotions in this situation would only hasten his decline.

Suddenly, with a single blink, he looked me straight in the eyes; and glanced to a piece of paper on the fine, mahogany unit that sat across from his bedside, slipped into a paper envelope. It was addressed with **William.**

I hesitated. Almost frozen, like a pheasant faced with the barrel of a shotgun. But, after a grunt from him, I relented and picked it from the table. In typical Brunel fashion, this odd letter had been written with a certain conversational vigour. Oh yes; you could always tell when Brunel had written to you.

You need to listen to me, Jacomb.

So it began. I observed it had clearly been written some time ago, though no effort to actually present a date had been made. Had Brunel planned to introduce this for long? Years? Our entire careers together?

I glanced back at Brunel and nodded, perturbed to the nth degree. Whatever the purpose of this stunted, distressing conversation was, it already felt important. As he pierced my eyes with his still faded, sorry looking glance, and I looked back to the letter, time seemed to trickle slower than the tarlike waters of the Thames.

If you are reading this letter, I am dead. If this is not the case, I am surely close to death. In any sense, it is essential that you take heed to what this letter states, and what it means to you, not to mention our professional fields.

I, and by virtue, you yourself, have been partaking in a colossal hoax that has permeated the empire. The world is not what you understand it to be, and much of our technological fabric is not of our own invention. It has seemingly existed before, and thus always awaited our discovery. At the centre of this grand conspirator's plot is a society. A society that you will encounter and no doubt draw the ire of.

There was a pause, tears sliding down my master's face as I considered what exactly I was reading. I could feel my eyebrow arching quite independently of myself.

When I am dead – and I am too bright a man not to recognise it cannot be too far away from us; you must organise a meeting with Robert Stephenson. It is imperative that you tell him your awareness of a man named Hargraves. You must get used to this name. Hargraves is a man you will cross repeatedly over the rest of your life. He is also the man responsible for much of my successes and failures. In that sense, he will assist your career and your business to an incredible degree. You must know him; but consider carefully before you work with him.

I wondered if it was useful to keep notes, or if I would be able to take this letter with me. Would it not be incriminating? I was still dealing with confusion and a feeling of immense tension. Even fear. I felt as I had been thrown into something I did not wish to be part of. My master was dying in front of me, and rather than be able to speak, I was communicating with a letter, in a completely silent room.

Hargraves is head of the Society of London Engineers, Scientists and Learned Individuals. I am a member, and Stephenson, too. The same, as I'm sure you will discover, goes for many of the empire's greatest minds. Hargraves is the leader. He is known as 'The Keeper'. You may not know him yet, but you will. Nothing is more probable. He will ask you for that book upon my bedside table.

Brunel's hand was shaking, and he remained silent, bar the odd guttural groan, but he still pointed towards the book quite directly. I noticed he had been biting his nails. This seemed a very unhealthy habit for a man on his deathbed - one supposes it wasn't exactly a priority for one bed bound.

You need to take this book. But do not build nary a plan within it, nor invest your finances. It is a book of nonsense engineering, William. A book of false creations. I have spent every moment making sure they are impossible. Hargraves will want the book so it may be passed to another engineer. Do not warn them. This book is built purely to buy you some time.

Brunel, by this point, had ceased writing the letter, and returned to it at a later date. It was noticeable not just in a change of ink, but his worsened penmanship.

This was, naturally, recognised only as I tried to distract myself from my own lack of understanding. I didn't quite understand what this 'extra time', or, indeed, his insinuations of any time constraints at all. Why did I require time between myself and this mysterious group? He was yet to actually instruct me. Typical of him, I considered, he seemed to be expecting me to fill in the blanks.

   'Where do I find this Hargraves, Isambard?'

I nearly buried my face into my hands at the realisation. It was futile to ask him. How could he reply?

Brunel's expression changed to a mixture of pain and disapproval; most likely as I hadn't called him Sir. However, as he wheezed, the circles around his eyes seemingly darkening progressively, the scornful look upon his face softened. To my amazement, Brunel's lips parted once more; and, although slurred, slow and deliberate, his final words to me were uttered. In typical fashion, they were blunt and intemperate.

   'He'll find you. Now go. Leave me to die in peace.'
   'Now, Sir, please - you don't know that will happen.'

His brow furrowed. And the room went silent again. Finally, the response – one that has echoed in my mind ever since.

   'I'm one of the greatest engineers of our time, Jacomb. Do you
   think I shan't recognise when the Reaper is at my door? Leave me.'

I stood from my chair. His behaviour remained stubborn and even rather infuriating. Despite his ill health, he seemed dedicated to ensuring he was difficult company. One would think that after so long being the great man's assistant it would have grown familiar, perhaps endearing - but to react so coldly in this situation? I walked towards the door, taking the leather-bound draughtsman's volume with me. I had just opened the door and was about to leave my master to meet his maker; when he spoke to me for the last time.

'Oh, and William?'
'Yes?'
'Thank you. You truly are...'

A pregnant pause - the sort that, in a theatre show, often proves so frustrating - followed. Brunel considered his words carefully. As carefully, of course, as his depleted mind could manage.

'...one of the wisest men I've worked with.'

I had to collect my emotions before I left the room.

Brunel's wife took me into the kitchen, where her tears were still being shed, and we soon settled with coffee - a drink I was not much a fan of, but greatly relished in such an exhausting situation.

Not a word was said. Time seemed to tick by with an eternity, and Brunel's favourite standing clock - a grand carven figure hewn in mahogany, presented to him by his father - clacked along with a noise almost deafening against such a tense, taut silence. What we couldn't have known is that Brunel's heart - despite its perseverance - was steadily decreasing to the great timepiece's pace.

I drummed my fingers upon the plain, red leather of the book Brunel had forced upon me. Mary's eyes kept darting to it, and back to my own expression.

'So what shall you do, William?'
'Do?'
'Don't consider me a fool. You don't marry a man like Brunel without a few educated observations. I know all about his book of

diagrams.'

There was another pause. I clutched my coffee a touch tighter. Mary sipped hers, but her eyes continued analysing me - awaiting my move.

> 'He wouldn't have told me to work this out if he hadn't have thought there was potential.'
> 'Of course.'
> 'He wanted me to find out what's going on, Mary.'
> 'Quite.'
> 'I suppose I'll have to-'

The door suddenly opened to the slim, twitching figure of the doctor, glaring at me, once again, with a greater, renewed sense of hatred.

> 'I think it's time this...' There was a pause. His thin moustache twitched.
> 'This 'gentleman' left. Brunel is dying. We've no time for this foolish chatter.'

He twirled on his heel and walked back upstairs. Mary looked at me, wide eyed. She frantically began speaking, and I felt myself leaning back in surprise.

> 'You need to leave, William. You have made your choice. And you must never contact us again.'
> 'Mary?'
> 'I've met Hargraves. If he feels I'm in the way, he will not hesitate to bring harm to my family. I have my children - and my husband's name - to protect. You will leave us, William.'

I didn't know what to say.

> 'Perhaps I-'

'No, William. You shall do this. I know that look in your eye. But you must leave us out of it.'
'I understand, Mary.' I didn't.
'Have a good life, William. Now go.'

The doctor was standing at the foot of the stairs with a particularly nauseating grin as I walked out of the kitchen, down the hallway and crossed the threshold of the Duke Street townhouse.

'No doubt I'll see you again.' His now familiar habit of pausing grated on me.
'...Sir.'

I turned to face him - only for the door to slam shut inches from my nose. The window pane set within it rattled; and my direct interaction with Brunel was over; with nothing more than a knocker quivering in front of my face and a book of useless plans - barring my many questions and a strange feeling in my chest.

I had the unshakable feeling that Brunel had brought me into something I didn't understand. I had a wave of nausea - a sort of nausea stemmed from anxiety and confusion - A lack of control as one would experience upon a rattling horse and trap with no reins. Blindfolded.

Later that evening, when I began leafing through this grand, beautifully drawn and rather fascinating - albeit deceitful - leather volume, I was not to know that Brunel had passed but an hour or so after my departure.

Storm clouds collected over London that night, and, as the heavens opened, I awoke from my sleep - and gathered a vague feeling that he had gone. It is a strange feeling - mourning a man subconsciously. That pit in the stomach telling you that something is so severely amiss.

Unfortunately, I am now very well acquainted with this.

When I rose the next morning, my decision was made. I would go against Mary's wishes, and try to pay them a final, respectful visit to the Duke Street townhouse - if only to see how Isambard was doing, for I still wished to cling to my naive optimism. I dared not consider that I would stumble upon the very man I was told to seek that morning.

And, I'm sorry to say, it wasn't Stephenson.

+ ENTER HARGRAVES +

I spoke extensively to Eliza that evening when we dined together; my fiancée, and the only woman with whom I felt confident in even the most private of matters. She often provided services as my secretarial assistant.

I, however, after much deliberation, sought to prevent her knowing the specifics of what I was about to embark upon - I greatly wished to marry her and saw no need to drag her into what seemed to be a most murky affair.

She proffered that, regardless of Mary's wishes, it was my duty as not only a professional but, more importantly, as a friend, to visit the Brunel household once more. A wise lady indeed - although I have no doubt that if she knew what was to happen that morning, she would have offered a different approach.

I strode down Duke Street feeling confident that, despite the misgivings of his family, I was doing the right thing. I had picked up a basket of fruit for my master - or, though it seemed unthinkable, his widow - and, naively, felt as if I'd see the lively little man who had designed the world's biggest ship back on his two feet.

The legion of press at the door proved me quite wrong - and, instead of continuing with my walk to the door of Brunel's home, I decided to turn heel and wait for the crowds to disperse. In the end, I found myself in one of the nearby inns. I took a cup of Indian tea - resisting the temptation to drink away my sorrows to the bitter demon that so sullied London - and watched Brunel's window, which was firmly shut with the curtains drawn.

I felt drained; empty. Almost vacant of emotion and occupied by my own reflection. I didn't feel so sad that my mentor and, I suppose, 'manager', had passed away - I was more than capable without him and, on a professional obligation, only took the assistant job for the incredible prestige and pedigree that came with it.

However, there were many other reasons to mourn. Brunel was such an unusual character; an eccentric of mind and appearance who sought to prove man's abilities. I do not only feel it was a loss to the engineering world - London itself seemed that little bit less interesting - less eclectic. The colours of the world around me seemed dimmer and lifeless. When you spend almost every day with a man creating the most wondrous of things, then suddenly lose that aspect of your existence... well, it serves only to dull it.

That was that; the greatest of engineers - the man whom had shrunk the world with his creations, and taken on the elements with vigour - that Herculean character passed away, unceremoniously, upon the fifteenth of September, 1859.

I briefly considered if I was mournful for a friend, rather than a colleague. Was I his friend? A foolish, but natural question for many in his trade, as he only ever seemed to be a social beast with those he worked with when it was for matters of work itself. In his elder years, he never seemed particularly eager to befriend anybody, and certainly not eager to judge his colleagues as if they were his social equals.

I suppose, in a sense, I had considered him a friend of mine, at least. We had friendly conversations, even the odd joke. He had been an enormous influence on me. But I had never heard him use the word 'friend' towards me.

Thinking about it, I'm not sure I'd ever heard him call anybody a friend.

I swirled what was left of my tea gently, gazing into the cup. I reminded myself briefly of the fortune teller's parlour trick, and wondered if I was even turning to such rudimentary measures myself for a moment of solace or reaffirming news. Needless to say, it never came.

Some hours passed, and the crowds of newspaper men with their notepads soon disappeared. The door to numbers seventeen and eighteen of Duke Street had not opened once - there was no signifier of humanity within. I knew, of course, that Mary had to be present. Brunel's body - my, how horrible it is to describe his physical presence as an inanimate object - would not have been moved yet, and the drawing offices that sat under their home would surely require some form of organisation.

Hark! A moment of clarity. The drawing offices! I could use my key and access there without having to even disturb his family. I promptly finished my tea and strode across the street - and into one of the backalleys that lead to those proud quarters. The drawing office was usually a hive of activity, well lit and with an essence of business even when unoccupied. But now, it was cold and lifeless. As if the very soul of the building's fabric had been taken away.

'Unsurprising.' I uttered, only to be met by the echo of my words. I was standing in this office for the first time without the intemperate engineer stood alongside me, smoking a cigar and, with not even an office boy's presence, it felt ghostly.

The relatively opulent offices bred nothing but unpleasantness and discomfort. In fact, for the first time in all of my years at that esteemed site, I noticed the immense, brown residue stains of tobacco smoke plastered across the ceiling. It occurred to me I had never had a clear view of the office's upper extremities.

I placed the basket of fruit - and a short letter of thanks and condolence for Mary - on the desk closest to the door that led to the Brunel home - and, for a few moments, tidied up those last remnants of his work of only a few days prior. Drawings for the Great Eastern, designs for new locomotives, tunnels and bridges... there were even plans for the home he was building for his retirement. I quietly categorised them - solemnly ensuring there was nothing a rival could make off with.

The office soon looked flawless - tidied enough to reduce Mary's labour and ensure all of Brunel's more confidential work was held where it should be. I was just about to clear out my own desk when a vicious hammering at the door echoed through the room.

Thump, thump, thump.

A terrible noise, a fist quite literally slamming against the glass paned door of London's most prestigious office premises. I straightened my cravat and prepared to meet whomever was so desperate to enter the building, and couldn't help but observe an enormous, dark shape behind the opulent glass doors Brunel had always so prized. (*He remarked once they were the finest glass from the oldest glassmakers in Paris. I regret to have never clarified the truth of this matter.*)

The black shape almost seemed to form the shadow of the reaper, and, while I was not usually one for such foolish superstition, the thought did briefly pass by that the creature had come for Brunel's soul; it would not be all that bizarre considering what I had already experienced these past few days.

However, as I came to the door the huge, lumbering shape - which now looked strikingly similar in shape to a bear - stepped away. I paused.

Thump, thump, thump.

The back door now ran out like gunshot - as if a huge battering ram was attempting to flatten the premises itself.

> 'Mary! You harlot, open this Goddamned door! Your husband won't do it for you, will he?'

My back straightened. My hands clenched into fists. Who would dare speak in such a manner to a lady in the best of times, let alone a widow? I decided to confront the figure through the door in which I had come, and did so quietly as to surprise whoever this appalling lack of respect belonged to.

Behind Duke Street was a broad alleyway, accessed via a gate, which allowed visitors behind the buildings. It was here the back door was situated: waste could be cleared by horsecart, Brunel himself could organise his personal carriage, and professionals could come and go with confidentiality.

This alleyway was blocked by the most disgusting visage of a figure I had ever seen.

The man was fat, enormous in fact - at least six feet in height and surely four feet wide. His facial features were tiny in comparison to the face they were set upon, his back was hunched, and his every inch seemingly unwashed and unpreened. He was wearing an expensive suit - Henry Poole, I observed, from Savile Row - which seemed to be quite ruined, numerous white stitches being obvious against the black fabric, which, itself, was covered in stains and spots of dirt.

I felt myself reeling back, only for his tiny black eyes to turn to me, piercing me harshly. I observed this hulking mass of a man was eating a boiled eel, wrapped in newspaper. I was already very scornful of eel as street food - quite why anybody would want to eat one of those grotesque aquatic serpents was lost upon me. To see a man gnawing at the flesh of one freshly boiled, in the street - with his mouth open, no less - made me feel fit to retch. He outright ignored me, and faced the door - which was still being struck by his fist in quick succession - as if I wasn't there.

The man was yet to acknowledge me beyond his glare; too occupied in his own obsessive hammering of the door and verbal abuse, not to mention the boiled creature in his oversized hands.

I stepped closer; but the culmination of his poor hygiene and his fish food repelled me. I noted some of the grease from the eel was seeping through the newspaper he held it in, and down his unwashed sleeve. I felt nausea take over me once again, and in my next stumble and the sound of my hand clapping over my mouth, the man's large neck - although little of it was visible - turned to face me, one of his tiny black eyebrows rising across those equally undersized pupils. I briefly wondered if a fellow with such frightfully small eyes on such an enormous head could have problems with his vision.

> 'You there, boy!' His speech was sloppy, addled with flakes of escaping mulch and spit.
> 'Are you referring to me, Sir?' I responded - bristling with indignation.
> 'Shut up and answer me, boy. Who the bloody hell are you? Where did you come from and what do you want?'
> 'I've come from the very office you're pounding at.'

I was still bristling. The man was as rude as his appearance was dishevelled. A very cold, grotesque sort of presence - quite beyond anybody I had met. He was very obviously wealthy. Why had manners escaped him so easily?

'The office, eh? And what's your business there? A rival of Brunel's, are we? Stealing documents are we? I've a mind to call the authorities!'

A smug grin appeared on his face. It made me feel even more liable to beat him rather than reply; but my curiosity towards this man, odious though he was, seemed to be rising.

'No.' I had already had quite enough of calling the hulking great figure 'Sir'. 'I happen to work for Brunel.'
'Servant? Office boy? Paper lad? Cigar carrier? Stop talking in vague terms and tell me who the hell you are.'

I was twenty seven years of age. Hardly a 'boy' or a 'lad'. This fool's demeaning terms seemed purpose plucked to infuriate me - I could feel my brow furrow towards him - but my glaring either went unnoticed, or, in his arrogance, was simply of no interest to him.

'I am Brunel's assistant, William Jacomb, and you?'

The man's expression, for the first time, ceased to be one of haughty arrogance and more one of confusion. He took another bite from within the eel's carcass and swallowed it in a hearty gulp. I had to look away from this little parlour trick and somewhat wished I had remained at the tavern.

'Brunel never told me,' he belched, stifling it in his hand, 'That he had an assistant. And I'm sure he would. Assistant to what, boy?'
'What else would I be an assistant to? His engineering, of course.'
'Well then.' I couldn't tell if the man's vile mannerisms were attempting to warm themselves.'I suppose, Jacomb, we had better get acquainted.'

'I've no desire for that, if you excuse me. Why are you shouting for Mrs. Brunel?'
'If you've no desire to get acquainted, Jacomb, you've no desire to know. Now get on with you; Mary and I have grave matters to discuss. And I don't mean Isambard's.'

How distasteful! He snorted in satisfaction at his own wit.
He resumed hammering at the door. I held my temples and sighed, trying to work out how I could relieve myself of this man's company without him pursuing the poor woman any longer. He continued as if I had already left - dubbing her with many unchivalrous words that I dare not apply to these papers.

Taken to the end of my tether, I finally grabbed the man's enormous fist - immediately regretting my decision thanks to the seeping grease from the fish in his hands.

'Very well, who are you? I wish to get acquainted.'

A smug grin reappeared on that glistening, perspiring, porcine face.

'I am a very valuable man; one who is a very valuable contact for any man in your trade, boy. And Brunel has something very valuable he was meant to give to me on his deathbed.'

Suddenly a grim realisation was beginning to gather. Surely this wasn't the man of the sophisticated society Brunel had warned me of? I was just about to suggest his identity when a trade-card was thrust into my hand. It took me a moment to register, but as I glanced to it my fears were made clear.

HARGRAVES
Head of the Society of Exceptional London Engineers and Individuals.

SCIENTIA EST IMPERIUM. - IGNORANTIA EST FRAGILITAS.
FORTITUDO EST IN SILENTIO.

'A society of engineers?' I had decided to fane ignorance. 'Fascinating.'

I couldn't help but notice there really was no utterance of a forename. Even for the time, this was unusual for a trade-card. Brunel's at least had his initials - though I always wondered if this was due to the sheer length of his Christian title. My own had my name clearly printed, as I'm sure Stephenson's did. The list went on. I made a show of slipping the card into my jacket pocket - but had no intentions of keeping it.

The man's chest blew up with pride - as if he needed any further inches on his torso.

'Not just any society of engineers, my boy. The finest, the most exceptional. The greatest men of the land, come together, in pursuit and execution of our combined, immense knowledge. Mr. Brunel was a man of the society.'
'He never mentioned you.'

Hargraves took another bite of his eel. I wasn't convinced he even chewed. He made dramatics out of a suddenly pensive nature, his eyes darkening. He tapped the bridge of his nose, and lowered his voice.

'We're a secret society, boy. We don't have to mention ourselves to anybody unless somebody else is worthy.'
'And you consider me worthy?'
'Not particularly; but I *do* know you know of Brunel's book of drafts. That makes you important.'

I rolled my eyes - and I was unsure if I was insulted by this man considering me unworthy or his immense lack of subtlety. My casual sense of rebellion - and ill manners to boot - was now ebbing away. He was exhausting to be in the company of; but I decided to make one last - if you'd permit - 'blunt' query.

'Well, even if I did, why should I give it to you?'
'Loyal to the end, I see. And young... neither a trait that this country holds in regard, boy. Come, I'll let you buy me a drink and we shall have a more... in depth discussion.'

I didn't even have time to protest - I was buying this man a drink, and that was quite that - despite my reservations I found myself being led back to the very tavern at which I had been mourning Brunel only a few hours before.

'Afternoon tea, I take it?'
'Don't be a bloody idiot.'

Evidently Hargraves was no more interested in traditions of the hour than he was his personal hygiene. Defeated, I took something stronger myself - a coffee. The foul, odious bear alongside me, regardless, seemed to glare at this with disapproval.

'Coffee, tea... women's drinks. Foolish beverages.'
'And absinthe is better?' I countered, glancing at the liquid in his brandy glass.

It had been expensive - being far less abundant in London than it was in Paris, and chosen by him with no request of my approval, of course. I had heard many rumours of this strange drink; that it turned people mad, that it embittered them. I had even heard it was only intended as a preventative of malaria. I certainly didn't think Hargraves had a risk of malaria. The only source of 'bad air' in his immediate presence seemed to be he himself.

'Absinthe is very popular on the continent, boy. Good for you. Also carries a fine kick.'
'I heard it was only enjoyed by ex-army drunkards.' I offered, trying my finest innocent smile.
'Well you heard wrong.' he snorted. 'Poorly educated. The continent is always a source of sophistication. All of which,

rightfully, should be ours.'
'Are you not a London society?'
'A society of gentlemen.'

He immediately followed this by a belch. The irony seemed lost upon him.

'London is no longer - no matter how we may try - the centre of the world that it once was, Jacomb. The use of London in our name insinuates our intentions; to bring us back to the centre.'
'By drinking foreign alcohol?'
'Impudent arse. No, not through alcohol, boy. We intend to use foreign and homeland techniques to improve our technological capabilities through and through - to become the aspirational targets of the world. To bring the future to our midst.'
'And how do you intend to do that?'
'If you join us, you'll find out.'
'And if I don't?'
'Then you can watch in envy; a minnow of the engineering trade, looking out from his stream to the raging rivers of progress!'

Hargraves swung his brandy glass enthusiastically, the most movement I had seen from him throughout the day. He was splashing some of the expensive liquor onto his shirt, before sipping the rest far too quickly. He belched again. For a moment, I feared he might be sick.

'Don't you realise the power we could bring to you, William? We have royal backing. We have university backing. You can't *not* join us.'
'I can, then. It was nice meeting you... Sir.'

I stood up from my table and adjusted my neck tie, nodding to him respectfully as I left the establishment. The result was a very large, very rude man glaring at me as if I had committed the most horrendous social faux pas he had ever witnessed. His pencil moustache curled with his lips, those little eyebrows digging deeper into the folds of his forehead. This was a man whom was clearly not used to being told 'no'. I tried my damnedest not to acknowledge my own discomfort.

As I walked quietly back down Duke Street, I noticed the funeral directors having arrived. It was a harrowing call back to the reality of my situation, and found myself standing in the middle of the street, watching in horror - as if the fact Brunel was deceased was a new discovery. I sighed, plunging my hands into my pockets as I watched the procession of black-suited gentlemen popping in and out of the town house with notepads, measure tapes and wood samples.

Mary eventually came to the door. She was already wearing black, and looked intensely tired. One figured a widow so recently bereaved was not in the act of regular sleep.She glanced at me with a weak smile of gratitude. It was hard to manage a smile. It was hard to feel positively about anything at the sight of the undertakers.

Of course, it was still a matter of concern that I had the book Hargraves so desired; but he had no idea where I lived, no clue as to my workplace - and certainly not the authority to go hammering on my door as he had the Brunel household.

I must have stood there in thought for a few minutes, only to be stirred by a man, atop his horse, shouting at me to get off of the road. I gave another reassuring smile - or at least the closest approximation of one I could garner - to the direction of Mary and went back on my way home, where Eliza was already waiting for me. She noted very clearly I was particularly quiet that evening; that I am sure of. But she refrained from asking questions - excepting, of course, the usual discussion of marriage, which always provided, in even the most trouble of times, a fine diversion for us both.

We spent much of the evening looking at tailor's catalogues wistfully. That suit would look wonderful on you, Jacomb - oh, my, look at that for the best man. Your father would look marvellous...

I decided it best to spend time with Eliza for a few days before making my first motions. I felt I had neglected her attention terribly, and she was very happy to see me still with her after 6AM, when I had usually started work.

The days of home milieu, the relative peace and quiet of frivolous trips to the park, or dining with my beloved, served to preserve my reluctance to get involved with this enormous system of crossed wires and cables. Whenever I may look off to my side at the huge man with the pencil moustache seated at his table, gnawing hungrily at seafood, or the very familiar, greasy figure reading his newspaper on a suffering park bench, Eliza would take my hand, and with it, my concerns, into her grasp. And my worries would soon fade away.

I feel it would perhaps cheapen my tale to delve too much into my relationship with Eliza, and I am making my most conscious effort to avoid it. Let it only be said that I adored the woman in greater capacity than anybody I had encountered, and had met her during my first few years as Brunel's assistant.

Of course, Brunel had voiced disapproval in chasing women - not that his reputation from his younger years was in any way clear - but had done so with a knowing smirk and often joked about me 'one day finally working up the stomach to actually speak to the girl.' His endless barbing is what had brought me to my relationship with Eliza in the first place. His relentless challenging of me had resulted in me being so desperate to prove him wrong.

I remember that knowing grin, holding his cigar and sitting back in his chair, pretending to read the newspaper, as I adjusted my shirt and left his office to meet her for our first courting.
As ever, he had known what he was doing.

Good gracious. Of course he knew.

Suddenly, the conflict in my head only worsened. If he had touched my life in such a way - as to give me all I currently had - was it not a traitorous act to deny his dying wish? My employer, no less - a man whom had no reason to give a proverbial penny about my welfare or personal life - had introduced me to my life's focus. Engineering, yes, but further to that, the one with whom I wished to spend the rest of my days.

I held Eliza closely, and stared directly at the enormous man on his park bench. It was Hargraves, all right. He spared no subtlety as he ogled the woman in my arms, then, with a vicious grin, shot me a wink.

My face paled. Our personal moment halted; though my grip tightened. I grimaced.

'William?'

Eliza's voice rang through me, like the chime of a bell, and brought me back to life; I hurried her back home with nary a word, my eyes over my shoulder constantly. My head suddenly felt somewhat lighter - and had regained a sense of focus. It was not simply a case of seeing through Brunel's wishes. It was a case of protecting my family. And, perhaps, although it was venomous to say... I would so take glee in seeing Hargraves lose his status.

Awkward coincidences continued; there on the door-mat of my London town house was a handsomely written, thick envelope - marked with a wax seal. At this point in time, after days of what seemed like stalking from the man himself, I had developed a strong sense that most unexpected events were due to Hargraves. I am, even now, unsure if that was cynicism, paranoia, or simple fact.

Right enough, that familiar Latin:
Scientia Est Imperium. Ignorantia Est Fragilitas. Fortitudo Est In Silentio.

With the letterhead proclaiming it was 'from the desk of Hargraves - The Keeper'. How he had found my address, of course, I knew not - what was certain was that this handsomely presented letter was indeed from that far less handsomely presented man - and would surely be unpleasant reading. To my surprise, as I'm sure you can imagine, the letter was smart, formal, well written and studious - everything the author of it had never seemed.

William,
I am very sorry and greatly indebted to you for your time at the premises of Duke Street upon the preceding Friday. My offer for such an illustrious young engineer as yourself to join our society remains, and I hope that, eventually, you shall find yourself taking this invitation for the good of the empire.
I remain, with pleasure, your humble servant.
Hargraves.

It had become quite clear how the society managed to function on any reputable basis; Hargraves, for all of his lack of social skill, was evidently a courteous man in print. I wondered how often it was he actually met cultured society in person. Even Eliza was quite taken by it, and it took a carefully orchestrated explanation to cease her questioning.

I found myself stroking my chin - a trait picked up from Brunel, no less - as I studied the letter.
There must surely be a hidden motive; a distraction?

Of course it was. I suddenly remembered my engagements with Stephenson.

'Eliza, do you recall where Robert lived?'
'Robert Stephenson? Of course, he invited you to his boat more than once.'

I cringed. He had indeed invited me to his 'House That Has No Knocker' - his luxury yacht, so used as to keep investors from knocking on his door, many-a-time. I dared not point out that I was prone to sea-sickness; it'd be found most comical to my peers that the assistant to the world's greatest ship designer should be subject to lacking 'sea legs'.

> 'Of course, William, if you took the time to read the paper, you'd know he isn't there.'
> 'Ey? Whatever do you mean?'

As I scrambled for the nearest copy of the London News, Eliza simply stirred her cup of tea, looking at floor.

Robert Stephenson was unwell, "Perhaps mortally ill", the newspaper noted. My face paled, and I almost felt like shouting with frustration. That was all I needed.

> *Stephenson was taken to his London home. He is presumed to be in bed.*

That settled it; to pot with Hargraves and his society - Stephenson was the key to unlocking it all, and I could not waste another day. Eliza only nodded in understanding as I glanced at her before walking out of the door. Once again, our situations and plans of marriage had become quite abandoned in my head. Impatiently - and without a moment to waste, I took my hat, the leather book, and stepped through the back door of my home as to avoid anybody who could be waiting there.

It always struck me as amusing as to how close Stephenson lived to Brunel's Paddington station. The two had often ribbed each other's technique when it came to the railways - Brunel's seven and a quarter foot gauge meant bigger locomotives, bigger carriages, bigger infrastructure - more space, smoother motion, faster trains, the list went on. In his typical form it went against the norm every step of the way, and in the process was one of the most expensive lines in the world, let alone the country - some speculating the total mileage of the Great Western Railway had cost more than railways double its length.

Stephenson, in his typical form, had a more popular - albeit less luxurious - option. Four feet, eight inches and a quarter was the gauge he and his father had developed and furnished much of the country with. It balanced the books; cheaper, more globally accepted, and still permitted a certain level of speed and stability. Companies found it easier to construct for, locomotives could be far more numerous in number at lower cost, and passengers could be carried more economically.

It was utterly characteristic of the two; and proved far too well - to Brunel's chagrin - as to why Stephenson was the country's most popular mechanical figure. The investors liked him just as much as the public; a hefty swing for an engineer to have behind him. I pondered this, quite silently to myself as I walked alongside Hyde Park, and began considering how this may affect a role in this bizarre society. Could it be that Stephenson was preferential to them, too?

I found myself rubbing my chin again, and with a heavy sigh, rapped upon the door to No.34. It was beginning to rain, and I took my hat off of my head as a sign of respect, only to discover the brim was already filling with water.

Stephenson's housekeeper answered the door - his wife had died a good seventeen years before - and almost immediately recognised me. It was strange how the tone so differed from Brunel's household in similar circumstances - the welcomes and atmosphere felt warm, and pleasant. Perhaps it was as Robert had not been drawn ill due to a terrible failure; the press had no interest in tearing his character, and there was no financial difficulty for the man to leave behind.

Regardless, my mood fell as a familiar, weasely little man with pointed features left Stephenson's bedroom with his case. The doctor from Brunel's home.

I stopped, as did he, and for what seemed like an eternity, we stared at each other in shock.

'I was not expecting to see you again quite this soon... Sir.' spat the little man, his whiskery moustache twitching as he looked over the frames of his glasses in a very reciprocated contempt.
'Likewise.' I countered, simply.

The housekeeper stood alongside, quite perturbed. His hands remained respectfully behind his back - but seemed ready to break free in case any fisticuffs should occur. The tension must have seemed tangible for him, as he remained motionless for what felt like quite a sum of time. At last, he cleared his throat.

'Might I offer the good doctor a scone?'
'You certainly may.' replied the wretched little man.

The diminutive, wicked doctor walked away from me - glancing at the book in my possession. I noted the upright and straight gait in his walk - as if his legs were the only part of him moving, and the rest of his body nothing more than a stiff jointed doll, as he stepped into the kitchen.

A bizarre fellow indeed.

This situation as a whole felt far too familiar, and I was almost inclined to leave - but the leather book in my grips and the thoughts swimming in my head refused to let my feet take the slightest step in retreat - and, instead, I entered the door of Robert's quarters.

There he was, sat, quite upright, in his bed. The relatively untamed waves of his hair were under a nightcap, a tired smile was on his face. His breathing was slow, and heavy - his sleepy eyes lit up somewhat at the sight of me, and instantly that grandfatherly demeanour he had always maintained in his advancing years filled the room. The atmosphere, once again, felt bright, warm, and pleasant - despite the rain outside, the Stephenson home felt like the epitome of comfort.

On the dresser, there was a small collection of photographic pictures; handsomely printed Albumens, all containing photographs of Stephenson, Brunel and many others standing alongside each other as friends in happier times. I tried not to give away my curiosity, but the knowing glance on Robert's face was all too clear.

> 'William. Oh, I almost wondered if it was arrogant to expect you visiting me. Please... take a seat.'

I did. And, before another word could be said, Robert's eyes had already caught upon the book in my hands. The knowing smile on his face had grown more obvious. He raised an eyebrow and looked at me, as if he already knew what my next twenty actions were going to be. A sort of smug, but utterly inoffensive smile. Again, grandfatherly.

> 'What's that you've got, there?'

I had a feeling he already knew - but, regardless, as he relaxed back against his pillows, I began to explain why I was at his home.

+ COLLECTION OF PHOTOGRAPHS +

My explanation went on for what seemed like hours, but Stephenson sat back quickly and listened to every word with that ever-thoughtful look in his eye.

His eyebrows would raise, he'd nod, he'd even shake his head - but still it seemed that not a word shocked or surprised him. It struck me as amazing how a man could seem so well educated and all-encompassing; especially when, like Brunel, he concealed an element of self-doubt and insecurity.

He lit up a cigar as my story came to a close. I couldn't help but be somewhat surprised, as I never knew he smoked; perhaps he simply didn't rely upon them as heavily as my master had. His cigar was far smaller than Brunel's favoured; at least, so one figured - he had often seemed to struggle to speak when smoking, while Stephenson could fairly comfortably.

'So, he finally told you. I must say, I'm shaken.'

(I noted he wasn't shaking in the slightest.)

>'He often dismissed it as being foolish to let you get involved into the 'hive', as he called it.' He laughed. 'He likened the lot of them to angry wasps. Never got on well, you see...'

Stephenson was frail, but his natural charisma was more than intact.

>'It's funny really; I was just looking at photographs of him and me. You're in a few of them... I was putting them in my scrap book. Nice to keep memories available. Would you like a cup of tea?'
>I held up my hand. 'I couldn't possibly. I can't really stay long.'
>'Nonsense! I'll get you a cup of tea made, we've got all night, Jacomb. I've a lot to talk to you about.'
>'Well, as you understand, I'm only here to talk about what Brunel sent me for.'
>'Jacomb, with due respect, Brunel's 'knowing best' was only ever the best for himself. The man's dead; what will he know? We all miss him; we all want to do the best for him - but until you join that bloody society you're not going to know a jot. Now how do you like your tea?'

Within the next fifteen minutes, we were already holding teacups and reminiscing on old times.

>'I must say; we all should have seen it coming.'
>'What?'
>'Brunel's death, naturally. He was never the healthiest man...'
>Robert stirred his tea, and seemed to be studying it intensely. His eyes rose again to meet mine, and he tapped the side of his head. 'But an incredibly healthy mind, Jacomb. At least; in his thinking. His emotions could be up for debate, you understand.'

He smiled as I nodded solemnly. As if he knew his little jokes would be taken seriously. Looking back, I think I only just recognise the humour. Oh, for the hindsight of many years!

'It always surprised me that someone so calm as yourself could be his assistant. You two were very different sorts of gentlemen; it normally takes someone so fiery as he was to even come close to taking him down a peg.'
'You were very different,' I observed. 'Why should it be argued for us?'

Robert stopped. He blinked, then nodded slowly, with a little smile.

'One supposes he had a habit of collecting those different to his own character. You'd be forgiven for it being out of the need for positivity.'

There was another silence. I relaxed somewhat in my chair, and studied my surroundings. The room had a great measure of mahogany in its furnishings. I observed it seemed to be flipped, horizontally, to the configuration of Brunel's bedroom. Fitting, perhaps. The warmth of the yellows, browns, reds and golds were also of direct contrast to the deep greens that Brunel was so fond of, though, the clock still tick-tocked with what seemed a ridiculous volume. I found it rather bizarre to consider Stephenson's health encountering anywhere near the risk that Brunel had been suffering.

It had been thirty years since the Stephensons had made such a legendary name at the Rainhill locomotive trials - with their first masterpiece proving the future of railways to be in steam haulage.

Robert, and his father, George, became wealthy men on this success - and Robert at only the age of 26. Not dissimilar to myself. How bizarre; to think that within only thirty years he was now a frail, ill old gentleman drinking tea and speaking of the past, as if it was antiquity.

My mind wandered as I mentally assessed him - but he remained very firmly on topic.

'Well, when are you joining?' Stephenson said, using his typical powers of observation and presumption.

He was no longer looking at me; too busy staring intently into his cup of tea as he stirred it. I found myself looking to my own tea, just in case there was anything interesting I missed.

There wasn't.

>'Frankly, I wasn't intending to.'
>'A bit optimistic to think you can do anything without joining, isn't it?'
>'I'm not sure what I'm even meant to do. What is this damned society anyway?'
>'The society is exactly that; a group of people working to a cause.'
>'You aren't being very helpful!'
>'Well as I said, you can't really do or learn something about a society before you're a member!'
>'...Very smart, Robert . But I was hoping for information.'

It really was incredible; his ability to smile, laugh and become so animated on the brink of death was a bizarre quality - a testament to his personality and what his philosophy manifested. It was clear as to why the Stephenson family was known for a positive temperament.

>'I'll tell you what I do know. But it isn't as much as you - or even I - might think. That society was set up by my father, and the other engineers that competed at Rainhill. It was intended to further progress the Empire's advancements using combined practises and knowledge towards the latest technology - in this case, locomotives. It was nothing but noble intentions, William.'
>'If that's the case, Robert, what has happened to turn it so sour?'

Now, Robert's face darkened. His voice hushed, and there was a pause. He nodded towards his door - that was still ajar - and watched as I firmly shut it. I sat down to a figure with a far darker look in his eyes.

> 'The advancement happened - and the book arrived. Along with... less savoury individuals. That Doctor is one of them. I can't stand him, the little insect. Let me tell you-'
> 'What book?'
> Robert's smile returned briefly. 'Sorry. Perhaps I should start from the beginning.'

That serious, thoughtful gaze returned, his eyes piercing nothing in particular at the other side of the room. He took a deep breath; evidently this would take some explaining.

Before he began speaking, there was an aching pause. I'm unsure if it was due to his own pains, for his love of Thespian art or simply to see how I'd react; with how I knew Robert, I felt quite convinced it could be any of those.

> 'This book... The book. They call it *The Eternal Tome*. A curious thing, it is, William. You could swear it was biblical in origin. A holy creation of higher power. I've only seen it the once; figured it was a company ledger or something. But it's far more bizarre.'
> 'Yes, yes, yes, Robert - but if it isn't a ledger, what is it?'
> 'I wish I could tell you! Imagine a book of plans, of technologies, of revelations, if you will. A sort of volume of discoveries. It describes technologies we've never dreamed of, and, indeed, many we have built. From what I understand, every man with the Society has produced some of these technologies. Suspension bridges, atmospheric railways... that sort of thing would be relevant to you. Locomotives, carriages, larger wheels for speed, smaller for strength. Then there's...the rest. It's, put simply, a book of blueprints for humanity.'

I was already disbelieving.

> 'You mean to tell me that everything we've discovered, everything my master has done...'
> 'You're oversimplifying it, William. Yes; we were often given blueprints. To translate them. If there's one thing Brunel certainly

wasn't capable of - It's being a charlatan. Frankly I think he went off-model with every project we gave him.'
'And yet the fact remains-'
'The fact remains, William, that somebody has done it all before. And much more than we have achieved in our lifetimes.'

I found myself staring, blankly.

'It's almost impossible, William, to overestimate what's within its pages. Things like vehicles powered by adapted lamp oil, incredibly destructive weaponry - larger locomotives with higher steam pressure, flight without gas balloons - new materials, and new energy sources!'

Robert became increasingly animated, even excited, by the revelations inside this supposed, mythological volume. I simply found myself dumbfounded.

'You've lost me, Robert.'

And thus, the excitement - it all disappeared. Instead, the old man smiled wearily and laid back against his pillows. The change was startling. I heard a slight rattle in his breath as he exhaled. The very room seemed darker, and greyer. Smog? Perhaps factory smoke above the street, I reasoned.

'I must confess; they lost me. A long time ago. It seems too good to be true, does it not? And yet, I can't help but question it all. Is it right to take the joy out of invention?'
'That's all about the situation to surprise you, Robert? All you question?'
'William, you must remember - it's been many a year. It's now simply...well, you'll pardon the pun, run of the mill.'

I didn't recognise any pun, myself. I smiled regardless. I fear it only betrayed my puzzlement further, as he patted my shoulder reassuringly. Part of me was beginning to wonder if the years had really been so kind to the eccentric old engineer.

'I don't suppose you're finding me very helpful, are you, William?'
'I have to confess that I'm not.'

Stephenson smiled in his way that I'm sure is now as familiar to the reader as it is myself. He took another sip of his tea, then a draught of his cigar. It took a little longer than he seemed to realise, and I twiddled my thumbs awaiting his next words.

'Not to worry. I don't understand it much myself, either. I'm not convinced any of us did. Books are books, Jacomb...they're meant to catalogue what we've already learnt, not what we're about to. It seems so - I don't suppose there's any better word? - Odd. Like a colossal misstep, fooling about with the powers of God, and the minds he's given us.'
'Quite.' That was all I could muster. I felt very foolish and inarticulate compared to the country's greatest living engineer - regardless of how oddly he came across.
'But as you've probably guessed, Jacomb... they have ears and eyes everywhere.'

I blinked, and nodded towards the door - and, thus, the direction of that horrid, weasely little doctor whom I had grown to loath so quickly. Stephenson didn't say a word, but nodded in affirmation. I felt myself go pale. I stuttered, but, eventually, my worries were released.

'Robert. Did they...'
'Kill him? No. At least, I wouldn't expect so. Brunel was a damned waste of money for them, but one of their greatest minds. One of the best of us. I consider him better than I was - not that I'd never tell him that. No, William. I'm sure they'd do no such thing. Brunel died of his own accord. I expect to be frank, you got that impression the moment you spoke to him.'

I couldn't argue. As much as I wish I was capable of doing so.

> 'But they will kill. They have before. Many less of a man. I can tell you that for certain. You. Family members. Staff. Children...'
> 'Is that a reasonable threat?'
> 'They are a threat, by nature. Reasonable, no.'
> 'And you think I have no other avenue?'
> 'You have plenty of places to go, Jacomb. But none of them would be in London, the Empire or, more's the pity, America. There are many avenues, but you won't find a civil one.'

I ran my hand through my hair, backwards. The clockwork deep within my mind was rarely challenged; here, it felt like every strut and spring was strained to an ultimatum.

> 'Disarm the threat, William. Join them and they cannot cause harm to you. To be perfectly frank, they'll benefit you.'
> 'You tell me this society will benefit me? After all you've just told me?'
> ' more than dare, I insist upon it. They do make a man wealthy. They make a man able to progress. You may even get a project stapled to your name.'
> 'I refuse. I positively refuse.'
> 'Selfish.'

Robert had a wily grin. He knew that would get my back up, and, indeed, it did.

> 'Selfish? I'll accept many jabs, Robert, but selfish? Never! I have nothing but support and nurture for my fellow man if they accept it - I provide charity! For you to-'
> 'If you have support and nurture for your fellow man, protect them. And yourself. And your trade. And what, mayhaps, of your master's legacy?'

I hadn't realised I had stood up from my chair, and it came as a surprise to myself that I had to render myself reseated.

'Do you smoke?'
'I occasionally partook when offered by my master, but...'
'Snuff, then?'
'Again, occasional.'
'You'll likely need to make it a regular habit for your life with the society, believe me...'

I noticed the stains on his fingers and the quiver in the hand holding his tobacco. The sight made me twist my lip.

'Is that... helping with your illness?'

He looked at the cigar. An almost regretful, sorrowful glance at that rod of tobacco leaf, as the tip smouldered in a quiet, red glow.

'There are many things that may help me, William. Tobacco is likely not one of them, but it helps one relax. Don't you ever relax, William? These doctors go forth about the plant a lot, but it feels damned fine for my head. I'd happily sacrifice a few years for a regular pleasure.'

He took another long drag - a curl of grey, acrid smoke left the tip of the cigar. A few specks of tobacco hit his sheets. It was clear that Stephenson, be it a smoker, was nowhere near the level of Brunel's regularity - even Brunel's finest bedsheets had the odd scorch and burn upon them, while Robert's were relatively clean and unscathed.

'I wish I could share your viewpoint on that.'
'You can. You likely will. Right now, you're young.'
'I wish you'd stop bringing up my youth, too!'
'Your indignation is an excellent asset though...'

I felt like a specimen for Stephenson; as if I was being used for study. One wishes I could say I took it in good stead, but I distinctly remember my back being up by this point of conversation.

'I hear absinthe is popular with learned gentlemen...'

I choked on my tea. The old man was looking out of the window when he said it, and he turned back with an unusually solemn expression.

> 'You met him, then.'
> I wiped my mouth on my handkerchief.
> 'Yes. Although I wish I could say that I hadn't.'
> 'Frightful, isn't he?'
> 'Robert, he's the foulest man I've ever met.'
> 'And I suppose you've seen a lot of him since?'
> 'Much to my displeasure.'
> He chuckled. 'Yes, unfortunately he's become quite a regular presence in my existence, too. Little wonder. He's never achieved a thing himself; he depends upon that Tome and his legion of creators. Treats us like servants. Everyone fears him on basis of reputation.'
> 'How, then, is he in charge? If he's never achieved a thing, how-'
> 'Fat, useless fool inherited the bloody thing.'
> 'The society?'
> 'The Tome. Though, in essence, he did both. He was slimmer, then, of course.'
> 'You are... really talking to me with sincerity?'

Laughter erupted. I was beginning to lose focus on what was a stupid question, and what was Robert's unnatural liveliness on his deathbed.

> 'Yes, William.' His face, however, immediately grew more serious. It soon looked quite grave. 'I'm speaking with sincerity. Sincerity of the highest order. You need to forget your thoughts on it and take it as pure, simple, fact.'

For what seemed like the first time throughout my visit, the old man looked me straight in the eyes. All humour - and, strangely, much of his colour - had washed from his face.

'The Book of Revelation exists, and it is a book of blueprints. Instructions and designs for the new world. It is heartily important that you get used to that. You'll be seeing much of those revelations. Everywhere you look. For decades to come.'

I felt a harsh chill through my spine. The room fell very quiet. I noted that Stephenson was gazing towards those photographic images, those little developed printed pieces that sat on his bedside table.

'It's strange, isn't it, William? These photographs. Little memories of the past. My father would have dreamed of these being extant in our profession. So much potential for capturing scientific discoveries, long since missed...'

He raised an eyebrow. It was a slow, deliberate motion. I noted his eyes seemed to quickly dart in my direction, to make sure I was listening.

'Yet, so easy to discard. So easy to lose. Thousands, perhaps tens of thousands, of pounds spent refining new forms of engineering. Yet, when you lose these things... they, and their idea, sometimes even the memory. It disappears.'

There was another pause. I glanced at the photographs. Then my tea. Then, back to him.

'Did you develop those yourself?'
'No, no. These were given to me. Beautiful, things. Given to me on a plate. Presented to me, to which I may do as I please. I can take them anywhere, tell stories with them. Tell my side of things. Explain the truth of every situation...'

I scratched my head - and when I looked up, realised I was being stared at by the old engineer. His fierce eyes - a trait from his father - pierced me. They were dimmed from his illness; but intimidating, all the same. He was challenging me to listen. Rather a curious thing, it was - seeing a man fade through so many emotions, stances and ways of speaking in one environment.

> 'History itself, William, is a revision. It's all written, rewritten and recreated over and over. You'll hear a great many stories. The key is to keep track. To record them. To write them down. You need to keep history recorded, my boy - keep things safe, well presented and well evident.
> You tell somebody a good enough story, and they'll believe anything. Scientists, historians, the press... that happens to be one of Hargraves' specialities. I'd recommend, pure and simple, to keep your photographs. Keep your words, and hold them to your chest. Write a diary, or memoirs... The common man; he is your ally. Not your peers, no - never your peers. They are rivals. It's purely the common man of the street who watches in awe.'
> 'Are you not my peer? Can you not be trusted?'
> 'There's not enough career left in me to further it, William. You know that as well as I do.'
> 'You know, Robert, for a man who's deathly ill, you seem to be carrying your wits about you perfectly adequately.'

Robert smiled.

> 'I may have neglected to take my medication. Another word of advice; don't take that of a doctor. Now, how about you give me a look at that book in your hands? Pour yourself a dram of something, let's see what rubbish the little man thought up!'

I don't know if it was the stress prompting me to accept a drink; but I did exactly that. And hours were spent looking at completely forged drawings, with inaccurate measurements. Some faux projects even featured crude remarks in Latin, and Stephenson pointed out one bridge that was approximately two foot short on its braces.

It quickly became a very entertaining affair, and for all of the terrible information and horrible confusion I had learnt, developed and now had buzzing inside my mind, I felt reassured that there were, at least, people on the side of relative rationale.

The only problem, of course, was that I only had one view of this being the 'correct' side. And part of me was still deep in thought that these gentlemen were nothing more than disgruntled employees; could my master hold such a grudge? Almost certainly. But Stephenson? For whatever reason, he seemed different.

As he sat there, sipping a cup of tea and chuckling away, there was still a certain innocence to the way the dying man seemed to be approaching the situation. An unusual, thriving mind that had no time to allow misery and death fill what the papers were calling his final days.

No, Stephenson was no disgruntled man. I couldn't think of any industrial hardship or humiliation he had faced in his twilight years. In fact, Brunel had often remarked upon it being 'A measure of the genius in maintaining a status quo.' Indeed, as petty as it may have seemed, I felt a twinge of jealousy in the place of my master.

Robert Stephenson and his father had innovated, certainly - but, despite his reputation as a pioneer, and the man who truly built the locomotive as we knew it - I felt he had strived to improve his technology nowhere near the level Brunel had. Yet here he was, sitting in a veritable palace, facing death with a fulfilled contentment. As I brooded, I caught myself, and went back to chatting with him like an old friend; but I had a strong feeling he knew of that harboured grievance.

Steadily, as the night went on, the tired old man began to slow. His hands had begun to quiver and look uneasy, and his voice seemed to be growing more and more hoarse. The smile never left his lips, but my growing cynicism and anxiety had me wondering if I was witnessing the man's departure.

He had only, on the 3rd of September - just over a week before Brunel's passing - fallen ill in Norway, when he had been present for the celebratory opening of the Norwegian Trunk Railway as guest of honour. He was considered, globally, a man of such distinction that he often found himself as guest of honour at international functions. That illness had often, by bizarre coincidence, been attributed to his visit to the Great Eastern when she had been stranded upon her dock - and he had fallen into the freezing riverbank's mud. This was another component to the persistent rumour as to the ship being cursed.

Indeed, if I was to be led into believing the same illness had now rendered him bed-bound, I couldn't help but consider that the world's greatest vessel now laid claim to the lives of the country's two finest engineers. Were I a man who gambled, I would place a handsome stake on the loss of the great ship's reputation. Perhaps it was selfish of me? To consider the vessel's reputation as being so precious.

    'Of course, William. There's one priority you can't leave alone.'
    'What?'
    'That Great Babe of Brunel's. That's his legacy, now. His legacy needs to be kept."
    "I'm surprised you feel so warmly to her.'
    'I'm surprised you don't!'
    'Robert, with due respect, I can't help but find her sullied. She's killed my employer.'
    'William, Brunel was already a dead man walking. If this hadn't have killed him, his next project would have. You know it as well as I do; the man invested too much into his projects.'
    'Expensive, maybe-'
    'Money is nothing. Blood, sweat, tears - the essence of the creator. That, my boy, is worth millions.'

I spotted a framed picture on his bedside table - hidden behind his decanter. I could easily make it out to be the Rainhill locomotive the Stephensons had created their fame upon; *The Rocket*.

The Rocket was not, at the time, facing a particularly elegant end. She was working on a mineral railway in Cumbria, and by all accounts was a shell of her former glory. There were persistent rumours that she would be due for scrap metal in the coming months.

Some said they were waiting for the death of her surviving co-creator.

> 'Believe me. If the Great Eastern is ever lost, you shall find yourself crying as if she were your own. She's Isambard's final thumbprint in the earth; you can't let that get washed away. If you want to preserve her, you need to work with her owners. Or rather, her owner's owners.'

He handed me a trade card. It was, I'm afraid to say, all too familiar.

HARGRAVES
Head of the Society of Exceptional London Engineers and Individuals.

SCIENTIA EST IMPERIUM. - IGNORANTIA EST FRAGILITAS. FORTITUDO EST IN SILENTIO.

I winced.

> 'It's your call, William. But I am confident that, should you gain membership, that terrible group shan't have a clue what hit it. You have that youth, that spark in your eyes. I see Brunel's effect on you. And I'm quite sure you're the best chance of justice - logic, invention and the future - prevailing.'

I took the card. This time, rather than discard it - like I had only a short time before - I slipped it into my jacket's inner breast pocket.

'You shan't regret it. But don't go to Hargraves. He'll come to you. He's particularly good at that.'
'I feel as if you are dismissing me?'
'Dismissing? No. I'm encouraging you. I can't advise you firmly enough to step out of my door and into the world. Or rather, against the world. It needs you to find its footing, Jacomb. Brunel saw it, and so do I. You've the right scruples. The right morals. And the right head.'

He smiled. This time, with such sincerity I couldn't help but smile in return.

'Oh, and Jacomb? Don't forget the book. I dare say I'm now wondering if Brunel would have been better off as a comedian.'

I was about to walk out of the door - before that thump of realisation struck me.

'You're ushering me out while on your deathbed.'
'Well, yes. It'd certainly seem that way.'
'When you're dead, where on Earth am I meant to go? Your inspirational speeches are a fine starting point, I'm sure, but how is one meant to know the next course of action?'

Robert took a long, deep draught of his cigar, and briefly disappeared in what resembled a miniaturised London Smog.

'I'd say the first step would be to pick up a newspaper.'

I stood there. Waiting for further instruction - but it never really came.

'I'll see you again, some day, William. Be it beyond these mortal restraints or otherwise.'
'Are all engineers so fearless when faced with death?'

A wide grin appeared on the old man's face.

'The successful ones are.'

Those words rattled though my head as I found myself roaming the miserable streets of London. I was not moving in any pointed direction: I was lost in that great, pulsating blood stream that the city's bustling population represented. The rivers moved slowly, crawling through their enormous channels in a thick, black treacle. The choking soot from factories was defiant to the whims of weather and time of day; continuously, the city was producing, building, expanding and pulsating into bigger, better things.

And yet, as I once again found myself drawn to it, Brunel's residence on Duke Street still seemed deadly still. Where the other high class residences of the address were alive with lights, people and industry, those two small buildings that made up Brunel's home and office remained dim and lifeless; the energy itself from the street was diminished, even with the rampant march of horse and cart. I had heard completely unsubstantiated rumours in the street already that the Great Eastern was to be abandoned, and that Brunel's estate was to end up for sale. I was already even hearing rumours of Stephenson's passing.

As I strode along the city, still lacking any destination, I found London's dizzying rush more and more difficult to acquaint myself with, and briefly considered if without Brunel, my profession would truly have any value to the world and its future. What was it, after all, without that great innovator leading us, the flock? And what would London be if two of the country's finest men of industry passed away in the space of one limp, damp Autumn month?

How long could a country that loses its finest sons truly continue with this cycle of construction, expansion and growth? To what end would our coasts fill with mortar, brick and the ubiquitous steel rail?

As the tumultuous processes in my head continued, I remained blissfully unaware that I had, in fact, traversed the quarters of

Gloucester Square and Westminster in an enormous circle - I had arrived at Paddington terminus - and the great structure that made up the train shed of the station's web of beautifully contorted iron and timber. This train shed had been the first project I had worked upon - the project that had enthused me into Brunel's working circle - and I considered it to be standing as a monument of our collaboration. While that enormous ship, the Great Babe, had proven a spectacular project, it was this glorious piece of railway engineering that still seemed so familiar and masterful.

I could spot the minor mistakes made by the navvies whom had helped construct her, I remembered the loose imprint of fingers and boots in the station's surrounding plaza, and the drunken brawls that often opened up nearby when staff clocked off for the evening.

The towering arches, pillars and glasswork rendered this fascinating epitome of a traveller's life into some kind of indoor city; a delicate system of nature that combined the growing dedication of mankind towards mechanics, with mankind's desperation to roam the land around him.

As I explored the building's platforms, each filled with travellers and the similarly intimidating lines that built up the Great Western's broad gauge locomotives, I recalled Stephenson's advice regarding the newspaper, and decided to take it. Every newspaper had Brunel's obituary on the stands - and I took purchase of a few engineer's monthly supplements. There were few engineers who actually purchased these; they were rather more used by students or armchair inventors, the queer sort that believed a falsified mechanical knowledge would make them the centrepiece of their local alehouses. I myself had not purchased a 'monthly' since university.

It was an odd habit of my master that he always bought the magazines most prone to giving him bad reports, criticising - perhaps, sometimes, rightfully - his tendency to seek glory and over-indulgence rather than the more economic methods that put an engineer into a positive light from his peers. He would seek out the flickering tongues of the judgemental and read them in great depth; often taking each word to heart. His arrogant exterior and knowing smirk was forever prone to falter from the harsh words of the community I always suspected he wished to belong to more intimately.

With my new knowledge of the dank underground that made up this group of the learned, I was certain there would be some kind of clue as to the society's feeling towards Isambard. Right enough, upon picking the paper and paying the however-many-pence it was at the time - my memory is not nearly so photographic, I admit, as this volume may portray - it became clear that they saw it as within their interest to voice disdain upon the man who had cost so many their fortunes.

I settled down in the Paddington station free house with the paper - I must confess I had taken ale purely to stem the flow of those chaotic events now rattling around inside my head - and took no pleasure in reading the obituary declaring Brunel's career 'unfortunate' and 'marked by arrogance'.

> *It is unfortunate that despite the great number of fields in which Brunel worked, the vast majority were nothing more than failed experiments. It is easy to see Brunel's mark in his magnitude - but, strictly speaking, difficult to see what, if anything, he has progressed in the field of engineering.*
>
> *His Great Western Railway presents little in its structure an engineer could profitably copy, and, beyond its earthworks, masonry and gauge, there is hardly a relic of its original construction remaining in existence.*
>
> *The man's great many legacies upon this earth are those marked by arrogance, and a lack of willing to bend to that ultimate cause of the engineering field - for a project to pay.*

The lack of financial success in his career means that Isambard Kingdom Brunel, despite his large impact upon this Earth, is a name synonymous with failure and the craving for only personal success, at the great detraction of his peers, colleagues and workers. He often quarrelled with his contractors and many of them consider themselves ruined by him.

The obituary went on, labouring the point within an inch of its life. I bristled. And was already planning exactly what I would have to say in return, when, as luck would have it, a gentleman sat next to be with a notebook and pen.

'Mr. Jacomb?'
'Speaking.'

There was a pause as the man readied his notebook.

'I was wondering if I could have a quick interview.'

I looked round to the man at last and swiftly realised this was no ordinary newspaperman. The chap ahead of me was one very particular gentleman - a man I fear many of you may have forgotten at the time of writing - who had become quite infamous in London; one mister Samuel Lucas. This gentleman, now in his middle age and with a receding line of wild, unkempt hair, with a natural confidence in his voice, was an ideal ally to have in this difficult situation; he represented everything that Hargraves hated.

Mr. Lucas had recently become editor of the **Morning Star**, a pro-peace, abolitionist, and damned near anti-authority newspaper that, at the time, seemed the purest definition of independent press. He was against monopolisation, fiercely opposed the slave trade and tried, in all quarters, to promote equality and peace in all respects - from business, to schooling, to crime and punishment.

I have no doubt that Brunel himself had likely had a few words, himself, for what it stood for; but the newspaper's lack of interest in monetary gain or authority made them flexible to their own means

- and naturally interested in preaching the opposite to the bound and purchased press.

It took no more than a moment to be to decide my answer, and with that, it had begun - my first steps of resistance. The society thought they could smear Brunel? I was surely the only man who could exalt him. And exalt him I did.

I quickly exchanged methods of contact with Lucas; and promised him far greater stories of Brunel to assist with the sale in his papers - provided, of course, he allowed us to maintain our alternative view.

Being such a liberal man, Mr. Lucas was all too happy to agree.

The response to this first eulogy began a scattering of positivity in the wake of the early hostility towards my superior.

It was not long before newspapers up and down the country were discussing the death of Brunel as a great tragedy to Queen and Country, following the trends of the popular press in the hopes of beating each other's distribution. We were, perhaps, one of the first groups to outright manipulate the press - and would be far from the last.

This had two purposes in mine and Mr. Lucas's mind - firstly, it showed our teeth against that great conspiracy's powers of persuasion. It planted the seeds of revolt.

Secondly, I now had the ability to find those willing to be on our side. I knew who to stand with; who to seek and join our resistance. I made it my personal mission to find out who, exactly, had the rebellion required to fight against those bastardising the truth - and figure out what their place was, to this great conspiracy behind all matters of our country's men of iron.

The very first man to come to mind was, of course, the chief engineer of Brunel's railway - Daniel Gooch. The mythical railway town - Swindon, in Wiltshire - was calling. The jewel in the crown of the Great Western Railway.

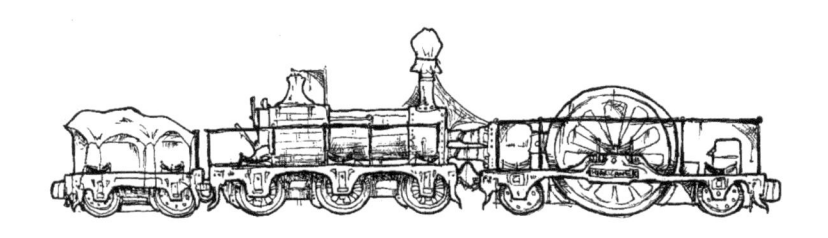

+ THE FIRST MAN OF IRON +

Two days later, I made my trip to Swindon – a town practically designed and built by Brunel, the Great Western Railway, and its chief locomotive engineer; one Daniel Gooch.

Daniel Gooch had been the superintendent of locomotive engines since 1837 – hired at age twenty, if memory serves – and was already established as one of the foremost locomotive designers in the country.

This was not all Gooch could be credited with; the very town of Swindon carried his mark, having been transformed into a thriving, perfectly organised community; what has become known as the Railway Village.

Parallel streets of small, but attractive stone houses, with matching community centres - the enormous Mechanics Institute resembled a grand cathedral - with an indoor market, accommodation, health professionals and a lending library all in its solid stone walls. The church matched the pleasing, stone aesthetic that made such an impact on the locality.

It was often said that the GWR's staff were rapidly becoming the best-educated, most pampered men of industry in the world; a steep level of class that would have put the men who put the Great Eastern's fire into her belly deep in a considerable awe.

Indeed, while the GWR had gained a passionate reputation for its work practises and the treatment it gave its workers, it would be foolish of me to attribute this progression of community to Brunel. Despite his considerable work in the town's design - including those distinctive stone houses - Brunel had come to have little to do with the railway or its operation since handing the reigns to Daniel Gooch.

As a matter of fact, the GWR - for all of its success now being boasted - was largely a work of folly for my master, outside of its infrastructure; he was no locomotive designer and his dishevelled experiments and bizarre flights of fancy had made up much of the railway's stock within its younger years; with limited (*to be generous*) to zero (*to be realistic*) success in many cases.

Gooch had turned the Railway's network, reliability and labour around with impeccable skill; he had committed what he dubbed 'motive standardisation' - this term was often bandied around, but for him it had practically become a catchphrase.

Despite his considerable youth, he had written a controversial - at least, for the recipient - report, which he had handed to Brunel only a few months after his hire. This scathing stack of papers and diagrams highlighted the efficiency, operational and economic failures in Brunel's bizarre and sometimes maddening designs; which had erupted into a fierce argument. The old man's stubborn ways, for a rare moment, failed, and he entrusted Gooch with the design and motive power responsibilities from thereon.

Make no mistake; not only was Gooch an excellent engine builder – he was also a good speaker. A man with the starting ability to stitch even Brunel's cynical words into a creative, fruitful, partnership – and, little did I realise, one of the closest and most durable friendships I had ever encountered.

Little wonder, perhaps, that he was a Draughtsman for Stephenson beforehand.

However, the sprightly young man was no more. It was becoming quite clear that one cannot work in railways without considerable ageing effects. Gooch was now very clearly greying, had grown somewhat stout in the face, and his eyes had clouded. It was also quite clear that he was rocked by Brunel's passing.

A grandfather clock in his Superintendent's office seemed to create an artificial silence. Despite the furore of the works in full steam, the static generator locomotive roaring away, driving nearly a mile of belts to lathes and levers, Gooch's office seemed silent, save for the loud ticking of the clock.

'He was a good man.'

He was adjusting his cuffs as he spoke. This was slightly odd, I felt – not least because his cuffs were already arranged quite beautifully in a draughtsman's arrangement – this being an otherwise peculiar double fold that left more of the wrist exposed, thus reducing the risk of ink spoiled shirts – or shirt spoiled ink – but in that Gooch, for all of the time I had known him, had never been particularly meticulous with his dressing arrangements.

His eyes darted up every so often; on the whole, he seemed particularly uncomfortable to discuss things.

I was the first to try and break this silence.

'I'm surprised to hear such eulogy from a man who met so much of his ire.'
'I suppose you heard more of his opinions towards me than I myself.'
'Frankly, he didn't speak much of you.'

Gooch considered this, and laughed in his deep, cacophonous voice – something trained for conversation in the chaotic noise of the workshops next door.

'A damning appraisal from him!'

I chuckled. There was the Gooch I had often heard alluded to.

'I dare say,' laughed the stout gentleman in his draughtsman's cuffs, 'That the only thing to gauge Brunel's feelings on a man was to hear how often he complained about them. I feel a trifle offended if his opinion was so negative he said nary a word!'

The engineer smiled and stood up, beckoning me along to an inconspicuous door in the far wall of his office.

'Come along, Jacomb. I'll show you the museum.'
'A museum? You've only been working for twenty years and you have a museum?'
'Ah – more of a graveyard really, one supposes. Have you ever seen a Brunel locomotive at close hand?'
'I don't believe I've seen anything beyond his drawings. You don't mean to say you've kept them?'
'Jacomb, for as long as there's a broad gauge railway, I'll keep them. These wood-clad kettles are living proof of Brunel's arrogance. Well worth seeing.'
'You don't speak highly of him.'
'Oh, no, I disagree. I speak of him. By *his* nature, that is speaking highly, isn't it? Why, case in point – how long did he take to speak to you about Hargraves?'
I jolted.

'We'll talk about that later. Now come, come.'

The room he led me to seemed like less of a museum, and would be better described as a large, out of use workshop - the original one of Brunel's construction, he explained. In the soft rays of the sky casting through the windows, stood many oddly proportioned pieces of metal and mahogany; grand pieces of beautiful - yet misguided - industrial, kinetic architecture.

'These are what remains of Brunel's locomotive designs, William. Every one, here, was a pitiful failure.'

He went along the vast room to light the dusty gas lamps along the walls, steadily illuminating the mismatched liveries and occasionally chipped, battered and scraped frames of these once-grand engines.

Many were partially assembled; some in pieces. Some even seemed to be under repair.

Like his office, the room seemed entirely silent compared to the chatter, clattering and industrial cacophony provided by the main workshops. A light breeze softly leaked into the room, catching the odd cobweb that adorned funnels and safety valves.

Gooch's wooden-soled engineer's shoes clattered against the hard, flagstoned floor as he lit the lights, casting shadows of the great beasts against any surface that took them.

'I find it odd.'
'That I saved them?'
'Well, partially.'
'And the other part?'
'Why you say Brunel was a great man, when you were the one who cleared his failures.'
'A locomotive engineer, he was not. A great man, he was. Brunel

would give anything an attempt, William. That is the makings of a great man; it's only a shame that in our business, an attempt is a very, very expensive thing.'

He lit the final lamp; before me stood a stout man in his railwayman's finery - surrounded by the corpses of fifteen engines, dimly lit and covered in layers of dust, cobweb and dirt. He gently stroked the dust from one queer motive, called *Hurricane*, and looked upon its monstrous structure in what seemed like a mix of affection and ridicule. He patted its side; once this engine would have been far too hot to touch. It was now ice cold, as it had been for some time.

'If Brunel was not a great man, he would have never touched the idea of a railway engine. The fact he tried and failed is a greater sign of his character. That determination, his dogged stubbornness - that wish to experiment and discover. No, Brunel's greatest expression was in his failures, Jacomb.'

Hurricane was a very bizarre locomotive; a queer structure of three pieces, creating a strange parade of wheels and pistons. Her front was a flat carriage, with two small axles and an enormous, ten foot pair of driving wheels between. This was connected via flexible pipes to the boiler, funnel and firebox - this was the second 'piece', which, if disconnected from the carriage in front, could be mistaken for an ordinary engine. Behind this was a standard coal tender. At nearly twice the length of any other loco in the shed, she was an eye catching, though confusing, beast. The enormous locomotive was clearly the favourite of its superintendent.

'Can you believe they tried to claim she reached 100mph?'
'Am I to take it she didn't?'
'No. Not a chance. She could barely haul herself.'
'And this was Brunel's idea?'
'No, no, William. Brunel was given the idea, and he agreed to experiment with it. The man who created her advised much of Brunel's flights of fancy with railways; his name was Harrison, if I

remember. Works on the other side of the country, now. This was his magnum opus.'
'And...what is it?'
'The idea was a light axle weight, a slow cylinder speed and a speed record. Not necessarily in that order, I'd wager. Like all of the engines here, she was an engineering folly. She was meant to be an express locomotive. Back then, Jacomb, nobody quite understood what a winning design could be, how it could be constructed.'

Gooch chuckled as he polished the locomotive's nameplate.

'She could go quickly. Very quickly. In theory, at least. I expect she could if her boiler was weightless... not the most appealing idea for an investor.'
'Or the society, I suppose.'
'Yes, Hargraves had his hand in the GWR's pocket. He was the man who insisted on a 'proper engineer' taking on the engines. That happened to be me.'
'Are you a member?'
'Good God, no. I think he wanted me to be.'
'Why didn't you join?'
'I'm a busy man, Jacomb. I can't imagine having the time to travel to London so often. Besides, you've met him. He's odious. He's absolutely insufferable. He's...'
'...Going to win every challenge I try to throw at him.'

For a moment, Gooch's smile slipped.

'You're challenging him?'
'Yes. Challenging the society.'
'You understand, that's going to be quite a challenge for yourself before they even feel it.'
'I understand. But it will become easier...'

Gooch grimaced pre-emptively.

77

'...If people join me in it.'
'I'm sorry, William. But I can't risk it; they could ruin me.'
'If they ruin Brunel, they ruin the Great Western.'
'You and I both know that's nothing but rhetoric. The trains will run, the engines will be maintained and the infrastructure firmly in place. If I join you? Then. Then, they could ruin the Great Western. Sabotage is not below them. Besides, for all we know, they could kill us both. We've got eminence, William, but we're not powerful in the way that Brunel and Stephenson are. We're disposable. To somebody like...them, unless we're a member, we mean nothing. We're as useless as luddites.'

Gooch walked back to his desk, and sat down heavily in his chair, resting his head in one hand, deep in thought.

'I can get you newspaper contacts. I can help you in your cause. But I can't publicly make myself part of it, William. I have thousands of passengers who could lose their safety. There are hundreds of employees in this very town who depend on the railway. It's too big a risk. I cannot afford to create scandal.'

I didn't say anything.

'You must think me a dreadful coward, William.'
'I find it respectable, Daniel. But I do feel you are evading my cause for other reasons.'
'This industry is fledging, William. My primary interest is in not only preserving it, but maintaining and enhancing it. I am an industrialist, but no inventor or revolutionary. Brunel created things. I simply manipulate tools and materials. I'm a mere engine broker. I'm not built for these conspiracies and national arguments.'
'It's not that I do not understand, Daniel.'
'I shall be supporting you, Jacomb. In my own way. And should things change, I shall be sure to inform you. As soon as I know nary a word, I shall present you with every fact. But for now...'

He adjusted one of the locomotive models that sat upon his desk; they had, I presumed, been built by apprentices.

'You may as well leave me to play trains.'

I left Swindon without any ally. I couldn't be angry with Gooch. I empathised with his position, truthfully. But I resented that my mission was a failure thus far.

He gave me a collection of trade cards and contact addresses for members of the press, and organised a ticket card for every mile of the Great Western Railway, ensuring unlimited travel at no expense. It was a generous gesture; something many would have likely never organised. But I had the sinking feeling that Daniel's position may be replicated across the railway industry. Besides which, Brunel had not exactly made many friends in this circle.

I needed to find somebody who worked with rather more independence. For now, our non-existent group was, like *Hurricane*, going nowhere - and with so little clout behind us, I was wondering if might require more people on our side before the truly great minds of Britain would be willing to join us.

I took the train home with my mind embroiled in thought; the beautiful scenery and pounding beat of Gooch's mighty locomotives did little to allay my fears and concerns, to such an extent that I barely registered the carriage's compartment filling with men in matching Savile Row suits. At every large station, another of them entered, silently.

The men all sat perfectly straight, their hands resting upon their briefcases. While their bodies and postures seemed terribly straight and angular, their heads, and all features upon it, were as round and pale as a billiard's cue ball. Their gazes reminded me irresistibly of owls, with distinctive bucked teeth, laughably small pairs of spectacles and pencil moustaches. It would be a humorous image if it were not so utterly bizarre to be faced with men in perfect coordination with each other. They were all utterly indistinguishable within their group – and not a single one raised even the vaguest eyebrow as they strode through station concourse and platform.

By the time we had reached Slough, the compartment was full of these strange men, with only myself breaking the continuous theme of bowler hats, black and white 'uniforms' and unremarkable pin-stripes.

The guard signalled, and the train slowly heaved out of the platform. By the time it had reached the open country, the gentlemen decided to speak.

'Mister Jacomb?' The first one asked.
'You clearly know who I am, or you wouldn't have each checked every compartment beforehand.' I countered. I was met by a pause.
'We were - ahum - looking for spare seats.'

If nothing else, these were less imposing foes than the likes of Hargraves and the weasely doctor.

'How can I help you, gentlemen?'
'We come from a rather eminent society of engineers. You have met our superior, we presume?'
'Am I correct to believe you are associates of Hargraves?'
'Indeed. He would like to once again, formally, present an opportunity for you to become a member of our little club.'

One of them snorted in a quick jump of laughter. The others followed suit, which did nothing to make them seem any less bizarre a set of eccentrics. Why had nobody noticed this bewildering group of people? It seemed beggar's belief.

'As a matter of fact, mister - ahum - Jacomb, he wishes to enhance his offer.'

The one sat directly across from me opened his briefcase, with his eyebrows raised - corrugating his perfectly smooth forehead. He handed me a familiar looking envelope, perfectly waxed sealed and extravagantly signed.

   'We're sure you'll find it *most* appealing.'

They waited for me to open the mystery envelope; seemingly as eager as a child at Christmas to see what was inside. I was significantly less excited about opening it. So I didn't; I simply slipped it into my jacket.

Two of the strange men looked at each other and raised an eyebrow.

Silenced filled the compartment, as it clattered its way towards London. I kept my glance fixed firmly towards the window, and the shadow of the train as it rumbled across the Western Line's countryside, snaking along hills with the silhouette of smoke trailing above.

Finally, I couldn't hold my curiosity longer - it was time to try speaking to these men on my own terms.

   'What exactly is your position to the society, gentlemen?'

The strange, owl-faced men perked somewhat.

   'We serve many purposes, Sir.'
   'You could say we are the backbone of the society.'
   'We're very much the men who get things done, don't you know.'
   'We send and fetch correspondence, far faster than the mail, you understand, and introduce the society to those without the luck of making Hargraves' personal introduction.'
   I smirked. 'You're responsible for making things more professional looking than that great brute, eh?'

The man across from me adjusted his collar.

> 'We are known for being somewhat more approachable.'
> 'But we take umbrage at him being called a brute.'
> 'He's a professional man; true, he may lack the form of business, but he certainly makes up for it in shrewd wit.'
> 'And profit.' Put in the one at the farthest end of the compartment. 'Not to mention his political power.'

I rolled my eyes, making no effort to hide my decreasing patience. This clearly offended them, as they all exchanged glances with furrowed brows and a twitch of their nose, rocking their tiny pairs of eyeglasses somewhat. The owl's feathers were ruffled.

> 'And I suppose you're all after those diagrams, eh?'

They each laid their hands on their briefcases.

> 'Brunel's draughtsman volume is of great interest to us, yes.'
> 'We will repay you handsomely, Sir. You'll see when you read the letter.'
> 'We'll no doubt see you soon. It's rare that anybody says no to an offer from the society.'
> 'Certainly; no true learned individual would ever turn down our opportunities.'
> 'And if they do, their careers certainly don't attract much longevity.'

I still found myself paying very little attention. I was growing increasingly cynical to these gentlemen, who irresistibly reminded me of street traders trying to sell good luck charms or cat's meat. Better dressed, perhaps, but their careers seemed no more dignified. It was only with their final line that my ire was drawn.

> 'Let alone their home circumstances.'
> 'Just what,' I bristled as I spoke; and ended my sentence with a rather harsh snap. 'Is *that* to imply?'

The man across from me was taken aback slightly, but maintained his smug persona.

> 'Well, Sir, such a rare, valuable object, being left at home...'
> 'How long can it possibly stay there without proper insurance?'
> 'You realise that it's your responsibility, as Brunel's assistant, to bring it to us.'
> 'And Stephenson's doctor did see it in your hands.'
> 'It's only right for you to give it to its rightful owners.'
> 'After all, it's not the only valuable object in your life. There are some precious objects you're far more..acquainted with.'
> I glared. 'Are you referring to my fiancée?'

The train jolted to a halt, just as I was close to raising my fist. We had reached West Drayton, and, with broad, buck-toothed grins, every one of the gentlemen left the compartment.

> 'We've had enough of your time, Mister Jacomb. Do make sure you consider that offer. If not, why, I expect that book will be leaving your home before the end of the month; don't you agree, gentlemen?'
> 'Oh yes. *Far* too many scurrilous men in London. Far too many opportunities for theft.'
> '*Far* too many ways in which a lady left at home could be injured...' said the final man to make his way through the carriage door.

I snapped.

Thump!

As he stepped from the carriage, I struck him hard to the back of the neck. He fell from the carriage, flat onto the platform with a clatter - his briefcase burst open. The people on the platform gasped, each stepping backwards as papers flew across the platform's surface.

The man climbed back to his feet, and turned to face me. His distinctive, sharp tipped nose was bleeding, and his face studded with small stones from the platform's surface. He sneered.

> 'This man;' he loudly proclaimed 'Just attacked me!'
> 'I did no such thing!' I spat. 'He just threatened my fiancée!'

He span to the other gentlemen.

> 'Did you hear me threaten his wife to be, gentlemen?'
> 'Certainly not.'
> 'Never.'
> 'You're the finest in chivalry; you'd do no such thing.'
> 'This man is clearly dangerous.'

The other people on the platform looked up at me fearfully. I backed into my compartment as they shouted for the police; but perhaps to my blessing, no constabulary arrived.

Instead, a familiar, enormous shadowy figure lumbered onto the platform. It was none other than 'The Keeper' himself. Hargraves stood, chewing on some tobacco with his mouth characteristically open. His speech was polished, formal and even polite - although his suit was still in a terrible shape, his hygiene still lacking, and his breathing laboured.

He raised his arms to attract attention - straining the white stitched holding the sleeves together within breaking point. With his size and manner, he quickly attracted the attention of the crowd that was forming in front of the train.

> 'Ladies and gentlemen, these men are within my employ, and I'm ashamed to say are very heavily inebriated. They no doubt said something insidious to my friend in the carriage. Pay them no heed; I shall see that their wages are docked.'

All of the men fell silent, and Hargraves instructed each into the stagecoaches parked outside the station building. He gave a large grin towards my direction, wiped his greasy brow, and left the platform.

The station was silent. Ladies gave side glances towards me; gentlemen shook their heads in disbelief. The station staff, naturally, recognised me, and looked away, trying to hide their shock.

The few moments that followed felt like hours until, at last, the train left once again. Adrenaline was coursing through my veins and my knuckles were sore from the impact. I was in no regular habit of striking a man, and I felt a mixture of exasperation, shame and excitement from the altercation.

Worse, however, I had lost my posture. I had shown how to evoke ire; displayed my weaknesses to Hargraves and his society. I was beginning to wonder if the entire situation had been planned.

I feared for Eliza; and worried for my career and reputation; not to mention, the safety of my home.

I found myself looking constantly over my shoulder as I walked to my next connection from Paddington station. I expected to see Hargraves following at close quarters. Men in bowler hats skulking around corners and alleyways. Instead, I was met only by London's thick, soot addled mist.

I sank, that night, into a restless, tumultuous sleep - drowning in my own thoughts and considerations.

It would be a better day tomorrow, I reasoned.

+ THE OFFER & FINAL FAREWELL +

Dear William.
After discussion with my colleagues, I would like to, once again, offer you a place in our most prestigious society, and a reward for the return of Brunel's draughtsman's volume - something of great financial importance to us.

With no further questions asked, we will happily accept the volume and your membership with the reward of an annual grant and, as a debt of gratitude, would happily pay the cost of your upcoming wedding plans - provided, of course, the society may be present as guests.

I eagerly await your response.
Yours sincerely;
Hargraves.
Head of the Society of Exceptional London Engineers & Individuals
Scientia Est Imperium.
Ignorantia Est Fragilitas.
Fortitudo Est In Silentio.

I quietly drank my tea as Eliza read aloud. I felt exhausted and had not been happy to find her curiosity diving into the letter.

I was to be even less happy at her response.

'I think you should take his offer, William. We could finally be married! You could advance your career - be just as eminent as Brunel himself. Think of the money you could make!'

I held my face in my hands. This was no call of charity from the society. Any act of charity from that man seemed to be sat purely in the realms of the impossible.

No, this was no good willed helping hand. It was a cynical move to demand my wife's involvement in this situation. An insipid letter for insidious purpose, with plotting and ploy dotted over every i and at the end of each sentence. Anybody who knew Hargraves would surely feel nausea from a momentary glance of such a letter.

I found myself glaring at the fine, silk paper in Eliza's hands - until she spoke up once again.

'William?'
'I'm sorry, darling. I can't.'
'You can't, or you won't?'
'I can't. You don't know who these people are.'
'I know what they're offering you, William. And it's everything you want.'
'It is.'
'Then why say no? Why throw it all back?'

I didn't reply. Eliza continued, however.

'Rich men, paying for your expertise? Don't be a fool, William! We could be married before the end of the year! We could

honeymoon in Egypt!'
'I can't, Eliza. You cannot question it; you simply have to recognise it. I cannot allow myself to get tangled up in that snake's nest.'
'I think you're a damned fool.'
'I think you should *hold your tongue* if you don't know what you're referring to!'

I pounded the desk and raised my voice, and immediately shrunk back upon the realisation of what I had just done.

For the first time, I had shouted at Eliza. No mere snap or growl, but a bark of authority and demand.

Instant regret hit me, and I stood to apologise to her the moment clarity hit me – only to hear the door to my office slammed shut behind her.

The rest of the morning was a dull, silent one in the home as she tried to avoid speaking to me except where necessary. I burnt the letter that very same evening, and later recounted to Mr. Lucas of *The Star* at the Dog and Fox pub, close to my home in Wimbledon.

> 'A difficult situation indeed.' He spoke through teeth gripping on his cheap, battered cob pipe. 'But seems quite characteristic of emotional games. He knows what shall happen; your lady will support them more than your views; as she values marriage so heavily.'
> 'You wouldn't have believed it, Samuel. The things that have happened so quickly. It's been unbelievable. I may as well check myself into Bedlam before it forces me there.'

Samuel smiled.

> 'You've given no further thought to Stephenson's advice?'
> 'To join them? Certainly not.'
> 'I fear that's the only way you can guarantee safety. There has to

be some form of rebellious sect in that group. If there are learned individuals there, there will be independent thinkers. Nothing is more probable.'

I rubbed my temples. Samuel puffed on his pipe and watched me analytically.

'Your financial situation. How is it?'
'I'm in decent stead from the Eastern.'
'Decent enough to maintain a career without society backing?'
'Yes.'
'But your marriage, then?'
'That is, regrettably, on the side lines.'

Samuel looked up at the oak frames of the old inn thoughtfully, still puff-puffing away at his leaky cob pipe.

'There are a lot of things that are easier with a support network, you know. A roof is nothing without its beams.'
'And I fear I shall be nothing without my principles.'
'Maintain your principles; and you may lose your most important pillar. By which, I mean your fiancée. The fact of the matter is that, while you are a member of the society, you will be safer than when you are not. A sickening truth, perhaps, but an essential one.'
'And I dare say the more headlines you'll get, ey?'

Samuel smirked.

'I'd be lying if I said this was not a mutually beneficial partnership, William. The Star is not in positive financial straits. But my beliefs are quite sincere.'
'How many copies of the Brunel issue did you sell, exactly?'
'Some thirty thousand. Not an immense amount by the wider press. But it serves both of us.'

'That seems like a very minor portion of London, Samuel.'
'It is. As a matter of fact, the Star only just broke even...'
'And you believe it shall have an impact?'
'I know it shall.'

He sat his feet up on a chair sat across from him.

'The smallest group of people can make the biggest impact, William. Dissent grows. It spreads - and I have no doubt that within time, Brunel shall be more celebrated than the rest of the society put together. And it shan't end there.'
He grinned. 'If a single five foot man in a top hat can convince men to invest in a seven hundred foot ship, I'm quite sure we can convince people to invest in his legacy.'
'Remarkably confident for a man with no politics.'
'...And you're remarkably reluctant for a man with such an impressive opportunity.'

I sat back slightly in my chair.

'Is nobody supportive of my decision? Stephenson, Eliza, now you...'
'Brunel might have been. But he was the definition of an independent thinker, ey?'
'He was that.'
'I did some digging, you know. Russell is a member, too.'

I pounded the table with my fist and sighed.

'Bloody brilliant. Marvellous. All I need! Would it be a quicker process for you to tell me who isn't a member?!'
'Probably. It's not an easy thing to uncover, but there must be thousands of people in Hargraves' little group. It's a messy series of false companies, investors, identities...'
'All going back to a bloody book.'
'The...'Tome'; that is a curious one, I admit. Seems very unrealistic to me. Some sort of ancient book with plans of the future? No, I

don't think so. Stephenson must have been mistaken. It must be a metaphor, an allegory...'
'The man with no politics is taking a sensible approach?'
'The engineer and scholar is taking a nonsensical one?'

I laughed and took another swig of my beer. My smile quickly faded away as I went back to thinking.

'In any sense, Samuel, I shan't find out, I suppose.'
'No, not without joining.'
'And I suppose I shan't be getting married, either.'
'Or much in the way of work opportunities.'
'...Or connections...'
'Perhaps, Jacomb, if you are so resolute, you should look into starting your own firm, and quietly study these things on the side, eh?'
'You might be right.'
'If nothing else, you have the Brunel pedigree. It must be worth something.'
'Bankruptcy. It's most certainly worth that.'
He tapped his pipe against the table and chuckled.
'Well, of course, if you decide to do so, we'll provide advertising. As little as it may help.'
'I appreciate it.'
'Again; it's mutually beneficial, William. And I do feel that I am on the correct side of the moral fabric in this situation.'

The discussion continued for the evening. Thinking of possibilities; considering the next move of the society and how best to approach this new strategy. But the vague sense of danger I felt in the pit of my stomach remained. It took a lot of careful consideration, but from that conversation at a little coaching inn near Wimbledon common, I had made the decision to start my own consultancy.

The letters from Hargraves did not cease. Week after week, further correspondence swamped the home, and week after week, Eliza seemed to grow only more agitated by my lack of response to these grand offers of marriage and fortune.

I could sense the increasing urgency to Hargraves' communication. I could sense his malcontent, and his shortening patience – what little of it he already had. And it seemed only natural to move Brunel's draughtsman volume away from our home and to a safer location.

The book was moved to the deposit boxes of my local branch of the a Union bank; and there it would stay until I had sought a solution to release the society's grip on my person.

It was on the 20th of April that the city of London lined its streets for a final farewell to the little man who had built the most impressive machines, bridges and rails of his day - and did so with vigour. Thousands, armed with flags and hats, toasted the engineer whom had built so much of Britain's industrial enterprise.

Brunel was carried in a fine wooden coffin, with gold ornaments and handles, with his family – avoiding my gaze – behind in their black wooden carriage. I had been invited by the creditors to have a presence in the funeral procession; but had decided, at Eliza's behest, to avoid it.

Hargraves was clear to see in his rather laboured, battered society carriage, only a few vehicles behind the family. He briefly shot me a look - but one supposes that, even for a man so unscrupulous, he recognised the bad practise in confronting me at such an event.

Instead, I got to see the many hundreds of London's working men and women standing in mourning at the loss of one of the country's most esteemed engineers. To see the poor and rich rubbing shoulders in mourning was a remarkable thing. To hear of the ordinary men who kept the trains running all stopping to celebrate his life - to hear of a member of the elite so respected. It was an almost otherwordly situation.

Many spoke of being present at the Great Eastern's launch. Many spoke against John Scott Russell, and some mentioned how much of a shame it was that the ship had been such a difficult project for Brunel - how regrettable it was to see such an impressive vessel fall subject to misfortune - a harsh contrast to those who mocked and derided her failure in the past.

Creditors wiped a tear from their eye; friends and relations said nothing, quietly ashen faced at the loss of their peer and loved one. The public saw the loss of an iconic figure; one who they felt had truly changed the world. A member of the elite whom got his hands dirty; whom faced the brunt of difficulty with vigour. It was a rare thing to see as wealthy man so well respected due to his work ethic.

Brunel's assistants, and contractors - the staff with whom I had so often worked with - were all present in Sunday best, quiet and solemn. There were many familiar faces - but no Scott Russell, no investors and no bankers.

This was a new perspective to the often criticised and commonly mislabelled Napoleon of the engineering world. It was the perspective he had deserved, and some of the crowd - including myself - followed to the rather humble and unpleasantly harsh Brunel family monument in Kensal Green Cemetery.

Throughout Duke Street, much the same as its neighbouring areas, shopkeepers and restaurants around the area closed their businesses to show respect over the loss of the little man who had built so much of Southern England to glory. The metropolitan area had closed to pay their regards to the working man's idol.

While many monuments in Kensal Green were impressive, ornate or detailed carvings for those interred there, the deep family grave of Marc Isambard and his wife - Brunel's parents - consisted of no more than a white marble block and kerbstones. My master had firmly instructed that he wished to be buried with his parents, and, while the grave was of no grand or attractive construction, it was fitting that the Brunel family should get the opportunity to remain so close even in death; their working relationships had been every bit as intimate as their father and son dynamic.

The crowd around the grave held their umbrellas tightly as the rain fell, met with pure, reverent silence as the last rites were held. The skies were darkening, and with it, the atmosphere of our great city.

One could almost swear that, without Brunel's presence, London was darkening and slowing. The march of progress becoming a slow, ambling hobble.

There was something remarkably odd and unworldly about the funeral and the world that surrounded it. Perhaps I was simply disassociating with the facts at hand - perhaps I had grown paranoid and fearful, painting grandiose visages in place of the dour, bleak reality.

I looked up - and was brought back to reality by a small reassurance.

Mary glanced towards my person, and offered a faint, kind smile. I only presumed it was due to me keeping my word of staying a safe distance from the family. I wondered briefly if they were aware of my work to clear Isambard's name. Whatever the case, my chest swelled with pride over that brief bit of recognition from his widow in even the most depressing, sensitive moment.

I remained throughout for the ceremony, and noted with interest - and relief - that Hargraves, indeed, none of the society members I had met, or were aware of, were present on the lowering of the coffin. Presumably they had already retired to some overpriced bar somewhere for Absinthe and cigars.

The coffin was lowered slowly into the deep grave, laid atop of his mother and father. The sky rumbled, the rain becoming a downpour - and, as we all began to leave - sodden, miserable and deep in mourning, I had many mixed feelings on the finality now presented to me.

Yes, my master was now truly no longer of this earth – but in contrast, I had grown aware that his legacy – no matter of how the society attempted to tarnish it – was safe, sealed and thoroughly secure.

I slept, for the first time, rather soundly that evening. Despite my sadness, I had received my first sense of reassurance. My next steps were to move into my own business, and try to work independently for the first time.

The days of the Jacomb Consultancy found their infancy.

+ THE CLUB +

By the 1st of October, my consultancy firm had opened in Westminster - and I found myself immediately met with an influx of work from parliamentary concerns who wished to carry the knowledge and interest of Brunel's teachings upon their projects and infrastructure.

While Brunel's business interests may have largely resulted in bankruptcy and insolvency, his teachings and his knowledge remained well respected and in firm demand.

While it would be exaggerating to say I made a high income, a steady influx of success began to ebb into the Jacomb Consultancy, and, stemming Eliza's own concerns and upset, we began to raise money - developing savings for our marriage and our first firm set of plans.

For at least a while, the society and the Great Conspiracy, as a whole, left my mind, and Brunel's falsified drawings remained safe in a safety deposit box, under a false name.

Eliza pointed out how strange it was to hide a purposefully useless book from the society; how futile it seemed to be when it would give them no useful practise.

She had become more than aware of the letters flooding in every day, all characteristically polite but deferring into more and more urgent choices of language. By now, there was some three pieces of correspondence a week, all of which I had taken to keeping in the top drawer of my work desk.

She was not unknown to prove her strength and mind, and in this situation had every intention of trying to guide me to what, she believed, was a more sensible path.

> 'It seems you're only keeping this from them out of arrogance.'
> 'Far from it, Eliza. It's my bargaining tool.'
> 'And it's dangerous. If they spend so long trying to get their hands on it, only to find it useless, they may well try to get their revenge.'
> 'For all they know, I'm completely oblivious to its true nature. They may be a large group, but they aren't able to monitor us constantly, you know. Small mercy as it may be, I still have my privacy. And, most importantly, I still have you.'

Eliza embraced me, head pressed close against my chest.

> 'I'm scared, William. I don't like this situation one bit. If Brunel was here I'd tell him exactly how I feel about it.'
> 'Brunel did not decide for me to confront them. This is a situation of my own creation, Eliza. If there is one person to blame, do not blame the dead man. Blame the one who is working deeper into it.'
> 'Very well. But I have told you exactly how I feel about it; and yet you ignore me.'
> 'Eliza. You are the most important, most valuable and most essential part of my life. Don't you ever forget that. But this; this is a situation grander than any of us. It's something that affects everybody in London, and beyond. It's my moral duty to see it

through.'

She smiled, meekly, and looked up to me.

> 'You engineers are obsessed with completion. It's a damned shame. But if it is truly so important, I shall remain by your side. Provided you guarantee our wedding.'
> 'I swear on it.'

Her smile warmed, her embrace tightened. And, once again, for only a fleeting moment, I forgot my worries and the tumultuous activity surrounding our lives.
It was a strange experience, returning to work, and I found myself unwittingly following the regime I had grown used to whilst under Brunel's charge.

I woke at 5AM, left the townhouse at 6AM, and took the coach to inner London. On the way, I'd pick up the paper, a package of his favourite cigars - which I would now immediately return upon the realisation that Brunel was not there to smoke them - and would enter the office promptly by 7:30AM. By this time, he was usually sat at his desk, poring over his letters, notes and own works of writing, producing clouds of tobacco exhaust.

Instead, the desk was mine and I'd do much the same in his place. The work of a consultant was one of intensive paperwork and filing - much less the sort of pioneering drawings Brunel was so esteemed for - and many hours would be spent quite deep in the office, archiving and sending messages with frightening levels of paper and parchment.

I had also given Brunel's more sarcastic teachings much thought, and used many of his rather fiendish tactics to make myself known.

The consultancy's proximity to Westminster was a carefully planned aspect. Many engineers planted their roots in this area of London, for it permitted a friendship - and preference - among government ministers, should a chance meeting take place at one of London's bars. I charged lower rates; met personally with little bureaucracy or red tape. There were no wide eyed, round-headed men in pinstripes and bowlers – only myself and a few office staff. In this sense, we were bound for more popularity than the society's awkward communication and arrogant owner – not to mention their monopolist pricing.

Brunel had always taught me how to spot a man of parliament. They were nearly always portly, walked a certain way, and dressed with certain knots in their ties and cravats.

They always wore dark colours; always spoke properly, and many seemed to be permanently miserable, despite sitting atop the empire's wealth and power.

Brunel insisted this was to keep up appearances to the peasantry; to this day, I'm unsure if this was a joke or serious accusation.

His advice, for all of the satire it may have intended, was positive. Within only a week, word had spread, and I had become a popular engineering consultant for the rapidly burgeoning country's infrastructure.

To what I could only presume was Hargraves' fury, my convenient location (*and far more positive company*) was making me a regular choice for informing parliamentary decisions. Things were looking up; and by October the tenth, I had already been invited to the Athenaeum Club; a place for which Brunel had previously had membership.

The Athenaeum Club was an odd place; a luxurious gentleman's club in the finest décor, and a beautiful building which sat distinctively on the Pall Mall street in its cubical shape with pillars and ornate stonework. There, learned gentlemen in the literate, scientific, medical and artistic fields rubbed shoulders with a mutual respect.

I was most certainly one of the younger members within the building's walls when I first entered that evening. The world of engineering was not well represented in the club - the two main members to the London locality in this field were Brunel and Stephenson; the latter of which was still bedridden and showing no signs of improvement.

Brunel's portrait was already hung upon the wall dedicated to those who had passed, and I was given a warm welcome by many of the city's great socialites. Imagine my surprise when many of them began discussing Hargraves - and the society itself.

The first I heard on the matter was from a man whose name I never particularly learnt. He was elderly, pink faced and husky, with an expression that looked remarkably like that of a bulldog. He spoke gruffly, with a slight slur and a deep tone. He sat back far in his chair - I figured that this chair was the only one he sat in, as it seemed practically moulded to his shape. The aged, harsh - but dignified figure was clearly a higher member of the club, and barely looked up as he spoke; almost constantly fiddling with wooden dominoes.

> 'Did you hear he'd started a smear campaign? Against Brunel, of all people? Bloody fool. That Hargraves will do anything to bastardise the gentlemen of industry. The sooner that fat, bally brute meets his maker, the better, I'd say.'

A murmur of agreement filled the bright room as men pored over their books and whisky.

> 'Quite right.' Spoke up Dickens; one of the leading authors in the gentlemen's club; and one who often found at least some opinion on every matter that struck him.
> 'I may not be an expert in engineering, but I know a work of art when I see one. Brunel's designs were exactly that. A sorry state of affairs it is, that Hargrave's little internal politics should rule over Brunel's legacy!'

'The fact is,' another man pointed out over a pinch of snuff, 'I don't think many of us could imagine pushing a seven hundred foot vessel into the Thames, let alone make it sail. I dare say most in Hargrave's squalid little gathering couldn't do it.'

'Not to mention;' Dickens put in, 'Those Crimean hospitals of his. How many hundreds of lives has Brunel saved compared to those few lost on his projects? The amount of soldiers that owe their lives to his hospitals! His work practically makes him a humanitarian.'

The snuff taker nodded sincerely. 'Without a doubt. Intemperate, perhaps, but Brunel was of great importance to that society. If Stephenson passes, who else does Hargraves, really, have to his name? They're all hangers on.'

'How is Stephenson? Does anybody know?' asked one of the younger members, who, I'd wager, was still a good fifteen years my senior.

The husky, pink faced gentleman shook his head as he chapped his dominoes against the lustre of the mahogany table.

'I don't think we'll find out until the funeral. You know how he is. He'd only come once a month when he was healthy. Rest assured though, there'll be disarray. I dare say Hargraves will do anything to improve his bloody membership the moment Stephenson is underground.'

Another murmur of agreement.

'In fact, if I were you, gentlemen, I'd not be surprised if there were a sudden spate of mishaps; part of his bloody security racket. We all know he can do it. We all know he probably will.'

He took a long, rattling breath, exhaled and looked at me with his harsh gaze.

'You'll be the target, William.'

I raised an eyebrow. 'Why me?'
'Please, don't treat us like fools. Of course he's offered you a place. The fact you're here proves you didn't take it. Do you intend to travel by train in the next few weeks?'
'No. I have too much business in London.'
The old man nodded. 'Good. Keep it that way.'
'For how long?'
'Until you feel they've lost interest. Or until, most importantly, you feel secure. Hargraves is a brute; he'll use deadly force to coerce you into joining him.'

Mr. Tyndall, an eminent surveyor, sat nearby in his typically flamboyant, prim posture - one that matched his growing, sophisticated interests in science and physics - but in direct conflict to his recent daring expedition to the Alps. He was a naturally curious, outspoken man of slight built but enormous charisma, with a naturally long face that seemed permanently lazy and distracted; this gave the impression he wasn't listening. His quick chime-in was proof otherwise.

'Let's face it, gentlemen; he uses deadly force in every endeavour. We're lucky there are no politicians here this evening, or we'd all be done for.'
I couldn't resist prying further. 'I thought that this club had no political bias?'
'Politics, no.' the old man placed a domino on the table.
'Politicians, yes. We may have no bias here, but money talks, William, my lad. As does scandal. Hargraves has much on the politicians inside this club and out. It could be anybody from the commons' office boy to Lord Palmerston himself; you aren't safe if the government are involved. Or listening.'

He started chapping his dominoes again; this time out of frustration. He almost seemed to be audibly growling.

'I wish I could give the bastard a piece of my mind. If only it made any difference. The only way to affect Hargraves is by hitting him

where it hurts.'
Tyndall joined in the growing chorus of discontent. 'Quite right. But if his only other great engineer is dying, who else is of substantial enough credit to hold a real defence? We can't expect all of his members to up and leave so suddenly, can we?'

All eyes fell on me.

'So.' The old man said, looking up at me once again with his piercing, hawk like eyes. 'What's your plan, Jacomb?'
'Why do you feel I must have a plan?'
'Of course you do. Your engineering sorts always do. What reason do you have for denying membership? What is it Brunel has told you? And more to the point, do you need our help?'

I rubbed my chin as I considered my answer.

'I'm not really sure how much I should tell you all, gentlemen. Let it only be known that Hargraves is more powerful than he may appear to you. He's got far more than politicians backing his little group.'
The pink faced bulldog groaned. 'You know how to lighten a situation, William. How? He's already a rich man with engineers in his pocket. What makes him more powerful than that?'

I was rubbing my chin again. I had to approach this strategically.

'Those engineers have the next forty years of progress mapped out with him. He's in charge of the lot. He's at the centre of every major construction project, and every major civil engineering project. Right up to the next century.'
'Sounds sinister.'
'Sounds like a bloody disaster.'
'Sounds like he's going to become the wealthiest idiot in the empire, to me.'
'This arse of a man.' Spoke the Bulldog - who I was beginning to

realise had a particularly harsh vocabulary, even for what I had grown used to in shipyards and construction sites. I figured he had to be an engineer or a sailor, himself. 'Is trying to build a monopoly on the Kingdom's very infrastructure. Before you'll know it he'll be trying to force the railways into one. He'll start selling firearms. I wouldn't even put it past him to start trying to manipulate trade.'

I sat down - for the first time in this conversation - and thought intently.

> 'We need promotion to the cause. We need to spread the word without him noticing.'
> 'Quite. The moment he realises you're responsible, he'll double down on trying to intimidate you. I can't make it clear enough, William - you cannot, under any circumstance, travel. You need to keep yourself undercover as much as humanly possible. You'll have already ruffled feathers with your consultancy taking so much of Hargraves' business.'

The other men murmured.

> 'We do not have many engineers amongst us, William - but we have scientists, writers and architects. We have philosophers and we have statesmen. All of us will work to help you. We may not be 'men of iron', but we do have voices, and if dissent is what you need, dissent is what we'll provide.'
> 'It's a fine start. But you realise that's not nearly enough.'
> 'Of course it isn't. But you have to be patient, William. Play the slow game. It takes time to really gather resources and people against something that's had its claws dug in for so long.'

I scratched my head as I listened intently. The more I considered, the more I was excited at the prospect of having some of the country's leading citizens behind our resistance.

'Brunel was an arrogant, pig-headed, intemperate man. But he was our friend. An Athenaeum. And, more's to the point, a man of the empire.
It's our national duty to protect society; we've spent our lives trying to enrich, educate and improve it. Our ultimate priority is in seeing the world around us improve, profit our fellow man and educate him.'

A pause followed – and an extremely slight, wry smile upon the bulldog's face.

'And the rest of us are bloody politicians.'

+ ANOTHER FAREWELL +

Stephenson died on the twelfth of October; and his death's timing so close to Brunel's did not go unnoticed by me, the club, nor Mr. Lucas.

The clubhouse was silent on the day of the report; save for the clink of glasses, or the inhaling of snuff. Occasionally men would rustle their newspapers.

> The Bulldog coughed as he spoke up. 'Rumour has it the Queen wants Stephenson's coffin to march through London.'

> 'It's a fitting honour.'
> 'I Can't imagine how furious Hargraves will be.'
> 'I wouldn't be surprised if he was behind it.'

Silence. Except for dominoes.
Tack. Tack. Tack.

The bulldog chapped his dominoes on the table as the fireplace - for the evenings were growing cooler now by the day - crackled in the middle of the room's eastern wall. The warm atmosphere felt familiar, and homely to me now - so you can only imagine the contrast with the cloud of dread and despair now hanging over every member's head.

I returned home from the club house that evening to Eliza's opened arms, and embraced her. Stephenson was a man who had endeared himself to me since our meeting, and his regular correspondence - in now characteristically shaky, uncertain handwriting, sat alongside my desk, often congratulating me on my progress and telling me quite how proud Brunel would had been.

He had been very complimentary towards the club and their advice, too - and had stood behind it at every avenue, though echoing their warnings of avoiding becoming too close to the Hornet's nest.

Now, he - one of the last, one supposes, truly sage like engineers I knew was gone. And the fight for Brunel's name was now one with one less ally; one less 'man of iron'.

The empire had no plans to allow the Industrial Age's favourite son to pass to the next plain without a great deal of commemoration.

The funeral was an incredible proceeding. More like a procession or festival than that of a Funeral as thousands paid their respects. The entire country mourned his passing, and I had received word that even Newcastle, Stephenson's city of birth, had closed to a standstill out of respect for their most successful child.

Locomotives, ships and factory boilers hooted their respects as the coffin was led down the streets of London, with fourteen mourner's carriages, including one dedicated to the unmistakable silhouette of Hargraves, rattling behind. Trains would stop on bridges over the procession to hoot and cheer, and the canal basins of The Thames had all ceased work to join the chorus. My, what an atmosphere it was.

Stephenson was interred inside Westminster abbey; fairly close to Brunel's home, and was done so in the manner of a public rather than private affair, with the Lord Mayor of London present in his full stately attire. You would be excused for believing it to be in celebration of a world leader.

He had been memorialised with a large, dark grey marble floor slab; with a stunningly detailed brass accented border, and portrait of him laid in state upon it. By all regards, it was a handsome memorial. Some even claimed it fitting of a royal further than that of an engineer; and to see - as many put it - a 'working lad from Newcastle' buried at Westminster caused a swelling of pride amongst the working class populous.

I feel rather detestable in that my first emotions relating to the funeral procession were ones of jealousy. I suppose it's testament to he and Brunel's own conflicts; the popular man had, in essence, overshadowed the death of the true innovator and daring leader. The financier's gentleman had overtaken one of science, tact and - most of all - constant experimentation.

I spent a few days out of office to consider my thoughts; to ponder my worries and concerns, and spend time with Eliza.

Throughout this time, I found myself regularly meeting Mr. Lucas, and discussing my feelings with him; we soon became excellent friends, as did many members of the Anthenaeum's club - though I made sure to not immediately link our affairs, feeling the pro-peace statements in the Star would link too unevenly with the factuality of a heavily capitalised club culture.

However, I could no longer shake my feelings of unhappiness and distress as the Tome continued to haunt my mind. It was, as far as I knew, only a subject known to myself, Stephenson, and Mr. Lucas -

that, of course, and Hargrave's cronies.

Eliza remained largely oblivious to my developing distrust of the world or my rather incendiary tactics. She only enjoyed the growing levels of company and friendship we found ourselves within, and watching our savings grow nicely to pay for our future wedding.

She was, however, still very much aware of my worries. She was far too intelligent to ignore the emotions of her fiancée – but knew that the life of an engineer was a difficult one, and spent no time trying to add to the stress and concerns.

My feelings were fairly clear to me. I had always been encouraged by Brunel to shoot directly for the target I wished to achieve, and attempt to do so in the most bombastic, creative manner I may. I had not only failed to keep this advice, but found myself doing quite the opposite.

Of course, Brunel's impatience, in many ways, had rubbed off upon me. In less than three weeks since his passing I had, in retrospect, achieved a great deal of things, tasks and duties. But they all felt very minor, hopeless and unproductive in the face of the task that now dominated my waking moments.

To make matters worse, my thoughts kept returning to this dreaded book that had become the centre of my worries and concerns.

If this Eternal Tome did exist – and all information given seemed to allude to the factual nature of what I had been told – then it can only be concluded that the entire of the engineering progression of the empire was not only fraudulent – but, more importantly, a fabricated, false creation. By virtue, my master – the man who had been the most esteemed engineer of his day – was a fraud. His fame was a falsehood. My education under him was a falsehood.

The very idea was boggling, yet only worsening as it ran through my head.

I took the Athenaeums' advice very seriously. For the next two months, there was no railway travel. I remained at work in my office; quietly travelling by an unremarkable horse and cart, hired under false names, and making no whispers that could be directly attributed to me.

The club's membership, too, with their obvious interest in the matter, worked wonders. Reports in engineering monthlies, articles with suspicious flair that matched leading authors, unusual statements alluding to the failures of less savoury engineering communities - one report mentioning Absinthe addiction even cropped up in a scientific journal.

These fighting tactics were fitting to the work of Hargraves, a natural pushing force against his own quiet, dirty tactics - and underneath them, the Jacomb consultancy steadily developed and led itself into great success.

One of the few things that constantly raised a grin in me, during these times, was the thought of Hargraves reading periodicals and gnashing his teeth, or going into furious rages as his reputation - and that of his society - began to decline. I was comfortable in the knowledge that, eventually, he would have no choice but to beg for my membership. Then, my true duties and promises to Brunel could finally be fulfilled - and I could seek the true decimation of the terrible man, his unsavoury cronies - and, most importantly, achieve justice for Brunel and topple the unnatural forces that seemed to be ruling the empire.

   'Still concerned about the book, eh?' Mr. Lucas spoke up as he chewed on the stem of his cob pipe.

I snapped back to reality, and my pint of bitter.

   'As I was saying before you left me... Trust me, William. The

feelings of jealousy are natural. I'd be surprised if you weren't. Feeling jealous of a mentor is no unusual thing, even if he was a good friend. The fact is that no matter where you are interred, you're still deceased. Stephenson, Brunel, God rest their souls, have no doubt gone to exactly the same destination.'
He smiled reassuringly.
'Perhaps it's some enormous workshop in the sky or something. Actually, there's a how to do - tell me; have you visited his workshop since?'
'No. I understand it already has a new owner.'
'Hm.'
'Hm?'
'Well, simply speaking, it doesn't. Mary still lives above it. Haven't you heard who is taking the office itself?'
'Obviously, not. You can tell you're a journalist.'

He tossed a small group of papers to me. A familiar face stared back from the correspondence with a particularly unusual gaze.

'Chief Assistant Brereton. Does the name mean anything to you? I don't believe you crossed very regularly.'

Chief Assistant Brereton was Brunel's favourite of his staff members. The other men in the drawing office knew him well and he was, by all accounts, a very difficult man to miss. He was a slight taller than Brunel, slim and largely bald. He rarely wore any kind of headwear; more unusual, however, was his distinctive, large black eyepatch which, I was told, covered a rather horrific scarred socket and missing eyeball that had been taken by a disaster during the Great Western Railway's construction.

He was effectively Brunel's railway assistant; the man who had helped tender and construct most of his structures in rail and infrastructure, and had done so admirably. We had all respected him immensely - however, I had indeed rarely crossed him - Brereton was more often travelling to his railway work sites, or sitting in Duke Street while I was overseeing the Great Eastern's construction.

Thirteen years my senior, Brereton was also a bit of a difficult man to find information on. He lived an almost hermitic existence, his address listed firmly as being Brunel's office rather than his home - wherever it may have been. He was, from what little I had spent with him, perfectly amiable.

> 'I find it curious that Brunel chose you to reveal all of this, when Brereton is presumably the more qualified of you both.'
> I rubbed my chin, while Samuel puffed on his pipe.
> 'After all, no disrespect to you, William - but you have seen less than he can claim to.'
> 'Now you mention it, I do agree. It seems a strange decision. Perhaps Brereton is already tied.'
> 'I'd presume so. He worked with Brunel for so long; I find it unbelievable that he could be otherwise. If I were you, Jacomb? I'd make him your next port of call.'
> I sighed. 'I never thought I would have to make so many trips around the city in the space of three weeks.'
> 'You're practically a detective rather than an engineer at the minute, Jacomb. It'll cease eventually.'
> 'All of this for a man who paid me a few sovereigns a month.'
> 'We both know you work on this out of loyalty.'
> 'I worry it's misguided.'
> 'It could well be. But I question you genuinely believing Isambard may have been a fraud. It doesn't seem fitting to his image. I'm telling you, this "Eternal Tome" of theirs is a metaphor. It cannot be a physical book; the very idea is nonsensical.'
> 'Brunel did not work within metaphors.'
> 'Be that as it may; I refuse to believe Hargraves has some sort of book of blueprints for the future.'
> He went back to puffing on his pipe.
> 'I'm getting old, Jacomb. I've seen much in my time. But they've always remained strictly in reality.'

I watched the thick, suspiciously black smoke billowing with every puff on Samuel's pipe. The dim, orange glow of burning tobacco was visible in the pub's less than stellar lighting. Around us, the standard way of life in a licensed premise was continuing as ever; gentlemen drinking, smoking, playing table games or reading books.

The occasional newspaper or quiet political discussion brandished tables and barstools. Men of minor concern, and low income life - rough, ready and avidly drinking in each other's company. Relatively speaking, seemingly carefree and lacking any real knowledge of the city's darker underbelly.

> 'Don't let it fool you, Jacomb. These men are largely miserable. The class divide in London is worsening by the day; everybody knows it. The joviality here is one of the only avenues to escape it. That man at the end of the bar? He's been working a fishing boat for decades. He used to work on the Thames; not a chance of that any more - You've seen the water. What fish could live in there, except for eels? He's having to spend days at sea; at age 78. Is that a happy life?'

The old man, tucked into a corner, smiled toothlessly as he took another swig of his tankard. His grizzled old face was lit up into a dozy, unfocused smile - but every inch of his head seemed tired, haggard and drawn. His hands shook as he lit up his pipe; a cheap clay one, with a chip in its bowl.

> 'The young man on the other side? He was a shipyard worker for Russell. He probably even put in some work for the Great Eastern. He's jobless now, until another Hot-Riveter job presents itself. He's not even old enough to drink. He survives as a pickpocket, William.'

The timid, frail young lad covered his face with his oversized flat cap and winced every time he took a sip of strong, cheap ale. The barman occasionally shot him a glare, but did nothing so long as the young man paid him a couple of pence extra for his drinks and kept his face relatively covered.

His arms were bruised and scarred from goodness knows how many incidents. His clothes filthy.

> 'Believe me, Jacomb - nobody in this society is care free. The elite may sit comfortably, the warmongers live in luxury - but nobody is 'free' from worries, stresses and concerns.'

A fight broke out outside; two large, drunken coachmen beginning to resort to fisticuffs over a couple of shillings. An audience developed; Samuel watched intently, then turned back to me.

> 'This city and society is a powder keg, William. All it takes is a spark and it'll come crashing down. The entire country may as well be a pair of drunken brawlers.'
> 'Come now, Samuel. Such cynicism? I'm surprised; for a man with no politics you seem rather afraid of a world without it.'
> 'Politics?'

He scoffed, and brought his tankard down on the table. Leaning forward to me, pointing with his pipe - It occurred to me how fierce Samuel's opinions could be; should they get riled.

> 'Politics are a clear example. It takes only a few well-placed words to have the common man braying for war. It takes mere sentences to have them hating another. The newspapers have much power in what they print; you've seen that first hand. A movement, a major psychological and a major societal change can happen in only months. The power is as much in your hands as it is Hargraves', William. With a little tact, you could turn the population into beasts against the man trying to keep them captive. That includes any higher, authoritative power. People, in themselves, are not meant to be pawns. The issue you've got is that you simply cannot demolish a chimney without starting from the base; you'd have to work from the source of the corruption.'

I rubbed the bridge of my nose. 'You and your analogies, Samuel.'

This immediately disarmed him.

> 'It's a quirk, I suppose.'
> He chuckled, reclined back again and took another draught of his pipe.
> 'You might even say a natural weakness. I always fancied myself as a creative writer; until, of course, I found a cause to align myself with; peace. A life without politics.'
> 'And now I throw you into one very much to do with politics. You must think me a terrible man.'
> 'You seek peace and justice just as readily as I do. As any of us who aren't drowning in corruption tend to. There's nothing wrong with seeking justice, Jacomb.'
> 'If everybody wanted justice, everybody would have it.'
> 'Not everybody knows what justice is. You are, if nothing else, quite certain of your decision.'
> 'Well I'm not sure if-'
> 'You're pursuing it like a man quite certain enough, William. Now, get yourself off to see Brereton. Work with him. See what he knows.'

I nodded; quite vacantly. I was lost in thought, still racked with my doubts. With my second guesses and reservations about what it was I was truly up against. The fact was I seemed to be taking umbrage with this society on a feeling. A feeling; and the outright instruction from my superiors that this wasn't right. I was following their instructions, not my own. I was beginning to wonder if I was, myself, taking the wrong direction. Barking up the wrong tree; perhaps even stumbling into a very serious miscalculation. People seemed to be becoming more forceful in it all; more dedicated to the cause than I was myself. Actively getting involved - perhaps due to their own investments rather than an honest, good hearted wish for justice and righting a wrong.

I was being used by these people as a deputation. It seems rather selfish now, in hindsight - but at the time, confronted with all of this, and still in my youth, it was a natural emotional response. I was beginning to worry I was being taken advantage of. Lucas, perhaps, out of his journalistic intrigue; Stephenson and Brunel out of industrial revenge - my fellows at the club out of sport.

I was beginning to worry that this really was going too far into the unknown. I hadn't, after all, particularly asked for any of this. As it stood, the society's presence was, thus far, merely one of poor manners and over enthusiastic, negative bluster. Hargraves and his men were distasteful - but I found great difficulty in seeing any man as 'evil'.

With my current progress in my own career, and the ever-increasing workload, It was difficult to lay focus on the cause. Truthfully, Brunel's loss was beginning to recline in my thoughts. I wondered if I really was better simply producing the book for Hargraves and leaving the society be to its cause; whether it truly be positive or negative.

Perhaps I had been too quick to judge Hargraves based upon his poor social skills. Perhaps the doctor was simply ill tempered. Perhaps they really were more interested in generally doing good for the world than they appeared?

It had only been a month, give or take, and yet I was already considering a close to my story.

Yet, as Lucas sat there intently, smiling warmly and enthusiastically talking to me like an old friend, I almost felt as if I could not, realistically, back out of my involvement. I did not have the nerve to say no or to refuse to go further; whether for better or worse, people had put their trust, enthusiasm and, more importantly, faith in my actions.

I was conflicted, to say the least. And I still had little idea what my future in all this could truly be - should I choose to pursue it.

For goodness' sake; I was an engineer - not a detective. Not a reporter. I was increasingly worried that I had become wrapped up in a case for revenge. The idea of this underground, shadowy organisation felt bizarre and otherworldly. How was any man expected to believe what I had been told?

The obvious answer was, indeed, to meet with Robert Brereton and try to elucidate the truth. I was beginning to feel desperate for a realistic clarification, and hoped dearly I would receive it from the man in an eyepatch.

+ THE CHIEF ASSISTANT'S WOES +

Despite my developing misgivings, and increasingly busy work life, I found the time to visit 18 Duke Street in late November.

The weather had worsened early in Winter, and where there had once merely been wet cobbled streets, London was shrouded in thin layers of frost and ice. The natural flow of life in the pulsating, rapidly expanding city was still going in the ways so familiar. New developments were a constant, scaffold, masonry, wood and iron springing up around the city like weeds in the paving. Green spaces were torn up in the interest of progress, and the city's natural state of being was a thin blanket of soot, smog and filth, with crawling rivers every bit as dark and thick as the pollution London was growing so known for.

My routines were still in much the same way, and my life was beginning to feel stable and comfortable. It was appallingly easy to forget that Brunel had now been passed for over two months.

Workloads were still heavy, and murmurings were beginning of a particularly enormous public works project that would require my input. It was, effectively, now or never - find out the truth of this grand fight and join the scuffle, or truly dedicate to my own endeavours and forget this increasingly doubtful case of espionage.

I buttoned up my jacket tighter as a cold wind struck from the Thames, seemingly in time with the hoot of a nearby Steamboat. I briefly took a detour to the Westminster - the infamous 'Bridge of Fools' - which at this time was now beginning to subside and crumble perilously over the desperate flows of thick, inky water.

It was still unusual, at the time, to see much in the way of steam powered vessels on the Thames. The big stink of 1858 had only recently left our headlines, so it was a surprise to see a pleasure boat - albeit one in some state of disrepair - rattling under the Westminster bridge with an acrid fume and clattering of engines. In the colder weather, the fetid stench of the river Thames did not permeate as heavily as many expected from the city of London's arterial vein - ensuring the diminutive vessel took full attention.

The little tin bath held a tiny boiler barrel within its frame, a long copper-hued funnel spattering out soot and sparks as it forced its way through the river's resolute, albeit sluggish current.

It seemed to waddle along the water with an uneven gait, and I watched with interest as it peeked from under the bridge with a proud little hoot of its whistle. It would have, once upon a time, been a fanciful, modern addition to any wealthy man's collection; an elitist pleasure vessel - but it now seemed to be little more than an archaic novelty rattling through the city - though, overseeing construction on the world's largest and most advanced ship may have tainted my vision.

You can imagine my expression when, sat back in the seat at the vessel's rear, there was a familiar, ungainly silhouette.

Hargraves looked up at me, and gave a hideous glare so overcome with hatred that I could see a twitch develop in his right eye.

If he said anything, I did not hear it over his little tin-pot vessel's clatter. But that piercing stare was beyond intimidating; a piggish little glare similar to a wealthy landowner watching a poacher - a pure, unfettered disgust and hatred reminiscent of a fanciful couple gazing upon ants on their department store picnic blanket.

More intimidating, however, was the fact his glare was so unbroken. Even as his little vessel rocked, his eyes pierced mine with so much unfettered fury that he barely blinked.

I stood up, and slowly walked away, raising my collar to shield from the cold. I had no idea why Hargraves had been travelling through the city on his little tin vessel; and at this point, had no desire to find out.

The sense of discomfort from this distant encounter stuck with me for the rest of my walk to Duke Street - and remained despite the relative change in the place from my previous visit. Much in comparison to what it had been when Brunel had passed, the address was once again a hive of activity, and the offices' lights firmly glowing through the natural haze of the city's atmosphere.

I gently rapped my knuckles upon the office's caller door, and heard the clatter of the rush to answer deep inside the building's hall.

I had little idea of what to expect; so you can imagine my surprise when, as soon as the door had been opened, the man inside embraced me tightly and patted my back.

The excitable voice of Brereton was not an expected factor in my visit; the warmth and welcome even less so.

> 'William! Oh William, it's so good to see you. How the devil are you, my dear fellow? Come in, I'll pour you a dram. Good gracious,

I haven't seen you since before the Leviathan was water-bound!'
'Oh, I- ahem, yes, quite. It's nice to see you, Mr. Brereton.'
'Hush, hush, hush. I've no interest in formalities. Let us drink to the old man before we lay another word.'

Before I had a moment's protest, Brereton had served up a dram of his finest from the drinks cupboard that Brunel had eagerly left him.

'You know, William, before I go one step further -'
'Now, hang on, Brereton, I-'
'No, no, this must be done! Sit yourself down, get yourself some snuff if you fancy - I've a grand pile of the Leviathan's objects to hand you. Brunel was quite insistent of what I leave for you upon his death.'
'You were the executor, then?'
'In a sense.' He grinned wryly. 'Brunel had no trust for a solicitor to carry out his tasks upon passing, William. He always insisted a friend should allocate his tasks, his duties and his belongings.'
'Sounds accurate.'

Brereton chuckled, handed me the decanter - with strict instructions to help myself - and bounded off to the draughtsman's office what he so surely saw as rightfully mine. The office, I observed, was unchanged. Right down to the stains of smoke and clag upon the ceilings and fixtures.

I waited patiently - but a nagging feeling told me to explore the paperwork I had sieved through on the day following Brunel's passing, and see if anything had been conveniently misplaced or disposed of. I was immensely curious should any cover ups or transactions have taken place. Perhaps the joy and excitement was little more than a façade; a false sense of security.

I considered my place. It was an enormous faux pas to rifle through - what, in any respect, was now another man's office. But, I reasoned, I had contributed to some of the projects held within – surely I had right to see my own drawings and papers?

My mind was resolute, and I slowly began to pore through drawer, cabinet and cupboard for the substantial levels of paperwork I had become so accustomed to from my master's workloads. Scouring the considerable portfolio of Brunel's projects for something I might recognise.

I had never considered the idea of Brereton wearing Harrow loafers in his office rather than the more common engineer's wood sole shoes.

> 'I can assure you, William. It's all quite present and correct. Hargraves has seen nary a telegram from Brunel's estate.'

I jumped, and a few locked box files fell to the floor with a thump.

> 'I'm sorry, Brereton, I-'
> 'Don't worry.' He smiled and sipped his dram. 'I don't blame you for your concerns. I admire it. Don't think I haven't noticed your efforts against him, either.'
> 'So you know, eh?'
> 'I've seen his reactions first hand. I'm a member myself, you know.'

I jolted, and backed away slightly.

> 'Now, now, William. Please. My loyalty is with Brunel, not with them. I followed Brunel in and followed his hatred of it all. And shared it.'

On the desk in front of my seat there now sat a maquette of the Great Eastern, alongside stacks of prints and artwork, some of which I had signed together with Brunel in happier times.

The maquette, mind? That I had never seen before. It was a finely crafted, beautifully polished model of the great ship that was true to scale and painted within the finest detail to Brunel's choice of livery, complete with every slip of rope, chain and flag that had festooned the reality of her. The staircases moving around her paddle housing, the polished brass banisters and barriers – it was as if the real vessel had been shrunk to proportions no more than a foot in length. That, Brereton pointed out, summated to only a whisker more than a 700th in scale.

> 'She's a little marvel, isn't she? Almost as miraculous as the full size Great Babe.'

I gently lifted one of the brass anchor chains with a clean dip pen, examining that finely moulded anchor hanging upon it. The delicate little model was an extraordinary thing; rigged with twine and delicate thread from masts no broader than a matchstick.

His initials were engraved onto the mahogany plinth, that held the ship upright on arching brass stilts.

> 'How on earth did he find the time to make this, Brereton?'
> 'I'd wager it was a pet project when he decided on two hours of sleep rather than four. Frankly, I'm not entirely sure why he insisted you have it, Jacomb – you aren't a collector of models, are you?'
> 'I presume it's because I oversaw the construction of the real thing.'
> 'You must have impressed him. I saw Brunel at his angriest, and at his worst. We must be the longest serving assistant's he ever had. He may have even seen you as a friend.'

I smiled. Quite a reassurance from him; the more I considered it – and it had been on my mind regularly over the past months – the more I did feel Brunel and I were, strictly speaking, 'friends.' A sort of posthumous friendship as I developed a greater understanding of his character.

'Mary likes you, too. You must understand, she holds no bad blood against you. It's purely for her family's sake. Brunel instilled a healthy love of family despite his overconsumption of workload. She doesn't wish to part with your presence; but has to.'

'How would you know all of this, Brereton? A good friend you are, yes, but few have seen Mary since the funeral apart from her footmen.'

'She still lives upstairs in the apartment, my dear fellow. Something else he stipulated.'

'Then presumably, I should leave.'

'No, no. You stay. Brunel had plenty of paperwork and Mary knew as well you'd have to collect it someday. For now, there is plenty of time for a toast to departed friends. And masters. Whichever he truly was!'

I laughed and sipped my dram, watching the balding man with the eyepatch reminisce fondly.

'He was a slave-driver. That much is true. So desperately obsessed with flat, straight gradients. Bridges, tunnels, cuttings and embankments.'

'The longest tunnel in the world. The flattest arched bridge in the world. The most elaborate viaducts in the world...'

'I am proud of the railway, Jacomb. I can't deny that. Endless glory, endless beauty - endless luxury. But is it mine to be proud of? It has Brunel's name firmly attached to it. And now Gooch is engineer and I am architect to his great toy trains. Before I started I had a full head of hair, both eyes and a damned steadier hand. He often forgot how much so many gave their lives to his projects. He himself, too. I've never known a man so meticulous and obsessed; nor a man so outspoken and intemperate. I find it surprising he's made all of this Hargraves business so simple for you. That he was so kind to you upon his passing. I only received a letter thanking me for my service and appointing me work.'

'Well, he also gave you an office.'

'Truthfully, this office will never be mine. I feel as if I shall still be using it for his projects fifty years from now.'

He chuckled.

'Of course, as you know, by the time the Saltash Girder Bridge had gone up, he was sick of railways. Failing locomotives, pig-headed accountants, incompetent contractors... then the country's other engineers; going narrow gauge rather than following his schematics for speed and comfort. He left them for me to finish so he could move onto your ship. Not really much of an accolade; his 'billiard table' is a damned expensive, damned difficult beast.'

I smiled and sipped my dram. Brereton was already on his second.

'Believe me, Brereton. No more so than the Great Eastern has been. She's barely even fit to sail again; lord knows how they plan to make a penny off of her at this point. People are going to think of her as a real leviathan. A beast uncontrolled; a maniacal killer made of iron.'
'Fear brings spectacle, William. I'm sure she'll do fine.'
'That remains to be seen; but without Brunel's word on it I fear that the creditors will have nary an idea of what to do with her. I worry she may depart this world before I do.'
'Put simply - though I have little investment myself in the project - if it happens, so be it. There's little point flogging a dead horse; if Brunel made a poor calculation for the vessel, he has to pay for it. What you still fail to understand, William, is that although you oversaw the ship, you most certainly don't carry legacy from its construction. It's Brunel and Scott Russell's project. Not yours. You don't have your own reputation to stake, and Brunel is still, largely, a national hero regardless of the ship's issues or his shortcomings. And even in its current form as a Brunel project, I'd be damned if it isn't Hargraves pocketing what little income comes of it. The grotesque old bullock is only interested in his own society's purse and reputation, not that of individuals or name. And he's certainly not interested in emotional attachment, either.'

I turned back to the model of the Eastern, so lovingly put together by a man who, at the time, would have been slowly and steadily passing away.

'A bit of an anti-thesis to Brunel, then, eh?'
'Oh, yes - Completely against his own attachment to his projects. No wonder Brunel hated them.'

Brereton was talking as if the 'Eternal Tome' had never existed. What caught me more, however, was his seeming obliviousness to its very existence. He wasn't much of a liar, and I was finding myself wondering if I should ask him, rather than following my original purpose.

I observed Brereton's body language as he spoke; I must confess I had so distracted myself that I had ceased listening - so you can imagine that his next words took me somewhat by surprise.

'...Of course, Brunel and Stephenson often chatted with me about the society's deeper underbelly. Something about 'a book'. No idea what it was, mind; I rarely paid attention to that chatter, and, frankly, they both spoke so negatively about it that I never once gave thought to the idea of attending to the society's whims.'
'Ah. You never knew of their inner workings?'
'I knew only of them financing projects and distributing them to their membership. I never saw anything of 'a book' and I certainly never had it brought up to myself. My time in the society is spent in the boardroom watching old men get drunk. My investment was distant. I was practically an understudy, in Hargraves' eyes. '

Brereton finished another dram, rapidly. He was beginning to look somewhat distant, himself, and leant against Brunel's desk for the most basic of support.

'I must admit I hardly feel like much else, either. Brunel's railway this, Brunel's railway that. It seems petty, I suppose - but I have a feeling my only legacy will be a memorial plaque and that'll be all.

No doubt Brunel will have a library of books about him. I loved the man dearly, but damned if I ever did so much to be forgotten, William. I'd dearly love to see more behind my name as a singular engineer, rather than part of a group.'
'Brunel recognised you, Brereton. Quite heavily.'
'Oh yes, he was outspoken about my abilities. He was my friend. He even sent me to Italy... But he rarely spoke about other's reputations in any reporter's presence. We're being whitewashed out of history by his sphere of influence. It's a damned upsetting circumstance. I'm not getting any younger, William, and who knows the name of Brereton in comparison to the name of Brunel?'
'If you're so desperate for your own legacy, why not work more with Hargraves' society?'
'If you steal something, my dear Jacomb, you have to spend your entire life trying to mask over the fact it was never truly yours. I would rather work on my own successes – if such an opportunity ever presented itself. I confess, my own lot in life feels somewhat squandered under the name Isambard Brunel. Believe me, William. You do not want to go the same way that I have. Preserve Brunel's name, certainly – but do not spend your life on another man's vision.'
'And the society?'
'I shall spend every free moment I have with you, trying to take that damned grotesque mockery down to its knees. I tire of Hargraves, I tire of his financiers and I shall never show forgiveness for a man who wore Brunel's work ethic down to a stump. The man may be financially successful, but if he thinks he's an engineer he's not only incorrect, but even more arrogant than I took him for. He's the sort of man who reduces every scrap of honour to our field and our industry. And honestly, our field isn't even – particularly – so elegant or honourable. We work other men to the bone for our arrogant little dreams and grand plans.'

He rubbed his brow, face down in his hand. His façade of happy, joyful expression had gone – replaced by his cynicism, his disillusion, and his fear of being forgotten.

> 'I'm sorry, William. I shouldn't be unfurling all of this to a youthful man with his life ahead of him. Just, please...'
> He stood, patting my shoulder. 'Be careful with yourself. Take care of yourself as equally as you do our field. You have your life ahead of you.'

He glanced in the mirror. His distinctive eyepatch was impossible to ignore. His own remaining eye seemed to glance at it constantly.

> 'By God. I'd barely wish ageing on anybody. Let alone with what I've given in exchange.'
> He smiled weakly. 'I'll organise a carriage for you to take this paperwork home – and the 'Little Eastern'. There's a letter for you somewhere, too. I'll make sure you get that.'
> 'Oh no, Brereton – I've taken enough of your time and money. I don't think it's my part to do so any further.'
> I think he could feel my discomfort. There was a silence.
> 'While I may not currently be in my finest state, Jacomb, I still consider Brunel one of my closest friends, colleagues. And I remain indebted to this field.'
> 'Quite.'

He poured himself another dram. This time, I refused, and instead watched this curious man. Was his bizarre composure and obvious decline out of mourning, an overindulgence in alcohol, or was he truly experiencing such a crisis of identity?

Was this what laid ahead for a good, hardworking engineer if he has no guidance or legacy? I felt shaken – almost as if I had glanced into a mirror of the future.
Brereton was, on the surface, a joyful, optimistic and energetic soul.

He had often been celebrated by Brunel for his energy, his spark, his natural creativity and dedication to his job – not to mention his impressive abilities and complete willingness to lay everything on the line for his projects and Brunel's designs.

But behind this character, there seemed to be a husk. I was wondering how long Brereton's outspoken, pleasant existence had been a charade. The ego was clearly a sensitive thing for most men in our line of work - but in Brereton, it seemed to have withered like a rose patch in winter.

He smiled - again, weakly - as if he had realised how much he had given away to this visitor, and sipped another drink. I had lost count of how much whiskey he had now taken, and noticed his eyes sinking slightly from the impact of the strong, graded alcohol.

'I'll organise the carriage to deliver these things tomorrow, William. For now, it is beginning to get somewhat dark out. Even this area has the odd spark of late night crime and misfortune. You should get yourself home.'

I nodded, and stood up pensively. He shook my hand, but didn't stand to walk me to the door. He simply sat, alone.

One man and his decanter, in an office that wasn't even his own.

+ A TRIP TO TOTTENHAM +

Silence had much ruled the relationship between myself and Hargrave's cronies for the next two months.

We continued our gentleman's assault, I and the Anthenaeums - gentle, non-confrontational propaganda speaking of the issues with large engineering franchises, and promoting the use of independent engineers and consultants with free thought.

A boom in the more liberal sectors, as a result, took place in full vigour. The belt of industry had changed to a different drive wheel entirely, and the economics behind engineering itself had begun to improve.

Perhaps it is relevant to this that my own working life began to develop with greater vigour than even I imagined.

I had found myself involved in a most unusual development in the city of London; the Metropolitan Railway project - this had been a concept of much speculative interest in Brunel for many years, and under a good friend and industrial rival in his, one John Fowler. Mind! I'm sure many of my readers are very aware of the man; his perseverance and impeccable standards were very familiar to me – particularly in such an enormous undertaking.

The Metropolitan railway was the first fully featured under-ground passenger railway; one that sat comfortably under the streets of London, at shallow depth, and travelled between Brunel's Paddington terminus, into the centre of the nation's capital and the other major railway stations of the city.

The idea was a rather amazing one, considerably similar to Brunel's ideas in scope and enterprise – much ahead of what many believed possible in the day. Some even conjured incredible plans of under-ground cities, towns and hamlets, restaurants and cafes spanning a whole new level of the industrial world's diamond-studded crown.

Fowler scoffed at these ideas; he was simply interested in the construction of a railway, and proved a fine figure to build it. He was, at this time, in his forties, and beginning to lose his hairline – but he had a kind, approachable face and demeanour that was impossible to truly argue with or stand up against. His determination and energy was essential to his standing.

Investors and shareholders found the idea of an underground railway particularly exciting – and made sure that they put their money where their mouths were.

By my first month in the company, finances were progressing beautifully – the new levels of investment took me to finding a greater level of engineering apprenticeships, students and other bright young men to join the constant challenges now facing the under-ground railway's infrastructure and future; with high plans of a complete city spanning railway on the horizon, the need for bright young men to join the growing company was essential.

The date, I recall, was the twentieth of February. I had just spent a few days in the centre of Cambridge. My fellows at the Anthenaeum club believed this was a very foolish endeavour, but my professional needs had heightened, while the threat from Hargraves and the society had dilapidated into, what I felt, was a gradual retreat.

In those days, the route from Cambridge to London was nearly monopolised with the Eastern Counties Railway, providing a fast link with a through point at Tottenham train station.

While I had always been used to travelling on Brunel's broad gauge, the 'narrow' gauge of the Eastern counties still provided a certain amount of luxury via the first class. Fowler insisted that his engineers and consultants would only travel in First, typically with their own compartments to ensure comfort and the provision of sleep. For this purpose, he also insisted our first class carriage be towards the train's rear, far from the noise of the grunting iron beast in front.

I had left early in the morning – just after sunrise, and joined my commuters in the journey to arrive at roughly ten in the morning. All was more than comfortable enough, and I swiftly felt myself nodding off under the influence of the train's rolling motion and distinctive clacking of wheels against rail-joints.

However, one doesn't work so closely with railways without working out when something sounds – or, indeed, feels – incorrect, and the train's motion began to unsteady only a couple of miles from Tottenham.

Perhaps a mere bit of poor quality track; a slightly defective spring wearing down. Nothing too serious, I reasoned. But by the time we were drawing closer to Tottenham, I was beginning to find myself, perhaps naturally, concerned. I was the only one, it seemed, roused by the slightly uneven clattering of the locomotive's wheels.

I peered from the carriage window – and while my vision was not entirely clear from the smoke, steam and cinders that made up the locomotive's exhaust, I saw enough to haunt me.

The engine suddenly jumped, like an agitated mare, and a piece sheared off like a plane from wooden board, leaping out from under her chassis. The tire of the engine's leading wheel had rattled itself free, breaking like a pencil under the force of the train above it.

I watched, awestruck, as the fragments of iron were flung across the ballast behind the locomotive's thundering axles and increasingly rattling wheels, and hollered at the train's rearmost brake van to attempt in halting the train. The engine's crew had hurriedly shut off steam, desperately trying to gather control while clinging to the open cabin's handrails - but in this instance, the sudden loss of pace as the engine slowed was no positive. Instead, the train slammed against the locomotive, jarring it forward and further off of the rails. The great beast began to roll and flounder amongst the ballast as it tried to continue on its route.

The train's brakes finally began to bite, and screeched in agony - joining in chorus as people began to yell, shout and scream, trying to break free of the carriages as the centre of the train left the rails, jolted clear by the hammering weights in front and behind it. I held onto the carriage door, almost frozen in fear, and expecting nothing but death from a terrible, painful impact.

With a thundering sound I dare say I shall never forget, that several ton locomotive, wheels still turning and exhaust pouring from her, veered leftward - and was vaulted by the Tottenham station platform ramp. The open cab provided no shelter or safety for the driver and fireman, who fell - but had no time to escape what came next.

With coal and cinders flying from her, the engine bucked upwards in such a way that it was airborne for a couple of seconds - before crashing against the stone of the platform surface with a catastrophic impact of shrapnel, ballast and steel. Immediately after, it fell backwards, funnel over footplate, and, with a painful howl of escaping vapour, collapsed against the lineside, onto her senseless enginemen. They were killed instantly, and the locomotive was left a pitiful, twenty-ton flounder, caught on its back and completely flipped in direction, now once again facing Cambridge.

The tender, still half laden with coal, attempted to mount the wreckage, before falling itself onto the opposing railway line. The first brake van, immediately behind the tender, tried to continue on the same path – it lost its roof into the process, spilling the guard, his companion and passenger's luggage across the station premises. Both vehicles were almost immediately rendered and torn into wreckage – but this was only the beginning of the chaos.

A passenger carriage behind collided with the wrecked van's rear. The carriage behind this flew leftwards, mounting the platform, and the next fell from the rails – albeit remained upright.

I wheezed as the train jolted from the impact, windows shattering – including the one close to my hands – and was flung across my compartment as the rest of the train forced onwards – and crushed the frontmost carriage, passengers and all, into a pile of mangled, twisted cast iron and mahogany.

Finally, our vehicles lost momentum – and for a moment, everything was silent lest for the engine's misshapen remains hissing and wheezing.

I cringed, holding my wrist and inspecting my shivering hand, embedded with large shards of glass. Immediately, I reasoned, I had to see to this issue, and did my damnedest to remove the razor sharp shrapnel.

After this, I ripped a piece of the curtains, shook it clear, and wrapped it tightly around my injured hand to relieve the pain, and kicked through the now heavily jarred door.

Screams, shouts for help and the chorus of the failed locomotive's mournful wheezing made a frightening accompaniment to an utterly terrible scene, itself smothered so heavily in escaping smoke, steam and the odd flicker of flame that I could barely see the carriage I had just stepped from.

The guard from the rear of the train ran to me, battered, bruised and clearly shaken. Other passengers from the rear freed themselves in the same way and gathered towards the guard for instruction; some ladies frantic, and all – both men and women – horrified and shaken.

The guard stuttered, backing away somewhat from the crowd.

He was a young man – at least, younger than I myself, and clearly not truly aware of what to do with the situation. The superintendent of the railway, who so happened to be at the station, ran out and barked at the young guard to treat the fire, while everyone else tried to help the injured – and unlocked the carriages.
Horse and carriage in the streets drew to a halt and within time, tens of people joined us in trying to aid the train's stricken and dead.

Thankfully, being a relatively early service, the Cambridge train had lost only seven – including the driver and crew. However, a further nine had been severely injured.

The passengers and I attended the chaotic accident's scene for many hours. The driver and firemen had been killed – so the truth of the matter that had led to the disaster was impossible to discover; incinerated in the engine's spilled fire and coals, and mangled beyond recognition.

By the end of the day, those of us that had stayed on the premises were exhausted – laid back on station benches, trying to gather our minds after what we had witnessed.

The doctor had arrived, now assisting our own injuries, and a temporary hospital had been developed in the Tottenham station waiting room.

By the time my hand was finally being seen to, it had fallen numb - though at this point, I myself was equal to it. I had gone completely blank.

It was one thing to see people dying on the work site; that one thing was tragic enough. A horrific circumstance I encountered thankfully with relative rarity. But at least they were aware of the risks - they were paid, they were trained and they knew what negative results could come from a lack of attention.

This was different. These passengers were blissfully unaware of any negative circumstance. They paid their ticket to safely travel home, or to work, or to business - and now seven of them laid on the station platform, shrouded and awaiting identification.

The weather was cooling - and the last of the glass was soon free from my hand thanks to the doctor, who was now - painfully - stitching up the larger cuts across my hands.

I grunted as the final thread was strung through my palm.

> 'You should heal up nicely, Mr. Jacomb. You might even go without scarring. A very lucky escape; had you been in the first carriage...'
> 'I can guess what the result would have been.'
> 'Quite. A very different and far more tragic outcome, I dare say. We're lucky to have gotten away with the relatively scant scars we have.'

I looked out at the seven departed souls, meticulously laid and covered against what would usually be a hive of travellers heading to and from their homes. This was luck?

The doctor spoke to the Superintendent of the railway, who was heavily shaken - but, most of all, confused. As was the inspectorate from the engine's home shed. The two gentlemen were honest, hardworking men - and had no reason to disguise the incident's happenstance. They provided any and all papers; considered every circumstance. And while the inspection was in infancy, no member of staff could work out, thus far, what had actually caused such a calamity in such a standard early morning journey.

The locomotive's fire had now been doused, and the wreckage left to cool. It was a miracle her boiler had not burst under the pressure of the engine's terrible treatment by nature's forces, and her remarkably well preserved condition enabled investigators and technical staff to properly examine the metal beast's stricken wheels. I, too, observed closely with the company's superintendent, and was surprised to find the tire of the wheel had seemingly split, quite cleanly, from its harnessing.

> 'I can't understand it. We inspect regularly. The wheel has done thousands of miles, and never worn by a hair's breadth. It doesn't make sense, Jacomb. The shed boy inspected them only this morning, and every dimension was fine.'
> 'How long before service do these inspections take place?'
> The superintendent rubbed his chin as he considered. 'Oh, not very long. Normally two hours or so - it takes that time to build steam pressure. But we're talking about a length of cast iron, riveted to the wheel frame. It isn't a case of simply prying from the wheel - and even if it was, it'd be noticed. It'd be obvious.'

It should be obvious to the readers I am no detective; I cannot emphasise enough, for that matter, how unqualified I was to inspect an accident site. But as pieces of the wheel tire were collected and laid upon the platform, I was beginning to get the impression that something was amiss.

Eventually, I was permitted to leave - but the scene at Tottenham would take days to rectify; and the reputation of the Eastern

Counties railway had fallen swiftly. The newspaper reporters made their views clear, and the company's other enginemen were left scared and bewildered, with two of their kind lost to the wrath of their locomotive. This event would be the news of the day - with many more days to come.

I arrived home to a tearful Eliza, embracing me so tightly I felt quite sure my ribs would break. Not a word was said; only fearful exchange of glances and a silent, protective hold between us; ensuring we were together when we could have been torn apart so easily this morning.

My bliss and thankfulness for being able to arrive home was smothered by survivor's guilt - and the confusion; that tumultuous thought of what on Earth had actually gone wrong. What had happened to the train to cause such calamity?

It was a long time before I was fit to write again, and for a spell I was rendered unable to do any kind of consultancy work. As a direct result, I lost clients – and finances.

Glacial progress was a standard in the engineering world; but a consultant was expected to respond with finished paperwork in less than three weeks. With the event at Tottenham, I was no longer capable of working sufficiently to keep myself financially solvent. The men of the Underground Railway were happy to gain my verbal expertise - but my other clients were far less forgiving, and steadily dropped like flies; turning to other freelancers, or worse, that of Hargraves' employ.

We sat together only a few weeks after the accident, writing off bills and financial receipts... carving a sorry looking picture of our monetary future.
The wedding plans were ruined. Our office premises in peril. And now, even my home's status was beginning to teeter under the increasingly demeaning, increasingly aggressive snarl of creditors, who, rather than making reasonable concessions for our situation, seemed only interested in making demands towards our rapidly

emptying purses.

Eliza and I constantly tightened our purse strings. Constantly made allowances.
But, all too soon, the expenses of high end London property had bitten hard. Our evenings in front of bills, paperwork and stern letters had devolved into an atmosphere of hopelessness.

I rubbed the bridge of my nose and looked over our expenses, while Eliza read my letters.

'He's written to you again, William.'
'Who?'
'That Hardgreave fellow.'
'Hargraves? Just put it into the waste bin, darling. Thank you.'
'No, William. I shan't. How much longer do you intend to waste the opportunity when we're so direly in need of money?'
'I'm not willing to discuss this, Eliza.'
'Then I'm not sure how much longer this can carry on. I'm worried, William. How long before you lose your home? How long before you're in debt? How long before I have to go back to my family rather than wait for your situation to improve? William, I love you. But you need to keep our heads above water. You can't expect to live in London on a tuppence. We can't survive in this circumstance unless you do something.'
'Eliza, I'll be capable of writing again in a month or so-'
'That's four more missed payments, William! Four more weeks without a wage! Four more weeks of bills!'
'I know, my love, but what can I do?'
'You *know* what you can do! The prospect has been staring you in the face for weeks! Go to that society, ask for help, try and gain some kind - any kind - of regular payment and work towards our shared goal, instead of that of a dead superior!'

She went silent. A slim trickle of a tear made its way down her cheek.

'Please.'

It had been months since Brunel had passed away. Months; that was all it had taken for life to bring me up to an elevated position – and then allow me to fall back down again. Allow me to fall away from all I truly knew, and leave me in a position so desperate to refinance my own legacy.

The boiler in my head was officially dry of ideas. And something had to give, lest my entire life rupture.

It became clear that what had to give, in fact, was my pride.

+ THE LOSS OF LUXURY +

'You can't be serious.' Spat the old bulldog, fiddling with his dominoes on that fine, Gilded Mahogany table.

'Is your situation really so dire?'

'If I don't get some kind of financing, I shan't even be able to pay my membership cost here. Let alone the rent for my offices, nor the costs of my home. I have no other option.'

The murmurs of disappointment filled the drawing room of the Anthenaeum Club's Pall Mall premises as gazes were exchanged. The husky old man who seemed such an essential - if difficult - component of our meetings was, as could be typical, a man of few kind words, and fewer sympathies

'Let one of the doctors look at your hand. There has to be something they can do to accelerate your recovery.'

Dickens peered over his newspaper. 'The matter isn't his hand's health; it's the therapy for getting it back in full order.'

Dominoes cracked onto the table, and the bulldog gave one of his characteristic barks.

'If I want *your* opinion, Charlie, I'll ask for it. Hold your tongue.'
'I'm pointing out the facts. Jacomb has to be able to write, and write damned well. Not to mention his draughtsmanship. If he doesn't have his dexterity on his side he'd be better off as a juggler than an engineer.'
'And *I'm* pointing out that nobody asked you. Jacomb, why don't we finance you? We're, largely, wealthy men. We could cover your expenses.'
'I could never request it of you.'
'Then don't. Expect it from us.'
'I didn't train as an engineer to be a beggar. I thank you sincerely. But I need sustainability.'
'On your own head, Jacomb. But our offer is always in place, and it hardly seems like the alternative is preferential.'
'And where would it end? Paying for my wedding? Paying for my draughtsman's curves? I appreciate it - truly, I do - but it's a ludicrous idea; and not something I'm comfortable with. I don't see where the long term benefit would be for anybody.'

A murmur of agreement rattled around the table that made the drawing room's focal point. It was quiet, reluctant - but one of firm admittance.

I wasn't sure if this was really a victory I sought. In my own words, I had chosen my conclusion - I would have to contact Hargraves; encounter the veritable belly of the beast, and find myself officially part of that terrible society; that gathering of little liberty, financial monopoly - and, most disconcertingly - the grand falsehood that ruled our industrial age, and the mighty empire.

I explained my situation to Samuel that evening. He, in contrast, was substantially more excited than the men at the club's drawing room table.

> 'Of course, you'll have to tell me what you find. And take notes. If you can even provide a diagram or two-'
> 'You intend to publish it?'
> 'I'm more fascinated by virtue of what may lay within that business prospect, William. You could be entering Pandora's box; or a veritable, industrial palace. Never mind the newspaper – what of the spectacle?'
> 'What if the "Eternal Tome" is real?'
> 'Then by God, I'll eat a copy of my own newspaper.'
> 'And what if this is too enormous a presence for us to handle? What if the world truly is pre-planned? What if our impressions of our very society just…shatter, Samuel? Don't you understand the gravity of the situation?'
> 'I wonder if I understand it more than you yourself. Surely you feel excitement?'
> 'I do not. I feel only dread. Disgust. I dare say I even feel traitorous. I'm doing this because I have no other option. I'm doing this because my fiancée, my home and my future career depends on it.'
> 'And in it, you shall complete a pursuit for knowledge. Make the best of a bad situation; consider what lay ahead as an opportunity, not a curse. Consider what follows to be a matter of potential.'
> 'Your hopeless optimism is doing nothing to quell my concerns, Samuel. Why must you keep pretending things are well? Why must you stay so positive in the face of adversity?'
> 'My dear fellow, cynicism is the first sign that the circumstances are beating you. You show more power and strength in positivity. Use that to your advantage.'

I sighed, and took another drink. Samuel was already on his second, and I was busy convincing myself that this was enough to discredit his words in my mind.
The rattle of the pub's clientele was the same as ever it had been; unaware of each other's eclectic circumstance and treating their fellow men as equals and peers, regardless of where they were in life.

While I had taken note not to overly romanticise this little powder keg of London, this battered wooden barrel that made up a perfect ant farm of the classes in Wimbledon, it was difficult not to envy those who were innocent of our situation. I found myself watching them with curiosity and intrigue.

Samuel took a pinch of snuff and offered me to join him; I refused.

'Perhaps, Samuel, I'd be better off retiring and becoming a clerk somewhere.'
'Perhaps. But you'd never be able to afford a marriage to your dear fiancée. How is Eliza?'
'She's well. As worried as I am; as distraught about our situation."
'And your situation is...?'
'Penniless. At least, in practicality - I can afford my meals, my paper, our transport around London - but my rent is vastly beyond what we're earning.'
'Hardly penniless, is it?'
'It's below our usual lifestyle.'
'But several times beyond what so much of what London can claim to. Far be it for me to claim you privileged William, but count your blessings. I would say you're making a serious situation purely out of trying to keep your circumstance. Something that is not sufficient as an 'emergency'.
You were born in easy circumstances. You only know easy circumstances - that doesn't make them challenging. You're still an enormously lucky young man.'
'I know that, Samuel. Believe me, I do.'
'Then why do you fret so much?'
'Eliza is used to better circumstances than I can provide for her, Samuel. I'm not willing to sacrifice my future with her.'
'She may be concerned, but I highly doubt she'd leave you over such a trifle, William.'

I held up my hand, still bandaged - still painful.

'In my profession, this is not a trifle. It is a serious threat to my

employment. If it doesn't heal, it's a serious threat to my future.'
'And that future will be with her, regardless of what it holds. It's the way of things.'
'I can't expect even my closest loved ones to stay with a failure, Samuel. I'm not deserving of loyalty if I cannot earn a decent living.'
'Spoken like a true cynic, William. But you should have more faith in your loved ones. Equally, you need more faith in your own abilities, regardless of how capable you are of writing.'

Samuel got up to visit the lavatory. I drummed my fingers on the table, and looked at my lukewarm ale, silently, allowing myself some reprieve as I sank into a day dream - thinking of nothing in particular, aided slightly by the weak alcohol.

I heard a very light sound, barely audible against the pub's bustle, and looked, to my surprise at a fine vellum envelope, sitting against my arm.

I paid little attention to it; simply took it into my jacket's pocket, and continued on with the evening. By the end of the night, the ale had taken its toll, and I returned quietly home after another few hours of putting the world to rights with Samuel.

The temperature had fallen, and I spent my evening in front of the softly burning fireplace, watching the flames, deep in consideration.

The room slowly darkened as the fire dulled over the evening, and the warmth dissipated as the flickering orange glow ebbed away.

Within only a few moments, I fell asleep. A restless, awkward sleep - the sort that was utterly impossible to enjoy; a difficult, tumultuous experience that was broken by the constant throbbing under my temples, like the thumping of a steam hammer - reminiscent of exactly those that had brought the Great Eastern to water less than a year before.

I stirred awake at 2AM. In a sudden moment of clarity, I remembered the letter in my breast pocket and fumbled it loose, but, submitting myself to fatigue, left it on the dining table and set myself to my bedchamber, instead of reading it immediately.

I woke up with a headache, far later than usual that morning. Between my exhaustion, my nerves and the claws of the beer still gripping harshly upon my focus and concentration, getting dressed proved a tumultuous experience. The room seemed to tumble and roll around my vision as I fastened my waistcoat.

The questions began all too quickly as I reached the bottom of the stairs. Eliza had come to see me, and had made a point of rearranging my paperwork and making me a drink.

'So when are you going?'
'Going?'
'The letter. Your appointment with that Hardgreaves fellow. You left it on the table.'

I sat down and groaned, holding my head. I must have resembled a pitiful mess of a man; unshaven, tired, hungover, and with my shirt creased.

Eliza poured me a large cup of coffee. 'Your razor's in the cupboard, dear. Shall I give you a shave? And perhaps a hotpotch? Or would I be better off calling the undertaker now?'

She laughed and nudged me. She seemed far happier now there was what she felt to be a grand opportunity on the table. I was already in a sour mood; the very idea of having to meet Hargraves made my stomach knot itself and churn.

I glanced at the letter. Finely written, beautifully hallmarked – superb quality, silken paper. The very materials used to write the letter would have bankrupted many. We could have barely afforded a sheet of it.

As expected, the man himself had composed a light, pleasant tone that completely shrouded his personality. The pleasantries – or, rather, the knowledge of how false they were - near turned my stomach.

My Dear William;
Please accept this as your formal invitation to join our esteemed society. We wish to assist you in your poor financial stead in the wake of the Tottenham tragedy, and hope to finance and furnish your family.
You shall find us at House No.3, on Eccleston Square. We eagerly look forward to welcoming you.
Hargraves.

I read it back, over and over in my head. Then, of course, it struck me.

'Eccleston Square? Why?'
'Perhaps he's inviting you to his home?'
'Far too modest, my Darling. A man like Hargraves would only want the grandest premises in London. And it can't be a location for the headquarters. Surely?'

Eccleston Square had only recently neared completion; a series of houses called the Pimlico Project, designed by the recently expired Thomas Cubitt. I had never met the man - I was under the impression Brunel had, but with few positive words to say.

Unsurprisingly, he was in a particularly small minority. Cubitt was a beloved man in the city of London - an industrial pariah whom had built so much of our city's aesthetic and style. If Brunel had built Britain, Cubitt had designed London - with an outward profile of a kind, friendly gentleman whom believed in the importance of good work.

Eccleston Square, like most of Pimlico, was built in the traditional style of post-Georgian London. It was a pretty little middle class estate, with a botanical garden to the centre, not far from Buckingham Palace. It was a lovely spot, certainly - but with the grandeur and success of the society, I could scarcely believe a building there would be sufficient for its requirements.

> 'It is a very nice little bit of the city, William.'
> 'It's a little housing estate near a railway construction site, Eliza. I can't fathom why they'd want me there?'
> 'Well regardless; I'm sure you'll find it perfectly serviceable. Let's get you cleaned up after your evening on the terrace and organise you a carriage.'

She held my chin and smiled, gazing into my eyes.

> 'That mister Lucas and his drinking are leading you astray.'

She smiled; that usual, honest, passionate little smile. The sort no gentleman could really resist. And I submitted; immediately beginning work to ready myself - and retrieving Brunel's book of false plans that the society still treasured so dearly.

Within a few hours, I was walking towards the imposing construction site of the planned Victoria railway station, and the beautifully laid - owing to the West End's fertile earth - gardens and squares that made up the area of London.

Eccleston was still under construction - Cubitt had passed away only a year or so prior, and progress had been halted occasionally by everything from cholera to the city running perilously scarce of its favoured middle class. It was now back into vigour, with several squares in the Pimlico project having being completed.

The result was an impressive selection of grand stone houses, built in a similar image to much of Westminster and Belgrave. Some were up to five storeys high; a veritable mansion for much of London's population, but for the truly important - the truly wealthy, hardly appropriate. Certainly nowhere near the scale I had come to expect from Hargraves' level of excess.

I rapped upon the door – to which a butler answered. His face was thin and sharp, betraying a grand old age that manifested around his eyes, lips and non-existent hairline.

His eyes seemed permanently exhausted, barely open, and almost caught in a constant, squinting grimace – as if the smell of the Thames was constantly nestled deep into his nostrils. I figured that he was short sighted.

His suit, though of some vintage, was perfectly pressed, meticulously cleaned, with hints of red silk to the lining and a gentle paisley pattern across the black fabric.

The tall, slim old man raised an eyebrow as I showed him the letter from my chest pocket – though his eyes remained barely open – then, he nodded, and led me inside the hallway.

It was a standard home dressing that surrounded us, though hardly a grand or extravagant fixture. The wall coverings seemed poorly applied and ramshackle, and the lights were thick with dust and cobwebs.

You can imagine my surprise when I was led through this dank, unimpressive room into the home's lounge.

Under a lock and key, this doorway opened into a grand lounge in a deep red. The room was an impressive size, picked out in teak and gold gilding, flowing through into two of the neighbouring buildings.

   'Goodness'. I mumbled, only to be led to an archway in the place of the fire and chimney breast. 'I'd have never guessed...'

The Butler broke his silence with a deep, throaty voice that felt authoritative and foreboding. His rattling tones would do much to scare a less rational gentleman. I briefly wondered what his story must have been.

> 'Cubitt was an early member of Mr. Hargraves' society, Sir. The first few houses of Eccleston Square are solely for societal use. The same applies with the garden. The house holds many secrets, of course.'

He walked me down the stairway that steeply dropped into the house's chimney breast, travelling downwards by at least two floors, below the usual lining of the house's cellar.

Contrary to the hallway and the utilitarian purpose of this mysterious staircase, passage into the bowels of the property seemed only like an extension of the lounge; thoroughly polished, meticulously designed into an illusion of pure grandeur.

At the foot of the staircase stood a pair of mahogany doors, both holding an insignia on the central panel - a fearsome thing it was; a locomotive wheel with an all-seeing eye central. The wings on either side bore a strange resemblance to a vulture's. I was feeling increasingly intimidated.

The doors opened; leading to a vast room of individual chambers, spanning what seemed like the complete distance between Cubitt's London squares.

The largest was reserved for Hargraves, and from the rampant snorting and grumbling, I could tell he was either on premises, or a wild boar was roaming those mysterious halls.

The Butler walked me in and hurriedly left; leaving me staring down that long, dark office to the familiar, hulking figure who had invited me.

> 'It's been a long time, boy.'

His grin was every bit as rotten and crooked as I had remembered. He didn't get up upon my entrance, and instead continued writing his fine calligraphy.

> 'I heard of your issues since the railway accident. Such a shame. Naturally we had to help. Please, sign up your contracts and we'll get your accounts cleared. After all, what other option does an office boy have, eh?'

He seemed unusually polite - for Hargraves.

> 'Don't be an idiot. Sit down, William. Sign the paperwork; take a positive step in your worthless career for once.'

Never mind. There it was.

I sat down in one of the plush leather armchairs that Hargraves had across his office, cast in fine quality cognac leather and Mahogany frames.

> Hargraves reclined smugly in his chair as he put down his dip pen, meeting my eye at last. 'Far grander than Brunel ever had to his name, eh? This is the result of financial success, William. Speaking of Brunel... the book. Hand it over.'

I glanced at the large, red leather book with gold lettering and signed. Hargraves grinned as I finally relented.

> 'There. You can make a good decision once in a while. I could have made life very difficult for you for this, boy. Naturally, you did that yourself, instead. See how easier it is to collaborate?'

I felt like I was a child being lectured by a grotesque beadle; but in the circumstance, presumed it would be best to play to Hargraves' hand. Rather than a witty retort, I simply hung my head and listened obediently.

'Nevermind. Your salary will be very generous. When do you wish to be married, William?'
'Eh?'
'To prove our little society is no slouch or bluster, we shall fund your marriage, Jacomb. It seems only correct, eh?'

I was momentarily shell shocked as Hargraves spoke. It all seemed so easy; life's problems being solved in one.

Hargraves then belched. The illusion was immediately broken.

'We shan't intrude upon your work for the Underground railway, of course, but will expect you to work simultaneously for us. We shall need our insignia on your paperwork, your consultancy whenever we require it, your complete dedication to the society's goals and assistance in our research... in return; you'll receive generous amounts of funding, hundreds of pounds in public money, your dream wedding... and blueprints for projects, beyond your wildest dreams of science, technology and mathematics.'

I nodded silently.

'You'll receive some incredible secrets. That, I promise you - things nobody realises the elements can be harnessed for. We have an immense resource, William. One that I believe shall truly impress you.'
'The Eternal Tome.' I replied, matter-of-factly. I never once thought that Hargraves was so passionate towards the society's secret.

The generously sized jaw of the man fell silent. His eyes widened - and very quickly narrowed themselves as he looked up from his letters.

'Let me make one thing clear.' He snarled, standing and walking around his desk to approach me; a surprisingly imposing sight while sat in a chair in the man's office.

'That book, William...' he grabbed my collar and pulled me to my feet, until his searing eyes were looking straight through me, at the same level of my own.
'...Is our business. You do not speak of it. You do not touch it. You do not interfere with it. If you do, I shall see to it your every asset disappears from this Earth.'

I swallowed hard and tried to avert my face from his pungent, sickening breath.

'Now, you sign that bloody paperwork. You shall see that book when I decide. You shall not tell a soul.' He spoke through yellow, gritted teeth. 'I can wipe bastards like you right out of history.'

I grunted in response – and was thrown back down into the chair, which shifted under the impact – leading to me sitting on the floor, dazed, under the shadow of that horrible ape of a man.

'I shan't warn you again, William. Sign that paperwork. Or I'll break more than your hand.'

I raised an eyebrow at that last remark – but I submitted myself to the hands of fate. I signed the paperwork, under that hateful eye of the society's head. The gaze of several portraits on the red, damask papered walls.

The decadent carvings of pixies and nymphs in the wooden skirting rails, desks and dadoes seemed mocking and vindictive. A hundred smiles against my own miserable outlook.

I had lost my higher ground; my pride. I was no longer the independent consultant to queen, country and prosperity. Through that single signature, I was now a dogsbody. A pathetic understudy to the corrupt party that took credit for building our nation's greatest age.

I had raised Hargraves' suspicion – I had raised the ire of a man I was growing to fear as readily as I despised him.

I was no longer a young man in the industry he knew and loved. I was a young man taking on a tar ridden pit of bad practise.

I was no longer Brunel's Assistant, nor was I William Jacomb.

I was simply another member. Perhaps to my arrogance and discredit, what I most feared was the lack of recognition I could expect.

I thought back to Brereton and his concerns, which now seemed so accurate and reflective on myself. I sighed as I left the deceptive building on Eccleston Square - a changed man. A lesser man.

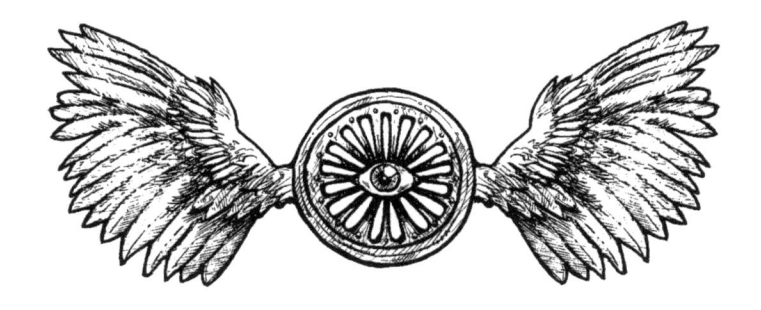

+ INITIATION +

The next few months saw my home furnished with a greater level of grandeur and luxury than we had ever imagined, as the society's generous payments began to roll for us.

Eliza was overjoyed, and even I found myself greatly satisfied - and most amused - by the levels of comfort we were now so settled with.

My consultancy work continued to full acclaim, and as my hand recovered, my output hit full belt with great vigour. I found myself happily, comfortably and reliably working on one of the greatest public works projects of the century - the underground railway that was to make the future of public transportation was now hammering at a pace befitting of the locomotives set to ride through those mighty tunnels.

The society, to my surprise, seemed to leave me quite content and in peace; scattering Brunel's unworkable diagrams, unknowingly, around their senior staff.

To make matters all the more positive, Eliza and I had now arranged our wedding date. Her family had given their blessing - and my own parents were overjoyed at the news. My father had often made a point of criticising our life together outside of wedlock, and with this development had taken far more interest in matters of our relationship - and my work.

My mind had been changed, quite firmly - the society was, for myself, a force of good. For three months we had now shared interests, and not a single inconvenience had struck me. I had received regular letters of congratulations regarding my progression and civil engineering, and even been invited to the society's mid-annual meeting in June –something, to my surprise, I was beginning to anticipate!

Not all, however, shared this oasis of contentment and activity that Eliza and I were celebrating. As I was explaining my excitement to my fellows at the Athenaeum Club, I was not quite expecting that familiar, husky voice to interrupt me.

'You're getting complacent, Jacomb.'

The bulldog didn't look at me as he spoke; instead he continued fiddling with his dominoes, a brow raised and his heavy jaw sullen.

'You're setting in too quickly, letting the society take hold of you. I'm telling you sincerely, you cannot trust people in Hargrave's position. You know how Stephenson, Brunel and ourselves spoke of it.'

I listened obediently, but failed to give the most important thing - self-awareness and agreement - to my fellows in the club's drawing room.

'Perhaps,' I replied indignantly, 'people are wrong about the society. Brunel could be a petty man. Who's to say he wasn't

towards the men at Eccleston Square?'
'And Stephenson, then?'
'He was a businessman. He probably had something to gain in his criticisms.'

The bulldog shook his head and glared. His strong brow was furrowed, his breath stilted.

'You, Jacomb, are acting like a politician.'
'And you, sir, are acting like you have some sort of leadership against me. You have not. I am following my own path, and as such, the most successful.'
'I expected a better sense of morale and scruples from you. Mark my words. You'll pay for it with your own head.'
'With the money I'm receiving, Sir, I shall be able to pay for it twice over – and still have a few guineas left!'

Crack! Dominoes clattered across the table and bounced against my chest, as the bulldog stood and stormed out of the room. He slammed the door – and a portrait from the wall fell, crashing to the floor and breaking its glass.

The other men, who had been watching silently, did not say a word. But slowly, eyes fixed firmly to the Persian carpet, followed his path, leaving me alone in that vast room, dominoes in front of me and only the fireplace crackling for company.

They were right to be furious, of course. After months of working in Brunel's memory, I had now thrown it back; dropped the concept of holding fort with my seniors and superiors. I was now working for myself and my own gain.

In my juvenile haste, I neglected to consider how I had just spoken; and left the club's membership only the next day to focus further on business matters.
I found myself poring over a series of draughtsman's drawings for a

local engineer who had contributed towards the tender for the Metropolitan Railway, when Eliza brought me the newspaper.

> 'It looks like they're demolishing Brunel's Hungerford Bridge, for the Charing Cross Railway Company. That's a bit of a shame, isn't it? Do you remember when we used to cross it to get to market, Jacomb?'
> 'The Hungerford? Demolished? It practically still smells of fresh paint!'

I took the newspaper, a sinking feeling washing over me as I read the article. The Hungerford Bridge was a typically Brunel example of a footbridge - an enormous, towering structure for such a simple purpose, and looked set to fall for the oncoming railway, replaced with a basic girder structure.

There was no mention of preservation or even maintaining the design precedent Brunel had set; no mention of trying to keep the area's character. The choice was a regrettable march of progress. Was this how Brunel's work was to be treated?

It had been open now for a mere fifteen years; and as the march of industrial progress had continued, the river around it had grown progressively more sullied with filth and smog, creating a Gothic silhouette in London's natural haze.
I mused what a startling sight it must be to the uninitiated as I strolled to the bridge early the next morning. A pair of towers, seemingly stranded to the Thames' current, bursting through the blackened, stench infested waters like bolts through a great corrugated iron plate.

I held my handkerchief to my face as I met with the bridge's iron gates, the exposed breeze pushing all manner of smoke towards me as vessels plied their trade.

> 'Saying your final farewells? It shan't be missed.'

Hargraves stood, having picked up an eel from one of the local stalls. As usual, he spat with each word, eating with his mouth wide open and a gentle wisp of steam rising from the freshly boiled animal.

'Good morning, Hargraves. You've heard the news?'
'Of course, boy. I signed it off. This bloody bridge has been obsolete since the railway arrived.'
'Seems a trifle sad, really. It's a beautiful bridge. Brunel was proud of it.'
'We've been waiting for his passing to demolish it, Jacomb. It stands in the way of progress. It doesn't turn a profit, nor does it serve a purpose; not since the market hall burnt down. It isn't good business to keep it.'
'It's not that I don't understand-'
'Then don't stand in our way.'

A mournful horn from a passing paddle steamer seemed to mark the epitaph of that grand structure as it passed under - joined in chorus by a vessel passing it in the opposing direction.

They slowly faded into the mist, their thin, trailing exhausts marking a cross that lasted only moments - then disappeared. A fitting headstone for the grand bridge and its final days.

A sign had already been erected to inform the public of the imminent loss. Market traders were to be the last ones to cross; a mass exodus of independent traders, put to pasture for the industrial giant's resolute, indiscriminate march.

HUNGERFORD BRIDGE UNDER IMMEDIATE CLOSURE
To allow the construction of The Charing Cross Railway Station and Bridge.

NO ENTRANCE is permitted for any members of the public.

Scientia Est Imperium.
Ignorantia Est Fragilitas.
Fortitudo Est In Silentio.

Some blamed a lack of specialisation, while some blamed high prices. In any sense, the traders saw the market's main artery as being forcefully removed for the demand of the railway.

It was a familiar experience for many in the country, and a familiar argument for those who sought to keep the railway's masters bridled.

Hargraves' next words would have likely felt just as familiar to the working men and women who had suffered at industry's hands.

'Remember, William. We don't work for your benefit. We work as one. We work as an empire. I'm not in the business of keeping a sentiment.'
'I know that.' I sighed.

I wondered if it was futile to make any sort of appeal - but figured, if nothing else, appealing to Hargraves' pig-headed grandeur and patriotism would be a useful step.

'But surely your society's accomplishments are part of your tapestry? The grand tale?'
'This was no part of our tapestry. Brunel did not work our rulings on this one. Like all of his bloody projects - trundling off to do his own thing with our money. My money. This country's money!'
'Am I not doing the same?'
'We prepared for more of his sort. We have more invested in your underground railway than you know, William. How goes the wedding plans?'
'They're going well enough.'
'August, isn't it?'
'August. My father is looking for the perfect venue.'
Hargraves gave a wide, rotten grin.

'Of course. We'll all be there. We'll be the financiers, after all. All you have to do is keep your neck in and stick to our rules. That means no more protesting our demolitions.'
'Plural? What else do you have planned?'

In response, the enormous beast snorted indignantly.

'And no more asking what the society has in order. You find out with the press, until we feel we can trust you. I'm sure you feel very important, William - but let me be absolutely clear. You're a pawn. A dogsbody. To us, you're a nobody. A nice name to put on the register. A well paid one - that, I admit. But one who is as insignificant as a guppy in the Atlantic.'

He picked at his mouth with a toothpick from his breast pocket, then flicked it at me.

'Now, swim away. Go back to digging up streets and planning weddings.'

Hargraves walked away, into the thick, murky atmosphere of the Hungerford area - leaving only myself, my thoughts, and a condemned bridge.

I felt like I had been taken down more than a couple of pegs too far - my pride had taken such a hit that I felt dazed and disorientated, lost in my own thoughts and sudden lack of self-esteem, where I had previously carried it in spades.

The next couple of days flew by swiftly; visiting churches in the evening and working feverishly on the Metropolitan during every other waking hour, signing what felt like thousands of documents every day.

Without the Athenaeum Club taking interest, my life became less social and more professional with each passing task and document.

The pace of the Metropolitan railway continued, destroying the old and covering it over, marching with a tremendous vigour in favour of progress. Passenger expectations were high, and there were rumours that Gooch was to be the locomotive engineer for what some were calling the 'miracle railway' - amusingly, very similar things had been said about the Great Western Railway once upon a time.

However, I felt a great sense of dread, despite my impressive levels of productivity - I had raised the ire of Hargraves; and with it I almost constantly expected the worst.

The feeling was constant - a strange emotion veering dangerously into paranoia. When my invitation to the society's meeting arrived, I wondered if my worrying had been for naught, and breathed a sigh of relief.

I wasn't absconded. There had been no threats. There had been no cause for concern. All that remained was to meet the rest of Hargraves' group; build my connections - and create a truly winning enterprise for myself.

The atmosphere as I walked to Eccleston Square that evening was bright and hazy. Summer was in full grip, now lit by glowing sunshine that, in London's great smog, added a strange, unyielding yellow tint to the great silhouettes of London's towering structures, narrow streets and busy pavements.

The smell of the river was almost unbearable, and demanded the use of a handkerchief to wander even the relatively well sheltered areas of Pimlico.

I rapped on the door, to which, this time, Hargraves himself answered - at first, with suspicion and a deep, furrowed brow. This intimidation quickly disappeared into a crooked, 'welcoming' smile - that, frankly, felt anything but - joined with a tight grip on my arm and a sharp pull into the façade's hallway.

The board room was filled with a murmuring chatter of aged voices, thin wisps of smoke floating through the join of the doors. It felt almost like a religious experience; a walk into a grand chapel of smoking incense and chanting monks. However, this wisping, twirling vapour was no patchouli; it was tobacco and opium.

'Take a seat boy. I trust you were unaccompanied.'
'Of course.'
'Good. Keep it that way in future.'

He opened the doors, releasing a cloud of acrid fumes of every vice one could possibly imagine. I maintained my grip on my handkerchief as I was led into the main chamber.

In the place of monks, there instead sat men. Businessmen in suits and tailcoats, coated in thick layers of hair oil - cheap scents, treatments and aging features.

'These, Jacomb, are the senior members of our grand society. They sign off every final action our society takes. Under my order, of course.'

A murmur echoed around the table.

Brereton sat at one end. He seemed rather surprised to see me - a grim expression of dismay at my own submission to his position. A position he found so dire.

'Who knows.' Hargraves boomed, holding his lapels with an - I assume - attempted mark of extravagant pride. 'Perhaps, one day, you shall find yourself among these great minds. Superb businessmen, all of them - leading the country forwards. Of course, the major work goes on downstairs.'

I raised an eyebrow. I was beginning to feel my quizzical glance was becoming a default facial expression. 'What major work?'

One of the old men - a portly, balding man who reeked of opium, and, more's to the point, of a government minister - spoke up. 'Do you have no imagination, boy? That's where development is underway on our country's future.'

'Everything goes on down there - we have departments. Everything from material testing, to chemical creation, to the manufacture of weapons.'
'Weapons?'
Hargraves gave a broad, arrogant grin.
'Weapons. One can't fight a fight for the future without the finest weaponry. I want this country to have the greatest arsenal in the world. After we sell it to the armed forces, of course.'
'You're monopolising war.'
'We're taking advantage of a free market, William. The same goes for our manufacture of metals for bridges, scaffolding... tunnel supports for underground railways...'

The portliest businessman lit up his pipe and smirked. I found the look on his face quite detestable - if Hargraves was not the true villain in the group, I laid my bets upon this man being the charge.

'...And the insurers of Scott Russell's shipyard during the Great Eastern's construction.'

I clenched my fists. I had never dared think that these people could have a presence behind the Great Eastern without my knowing; the very idea was frightful.

Hargraves looked me in the eyes. 'We were Russell's main creditors, William. We were who he owed money to.'

I spoke through grating teeth. 'He sold off our iron to pay off his debts to you. He brought Brunel so much stress it near killed him.'

'Yes; terrible business. Poor practise. Of course, we took Russell from our registers as soon as the catastrophic launch took place.

He'll never build a vessel again. But our policies as creditors are clear, and, I don't mind telling you, very profitable. It's a good business, William - you could be a jolly good spokesperson for it.'

Hargraves took a sip of absinthe - straight from the chiselled glass decanter; no glass - no sugar cube. He simply took it neat poured directly from that fine, glass decanter's throat. The other gentlemen looked uncomfortable.

He belched, returned the decanter and behind me, arms behind his back, in a clear reflection of his pomposity and self-importance. There was no doubt - here, he was the leader - the king.

'After all, William - we're much the same for your little underground railway. Most of London's railway connections have seen our generous bankroll. Isn't that right, Mr. Brereton?'

Brereton said nothing. He nodded and sunk slightly in his chair as I stared.

'And you see, William, it all stems from a single miracle. A grand miracle and our country's leading minds.'
'So I have been informed. All from a coincidence, eh?'
'Coincidence? Oh no, William. It was fate. People deem fate to be superstition, as a mere credence to the spontaneity of life. These people are idiots.'

Hargraves sat back in his chair - the largest at the table; not simply to accommodate his enormous figure - but to elevate him above his peers, to provide a grand, towering visage - or a grotesque mockery of such - to those who stood before him.

'We are here due to fate, boy. The world itself insisted we take the materials it offered to us. Fate is a parliament, William - it gives only to those who deserve it. The poor and the poorly educated are one in the same; it was essential for this gift to mankind not to be squandered. The wretched masses don't deserve to be part of our operation.'

'Hear hear!' applauded the portliest, pipe smoking businessman.

I was beginning to get the impression he was no different to the plotting vizier I had so often read about in tales of Arabia. In any sense, his face seemed to maintain that detestable, arrogant smirk no matter the situation.

The elitism here was astounding, and the sheer worship that seemed to be applied to Hargraves even worse; one could only imagine how much Brunel and Stephenson must have despised this bloated despot's empire and how it operated beneath him.

The stench of the London Society was beginning to truly infest my senses. Something was far more sinister than I had imagined. A society? Nay. This was nothing more than a cult of personality.

'I can see your scepticism, William. You seem to disbelieve the society's wisdom. The society's goals. What is it you find so unbelievable?'
'I find your society's miracle unbelievable, Hargraves. I know all about your little book story, and I think it's nothing more than a fairy tale.'

The men fell silent. Glances were exchanged, eyebrows raised - dialogue firmly halted.

Hargraves let out a deep breath. I was unsure if it was a belch or a submittal. The silence continued. It briefly occurred to me as to how often I now seemed to encounter silence in my endeavours. How I hated it. Silence had no place in a working man's life - that was something Brunel had insisted. Yet repeatedly, it seemed to provide the music for my scenery since my first encounter with a man's deathbed.

'Then you shall be shown our miracle, Jacomb. You shall be shown it, and you shall eat your words. Come with me.'

I was led down the staircase – out of the drawing room's view, and the view of the gentlemen behind us, still sat in silence around their table.

The darkness struck quickly, and before my eyes adjusted I had been rammed against the wall – hard. A meaty arm pressed firmly against my neck, and a putrid breath spat into my face.

> 'Mark my soul, you little runt – if you dare speak a word of it outside of this room, I shall destroy you. And your career. And your family.'
> I grunted. 'What on Earth am I supposed to do to your little legacy? What do you fear? What on Earth do you have to fear?'
> 'You're naïve, William. You underestimate the fragility of any empire. I will do anything to stop prying eyes and wagging tongues. That includes removing them. The Roman Empire. The Persian Empire. Our own British Empire; all were doomed to fail the moment they were established. It wasn't a mass failure. It won't be a mass failure. It was all due to a drizzle, a tiny leak – a pitiful crack in their foundations. And here you are. You're as small and as insignificant as they come. You're an office boy, an office boy for a dead dwarf who had big ideas and a knack for drawing-'
>
> I wheezed under his enormous wrist, squeezing ever-tighter against my throat. 'You're…really…so…vulnerable?'

The force against my neck tightened. I groaned and tried to grip his hand – digging in my nails; trying to release myself from that enormous arm.

> 'Vulnerable would be a lack of ability to erase my problems, William. You are not a vulnerability. You're a rat. A harbour rat

that's spent too long skulking around ships instead of doing business.'

He released me, leaving me gasping for air, crouched on the floor. His silhouetted form stood against the dim light of the drawing room above.

'You wouldn't benefit from a young, newsworthy recruit turning up dead, Hargraves. You'd be under scrutiny in the space of twenty four hours!'

Hargraves laid his foot upon my leg.

'Look around you, office boy. This headquarters covers more ground than Parliament and Buckingham Palace put together. I have projects that would benefit from human experimentation. Don't think I'm beyond it.
I've done it before, William. Serums. Chemicals. Furnaces. I have experience in erasing stray pencil marks. You'd never appear again. Nobody would find even a scrap of your pretty little lace cravat. Do I make myself clear?
You are not a vulnerability. You're a number. You're an easily erased little piece of graphite on my grand tapestry. You can be rubbed away in seconds. You're an arrogant, worthless, jumped up little paper shuffler; you can't deny my power, you can't deny my society's grip and you can't tip a single fruit from my apple cart. I will show you our miracle. But I want to make it perfectly clear. You shall not see daylight if I get the slightest bit suspicious. Our technologies can prove unstable, William.'

His foot released me, and he backed away - a horrible, wide, rotten grin catching what little light lined the corridor.

'Why, a train can jump off of the rails with barely the slightest tempering. I would know.'

The coin dropped.

'You?'
'Oh, grow up William. Surely even an office boy could work that out. It wasn't a tragedy; it was orchestrated. To the finest detail. It was an attempt at erasing a problem. Sadly our unstable technologies don't also guarantee the loss of one Mr. Jacomb at Tottenham Station. Shame, too. Imagine the payment your wife would have received.'
'You killed innocent people!'
'A worthy sacrifice.'
'Of all of the hideous, appalling, disgusting actions I've heard, I could-'
'Kill me? Get a grip man, you're no murderer. What on earth would you kill me with? A fountain pen? I have the entire country's wheels of industry, every railway line, every factory under hand. It takes nothing to create an accident.
'Let me be clear; this is your official warning. Stay within our terms, follow our orders, and if you try a single, slightest mutinous action, I'll see to it you're swept off of every register in the country. You're a dogsbody. You were under Brunel, you are under me, and you will be for your entire life. Don't cross me.'

I had to clench my fists in a desperate attempt to still the tremors of fear and anger running through them.

'Now come. I promised to show you the Tome, did I not? Or have I finally instilled the fear of your superiors?'
'I am not fearful.' A lie.
'Then you shall follow me into the chamber. Come.'

I did as I was told -and was led by that hulking, great monster towards an enormous, bolted doorway - deep in the dark, labyrinthine tunnels that made up so much of Pimlico's secretive heart.

The fine stonework seemed to drip with an eternal, echoing moisture, setting up a sinister, dank tone to what seemed like a dry, warm and well-built environment.

I considered briefly if that dripping was manufactured; an attempt to add imposition to Cubitt's impenetrable, subterranean district.

Hargraves stood by the side of those enormous metal doors, inserted an unusual key - then, using a strange, iron mechanism, not unlike that of a screw valve, slowly opened one of them into a broad entrance way – thinly lit with a dim light of gas flame, held in glass lanterns with a deep, red tint.

He beckoned me inwards and nodded. The boisterous, villainous man had become, instead, quiet, brooding and introverted.

I was not convinced. I felt like I was being toyed with. But my natural curiosity ruled. And I stepped inside.

+ REVELATION +

The atmosphere in the chamber was completely bone dry and unnervingly silent - save the soft, hollow hissing of gas being piped to the lanterns that gave their dim, red glow.

'It helps preserve it, you know. This book of plans is the ultimate resource for our country's future. It's essential to prevent even the slightest fragility.'

Inside the chamber's scant light, there stood only a glass case, no larger than a side table. Inside the case, there sat - quite comfortably, on a large, purple velvet cushion - a yellowed, tattered book. It was enormous; similar in size to the bibles held in cathedrals, albeit with many times the page count. It was adorned with thick layers of burnished bronze on each corner, bolted securely into the heavy calfskin endpapers.

The papers were foxed at every edge, with the odd hole or knot in the heavy leaves of paper - that more accurately resembled hammered tree bark than the refined product used across the country.

The writing on each of these heavy sheets seemed unusually accurate and clean; like the product of an advanced printing press rather than the written word or the product of stamps.

Occasionally, a slim coating of red dust was blown around it from inside the glass casing, from a large grill underneath the cushion's plinth.

> 'Clay. The Eternal Tome was dug from clay; we reason it's the only way to keep the pages properly. There are later sections and page dedicated to preservation and conservation – but those are well beyond our abilities yet.'

I glanced at Hargraves, who seemed swollen with pride – and a strange reverence for this unusual tome.

The Eternal Tome was open on an early page in the book's colossal length, displaying an unusual configuration of motor, similar to a static steam engine.

> 'They call it internal combustion, boy. No coal. Only gas. It's being worked on by a chap in Belgium, from what I understand. The book is chronological, I believe. The current page is where technology is – so we stay ahead of current development using this. Our tactic is usually to skip ahead by a year or so.'
> 'It's espionage.'
> 'Not so. This isn't an aspect of justice, crime or morale – you cannot spy on something that has already existed for thousands of years. It's perhaps a gentle bend in the natural order – but I don't believe in such things.'

A wheeze came from the grill underneath the book's mount, as another, pale red cloud enveloped the imposing, tattered volume into a hefty silhouette.

'You need to understand, my lad, that this is no mere book. It's a brain. A memory. Everything in the Eternal Tome stems from the past. It's a record of something long since passed. How, we do not know - and may never find out. For now, all we can do is show it the respect it deserves.'
'Where did it come from?'
'The canals; deep in a clay bank at the start of the revolution. My father found it; and had no idea just how important it was.'

I was walked out from the room, and watched as the door was screwed shut, an echo of the resulting clang echoing through the tunnels and arches of Pimlico's secret city.

'He was a fool, building in those damned waterways. By the time his precious docks and locks were finished, the railways were making them obsolete.'

Hargraves clearly saw no fond feelings for his father.

'He made us penniless; and figured the book might be worth something, even if he couldn't make sense of it. He put it up for auction. Nobody saw value in a big old book, regardless of the contents.
I did. I had been working as an apprentice, and figured the book's importance to the world. So I did the sensible thing. I took it, and made sure my father would not follow.'

He walked back towards the stairs that led up to the society's drawing room.

'I did it for the nation's good. I regret it, of course, but needs must.'

I didn't believe Hargraves had any regrets.

'I found a society set up by George Stephenson following the Rainhill Locomotive trials. I introduced them to the Eternal

Tome, and explained the idea I had - to bring our nation to the future. Naturally, we developed some concepts, sold them on - made an immense profit. And, well - it wouldn't make sense to keep knowledge a free enterprise, would it?
So I bought shares. I bought other fellows' interest. I pushed Stephenson and the other engineers out slowly, and by the time they had noticed, the society was already mine. Turning a grand profit. More than any railway could produce. Engineers, mechanics, architects, they were all eager to try some of these strange new technologies and techniques. It was a trial and error process, of course, working out where to begin - and how to reverse engineer. But we got there.'

Hargraves took a deep inhale of snuff as he lumbered along.

'By the end of the 1840s, we'd attracted the greatest minds of the country. And the world. And became the most profitable - ahem - gentleman's club that the world knew. And that, my boy, that was the gem -the stroke of genius. Nobody knew. We were an enigma, an invisible group working from the shadows.
No names, no credits, no signatures. Only cover companies, false bankers, and false investors - steadily turning pennies into pounds, and doing so with such a graceful, elegant movement that, if you so much as blinked, you missed every merger, every threat, every investment, and every insurance policy.
 We're unstoppable because every member of ours is completely stoppable, disposable and easy to silence. Money speaks, certainly - but silence can be bribed and threatened into even the most opinionated, headstrong idiot in our industry.'

Hargraves took notice that one of the red-glass lanterns had not lit, and fiddled with it, turning his back to me without the slightest concern. He continued on his monologue.

'Sadly it seems your master lacked any kind of loyalty. Any kind of positive character, in fact. I always suspected as much. But for him to send to send some kind of student engineer after my grand establishment, from the sheets of the deathbed my money paid for? Treacherous. Disgusting. Appalling.'

I could feel myself bristling under his constant insults. Unprintable thoughts and ideas were rushing around in my head – was I desperate to topple this man out of an honest intent, or because I so wanted him to fail from his self-established podium?

'Not to mention stupid. I don't know what he thinks you can achieve, but I hope our discussion has made the reality perfectly clear – you can't, and you won't.
I've built this empire over twenty years, William. It's practically been in place longer than you've been able to write your name. It's too large for you to overcome. You may disagree with my methods, but they're damned effective – and, for this nation, are the only way to keep us ahead of the rest of the world.
Destroy that, and you shall destroy our country, eventually. Now remember, put on your best face for the elite back in the drawing room, keep your trap shut and your eyes on that subsidy and wedding, eh? I don't want to have another conversation with you on this matter.'

I nodded – reluctantly – And followed him up the staircase and back to the drawing room, trying to still the shaking in my hands, and the wish to retch from my stomach. I returned to inquisitive stares, and a distraught, shameful Brereton, averting his gaze as much as he could.

'So, Jacomb. What is your conclusion?' requested that wicked vizier.

There was a pause. Hargraves slapped me on the back aggressively, hidden behind a friendly, chummy façade with a cruel mockery of a reassuring smile.

I swallowed my pride. 'I will be honoured to join you in the march of progress. What a miraculous thing you have down there.'

The gentlemen slowly began to applaud; soon erupting into what I recall Brunel as calling 'shareholder cheering' - when men seemed needlessly excited for the turning of profit; something that, in itself, was an impeccably boring fabric of their livelihoods.

I felt trapped, and quite unsure of how to approach this situation from then on. Everything about the Society seemed like a falsehood; a crocodile's grin, if you were. Waiting for me to slip or fall, so they may pick me apart.

'Now that has been settled, Jacomb, you must sign our ledger. After that, you're free to leave until we call upon you next.'
'This is all of the hospitality a new member receives?'
Hargraves gave a bellowing laugh. 'What, you expect a bottle of the finest brandy, some flowers and a rosette?!'

The other gentlemen chuckled.

'No, Jacomb. You sign, and you leave. We don't hassle ourselves too extravagantly. Only our senior members experience a privileged seat - and the scientists and engineers below our feet operate in entirely closed quarters. You get to continue in your own trades until your skills are required.'
The vizier blew smoke in my direction. It felt targeted to my face. 'Quite a favourable condition, for somebody so young and inexperienced. I should hope you'll be thanking us for years to come, let alone when your marriage takes place.'
'I can't wait to come along. I hope the wedding dinner shall be a suitably grand affair for our money!' laughed Hargraves.

An echo of 'shareholder laughter', as I had figured to dub it, echoed around the drawing room table, as I signed the long, creeping vellum ledger that slipped down Hargraves' fine, mahogany bureau.

The ledger was a bizarre thing; like an enormous indenture, or a finely polished financier's contract – with a rambling pretext concerning the 'kingdom's voyage of discovery' and our promises to continue the 'exploration of progress from the sacred tome'. Under it followed an extravagant line of inked signatures spanning some two decades. The deceased were marked with a red blot alongside the name – or so I supposed, from Brunel and Stephenson's names carrying such a mark.

I recognised the penmanship in the contract's design to be that of Hargraves; that fine, flowing calligraphy that made such an impressive impact to those within any professional endeavour. It was rather bizarre to consider such a seemingly complex operation not only sitting under a fairly standard London district, but with an epicentre revolving around drunken, fat, lazy men smoking opium and drinking foul, pungent liqueurs.

Hargraves belched as he looked over my shoulder at my signature. I wasn't sure what he had been drinking, but his breath was an odious thing, with an odd hint of angelica, bacon grease and expired seafood.

> 'Excellent. Now leave, Jacomb. Until we need you next, you're free to return to your post at the Underground railway.'
> The vizier gave his characteristic grin. 'It was delightful to meet you. I look forward to sharing a pipe with you sometime, Jacomb. Allow me to walk you to the door, eh?'

I tried to resist – but the Vizier pulled me along, to a suspicious glance from Hargraves himself.

The drawing chamber's doors closed, and the portly man - bedecked in the finest silk and velvet, I noted – walked me towards the false door that maintained the illusion of Eccleston Square's innocent purposes.

> 'So tell me." The Vizier muttered, "How much has he threatened

you?'

'I don't quite know what you-'

'I'm no fool. I'm more capable of reading people than the flimsy, wet handkerchiefs sat around that table. He's disgusting, isn't he, William?'

I stayed quiet.

'I've got many-a-deal for you, if you share my distaste for him. We could take over it all, Jacomb. If you aren't a scared little boy, like he'd have us believe, join me in overthrowing him. He'll barely be able to handle the shock.

'We'd be unstoppable.'

He tucked a note card into my pocket, and patted my back as he opened the door.

'Think about it. There are plenty of us willing to take action.'

The moment the door closed behind me, I couldn't help but shudder. My hand held the area of my neck that was subject to Hargraves' arm. My head was swimming.

The revelations seemed endless. The Eternal Tome truly did exist; the dictatorship of Hargraves' society, his cult of personality and his horrendous behaviour were all true. The wicked larceny that Brunel and Stephenson regarded him with -it was now quite believable.

Yet, there were men under Hargraves plotting against him; there were men far beyond Brunel's relatively modest staff working under him. There were profits at stake, people fighting for this bizarre, opiate-infested empire.

And yet, the first of all - that was the most confusing and laborious to me. That bizarre relic - with all of the grandeur and worn character of something truly historic; it was the source of Brunel's output - of Stephenson's railways - of the world's greatest engineering and architectural marvels.

Nobody seemed to ask the more bizarre, fear-struck questions in my head. How? *How* could this exist? *How* could this be happening?

It is perhaps telling of the British upper lip that nobody seemed, on the surface, particularly shocked or shaken by the existential quandary of the book's existence. Nobody questioned as to how these things had existed in the past. Nobody seemed scared or confused.

It was as if its existence was already in our subconscious; that we were simply following paths already laid ahead. The Book of Revelation truly did exist; and as Stephenson had told me – it was a book of blueprints.

Perhaps it was my engineering side; perhaps it was my natural curiosity, relative to my youth. I had to know more; and I had to discuss what I had discovered.

I arrived home feeling dizzy, that evening, after an ambling, aimless walk through Pimlico – searching for other traces betraying the society's existence.

There were none, barring the regular shapes and dimensions of those perfectly designed streets. Who would ever think so much activity was rife below?

The only evidence was I myself. I had burnt my bridges with the Athenaeum club, to my mind, and I highly doubted they would believe me with such a complex, disturbing and irregular story.

I had to find a way to communicate with Samuel that was secure, and unlikely to be monitored.

I sank into a restless sleep; remaining thoroughly unhappy with my circumstance. I hadn't wished for this situation. I hadn't asked for so much tribulation and difficulty.

And yet, here I was - entrapped - a dogsbody for a master I despised. Caught in the great London conspiracy with dwindling allies and nothing but a fat purse to show for it; something many would kill for the chance to experience in our unjust city.

Why, then, did I feel so desperate to sever this connection, and not harvest it for my fortune?

I figured I should, at least, reap the positive relationship for at least one of my few clear priorities.

+ THE WEDDING +

As Summer came closer, so did our society-funded wedding. Eliza was beyond excited - we could now live and breathe every day of our lives together with Church approval.

The wedding was going to be a grand affair; as Hargraves had promised, no expense was spared for his members - indeed, our families had found themselves without the need to contribute anything to our fund, and focused instead on giving gifts to our household.

My father was retired - and had been so since a relatively young age, having been quite the taskmaster in his younger years and amassed a comfortable circumstance for myself and our family. He was suspicious at best; at worst, he was constantly worried and guarded towards what I had gotten myself involved with.

He was a wizened sort of gentlemen- whisking sideburns across his face and a stout figure, though maintaining the defined cheekbones and slim facial structure the Jacomb family seemed to maintain.

He had a habit of rubbing a thumb against the side of his nose when he was unsure of things, I recall - and spoke with a gentle tone contrary to a sometimes intimidating visage.

> 'You don't speak to me enough about your professional affairs, William. I raised you to be transparent with me and now this... this, well, utterly bizarre group of builders and mechanics are responsible for your wedding rather than your mother than I? I can't even find this Hargraves fellow in public records.'
> 'You'll meet him at the wedding, father. He's relatively tame, I promise you.'
> 'You're lying to me. Look into my eyes, son. You're in trouble, aren't you?'
> 'Trouble, no. Nothing I cannot handle.'
> He sighed. 'A boy becomes an assistant to Brunel and he thinks he's capable of taking on the world.'
> 'You blame me for feeling so?'
> 'I'd be lying if I said yes. Just be careful, eh?'
> 'I will, father. I promise you - all is fine.'
> 'Fine, fine. So be it. But William?'

He took my hand, in both of his, and shook it gently with his firm grip, a gentle smile curling from cheek to cheek. I could swear there were tears in his eyes; a look of pure pride in the old man that would enliven even the most tired, cynical son.

> 'Make sure you enjoy this day. It's yours. And Eliza's.'

I had never lied to my father before; in this unusually intimate moment with him, I felt like I was doing him somewhat of a betrayal by claiming my career to be one of plain sailing.

My mind was clear, and my targets firm: to glide upon the waters ahead of me like that of a great ship; regardless of the endless effort, grime, soot, blood and sweat that propelled it; much like myself.

I could not let this façade collapse for those around me. I had come close; but I was now resolute. Secrecy and a smooth outset was absolutely paramount for my mission against Hargraves, his society - and my mission for a happy, peaceful, and just life with the woman I adored so dearly.

The venue was a suitably beautiful one; St. Johns, of Notting Hill - a towering house of God, only fifteen years of age, that was built to a traditional template rather than the modern styles of architecture now so familiar to Parish and Manor around London, a city insisting on the contemporary. The building's sharp, white Suffolk stone profile resembled a lump of quartz upon a rolling, grassy hill in the summer sunshine, and both Eliza and I had taken to regularly visiting together on our summer walks.

Business was still holding me tight in its grip, and paid dividends for my time and efforts - but it made the planning of our ceremony a vexatious issue between Eliza and myself. I had been running so late recently that it had become necessary for me to rush to a fine suit-hire company on Mayfair, indeed, the very eve of my Wedding. I had returned home to her scathing glare (though it held a certain amusement behind it) and tapping foot, much to my surprise.

> 'My darling! It's supposed to be unlucky for our eyes to meet on the night before the marriage-'
> She chuckled. 'You will be the unlucky one if you don't cease getting caught up in your work, Mr. Jacomb. I'm half worried we might end up with some sort of knob stick wedding!'
> 'Perish the thought, Eliza. Tomorrow shall be magical.'
> 'You're an engineer! You types don't believe in Magic.' She smiled, wrapping her arms around my waist and her head against my chest. 'For all I see of you these days, William, you could have married a hundred girls across London.'
> 'For all I know, Eliza, you could be married to every ruffian in

Parliament.'

'No need to use such offensive language, dearest Fiancée!'

We smiled broadly as we watched the clock perched above the mantelpiece of our home. How bizarre it was, to consider that our wedding was so close - after years of preparation and attempting to raise funds. Despite everything we had endured since the death of Brunel, we seemed to have only grown closer and more adoring through even the most perilous situations.

We both eagerly awaited the morning - but for now, we opted to part ways as tradition enforced, and parted with a kiss - before leaving me to prepare myself for the day ahead.

The morning before the wedding was a chaotic one - barbers, last minute tailor's alterations - even ensuring my hip flask was properly filled and a couple of cigars secured for myself and my father.

But the chaos? I revelled in it - the sheer excitement bounding around within me put steam and vigour into my stride, and I gathered my requirements with a beaming smile on my face - and the odd neighbour or acquaintance wishing me good luck for the day.

Not a single negative thought clouded my head - this was a day I had been desperately waiting for, for what had felt like an enormous part of my life, and, in my head, something I had more than earned through the poor treatment I had endured through the society now paying for the celebrations.

Not even the thought of Hargraves himself being present worried me; the only focus in my mind was for the future with Eliza; with Mrs. Jacomb - finally, one of the rewards for my hard work was upon the table.

The day beat on impressively, and within what seemed like a blink of an eye, my carriage pulled up in front of the grand, monolithic tower of St. John's church. The sun beat off of the white stone in thick, smoky beams, through a gentle blanket of white cloud.

But for a brief moment, I found myself wondering if this was a blessing upon our ceremony and future from the higher powers that be. I was still wearing a broad - if nervous - smile as I entered the church to talk with the vicar.

Samuel was my best man - of course, who else could I claim as being a close friend and counterpart through the past year? And Eliza's parents were already there to give her away when she arrived.

I had deliberately changed the seating plan to ensure Hargraves, and any other 'professional' contacts, were seated firmly to the rear of the grand hall, to keep them away from our families and the main proceedings.

I was sure most would have no part in trying to create business during our ceremony - but the idea of having Hargraves remotely close to my family, and, more importantly, my in-laws, was frightful to me.

Friends and family were soon arriving. Gooch had remained at Swindon due to his ever-increasing obligations, as had a few of my other professional friends and colleagues, but in all, a veritable crowd of fifty were soon present - to my surprise, it included Mary, still wearing black in mourning for Brunel's passing, and Brereton in his Sunday finest, trying his damnedest to blend into the crowd - something quite difficult with his eyepatch.

Behind them sat what I and Samuel had dubbed 'the bandit's row' - Hargraves, two of the Dealers, that odious vizier and one or two of the other detestable fellows I had met at Eccleston square.

Thankfully, they seemed to be taking their placement seriously;

although Hargraves was indulging himself in boiled sweets, which he crunched loudly with his mouth open.

I scanned the crowd for more familiar faces, trying my hardest to ignore that crunching of syrup and sugar from the largest inhabitant of the audience - before being snapped back to reality with the organist starting to play.

Eliza had arrived; and the future Mrs. Jacomb looked utterly radiant as she slowly walked between the pews - Hargraves looked like his eyes could have very nearly left his skull, the odious letch that he was - with the gentle, bashful demeanour I knew her so well for.

It was tempting to embrace her the moment she reached the altar. She smiled and held my hand tightly as the vows were read. I felt rather like the shy young graduate I had been when we first met, and found myself hopelessly stuttering with every line fed to me.

All the same, despite my sudden lost nerves and the incredible pressure I felt in front of fifty prying eyes, it went beautifully - cleanly - and without a single issue, much to my somewhat paranoid head's relief. It was, truthfully, the closest to a perfect day that, in my mind, I could have ever experienced since Brunel's passing. It made the difficulties, the arguments, the threats and more all worthwhile. As we left the church, I could honestly say that, for the first time in nearly a year, I and Eliza both felt happy - completely, and utterly, content.

I smiled and nodded to those I recognised in the pews - and tried to ignore the wide grin of the vizier and Hargraves' ogling of my wife. What was more difficult, in my eyes, was attempting to ignore the fact they were responsible for this happening at all.

We made our way back to our home in a luxury carriage - hands firmly entwined.

'William, it was perfect.'

'It was, Mrs. Jacomb. I couldn't be happier.'
'Will I start seeing you at home more often now?' She smirked, looking into my eyes.
'No promises.'
She laughed and pushed me. 'You're a terrible man. And I love you. Do you not at least have some time away from work for us to settle into married life?'
'One day; after that I shall have to get back to the grindstone, Eliza.'
'Such a luxurious career, William - digging holes and laying tubes underneath roads…all for big kettles to rattle around on. I'm sure it's all of your dreams realised, playing trains and sailboats…'
'Now now, let's not go mudslinging, eh?' I smirked.
'Do we have any plans for our evening, dear husband? Perhaps you can bribe me to silence…!'

I said nothing; simply held her close as the hoof-beats trotted us towards our home - which was finally sanctified in the eyes of the judgemental. At long last, we were a 'legitimate' couple in the eyes of the Lord - whatever that may mean.

Our evening was indeed quite a treat for even the most discerning diner - recommended by Hargraves. I would not normally take any recommendation from the man - but after all, I and Eliza reasoned, he was such a tight fisted old letch that we believed he'd only accept the best for so much as a guinea.

My father had given us a generous budget for our first married meal, and I had been conscious to ensure our experience was kept relatively quiet and reserved, in absence of a honeymoon.

The *Cafe de L'Europe* was Hargraves' recommendation for their three-course-and-dessert. I couldn't help but notice a similarity once again in Hargraves recommendation - his open hostility the rest of the world, but thorough enjoyment of certain customs and tastes he found convenient to him.

The De L'Europe was equally popular with Brunel. Brunel was, in contrast to Hargraves, always a lover of foreign custom and intensely world conscious. The fare of De L'Europe's was an enormous influence on his palette, and, Brereton informed me, his own finest choice for meals in both business and leisure - rather a contrast to our common meals of goose and beer at local pubs.

The restaurant, lit up brightly, occupied one of the old Haymarket theatres - creating a place of high ceilings and airy, natural warmth.

The Chandeliers, the tranquility and the exceptional service were an unusual change from our everyday lives of paperwork, business and my own concerns. I felt as if I was in another world. I had known Paris was famous for good food - but *this* good?

It was a proud place, serving only the finest hearty, Parisian fare, and yet provided an intimate, romantic atmosphere that truly made our evening complete.

No matter where Eliza and I seemed to spend our time together, the good natured, cheeky, yet contagiously relaxed lady I now called my wife seemed to be a completely natural part of every environment. A bright, luxurious gem - a diamond, no less, regardless of whether sitting in a dimly lit coffee house, or taking a luxurious dinner.

I apologise, dear reader - truly I do. I did so intend to keep my romantic feelings away from this work - but, in all of the powers that may be; I can honestly say I had never felt so sincerely in love.

+ DARK TUNNELS +

For the next year, my efforts were solely focused on the Underground Railway through London - working in close efforts with Mr. Fowler and his team of engineers to see the ultimate in modern, high speed transit for the city at the centre of the civilised world.

Or at least, this was Hargraves' view on the project. He had decided to regale me with a visit to a local fighting bar in Whitechapel - to view savages fighting for superior entertainment. Again; this was his view on what was in front of me.

To my eyes, it was nothing more than men shouting and screaming at two other men beating themselves to a pulp; all paying handsomely for bets and tickets. The men in this case were East European, and could barely speak English. Part of me wondered how people could even get into this industry -how does a place like this come to exist?

'One of my side businesses, boy. We get dogs in sometimes; a grand Saturday night, eh?'

Ah.

I rolled my eyes and held my hands behind my back the entire time as the battle inside the ring raged on with excessive brutality. I felt ready to duck should a stray tooth or splash of blood head our way, and winced as the two gentlemen continued fighting.

> 'They're brothers, you know!' chuckled Hargraves. 'These people are so backwards for a couple of extra meals. If they could speak a lick of the Queen's, they'd probably be good workers.'
> 'Then why treat them as entertainment?'
> 'They get paid, they get fed, and they get their opium - who suffers?'
> 'From the bloodied noses and fractures, I'd say they do!'

Hargraves took an enormous snort of snuff. I still found it bizarre to see how much tobacco could fit into his crooked, proboscis addled nose.

> 'A mere trifle, boy. Nothing to value. The bets are a good business; hell, sometimes over ten pounds a night. I have five or six of these gentleman's clubs around London. Gambling is good business. '
> 'I don't believe in gambling.'
> 'Of course you do. Your investors and backers have been gambling on projects for years. It's no different; you're the benefactor for their naivety or your convincing prattle.'

He didn't look at me once; simply leant against the wooden barrier around his cockfighting pit, casually. It was as if his constant insults and barrage of unpleasantness was akin to a conversation over a tankard; that the savagery in front of us was no different to watching cricket. I just shook my head behind him.

I have no idea how I was still being surprised with every moment I spent in the company of this arrogant arse. The fact remained that, despite now being a happily married man, under valuable employ and becoming increasingly wealthy under his rule, I loathed him so heavily I felt quite prepared to drop everything just to see him fall.

It was, perhaps, little surprise that the more I learnt; the more I recognised Brunel's position. I had taken to night time meetings at Duke Street, sitting at Brunel's old desk with Brereton and Samuel, partaking in a dram and discussing our lot in the world, or, more specifically, that of the society.

We were both becoming increasingly comfortable in each other's company, and now, with myself in the picture, Brereton was clearly feeling far more liberated with his own criticisms and umbrage. He, like I myself, was beginning to seem pessimistic and suspicious of our fellows and the world around us. Samuel often listened intently, giving his findings or occasional - albeit very valuable - input regarding the grapevine, and how the industrial world around us was reacting.

The meetings had become replacements for those at the Anthenaeum club, a proxy for spending time with my peers and explaining my plans and ideas. We had even considered trying to bring Gooch into the picture - but he had rejected due to his commitments in the Great Western.

> 'I hear the Great Eastern is having further trouble, William. Typically Brunellian issues, might I add.' Brereton put in, pouring himself another dram of single malt.
> 'Quite. I've been trying to avoid the subject, honestly.'
> 'Why should you? By rights, she's yours by proxy. I dare say even after your railway is completed, she'll be your largest and greatest achievement.'
> Samuel smiled. 'Ignorance doesn't stop the failure, William. It's not her engineering that's failing, you know, or her construction. It's her ownership.'

The Great Eastern was indeed proving a difficult endeavour for her owners. She was now repaired, and back under steam - but the Great Ship Company - a company that Hargraves was firmly behind the financing for - had quickly discovered that there was, in reality, very few passengers who wanted to cross the globe without refuelling. As a matter of fact, very few seemed to share Brunel's fascination for the East and Eastern trade whatsoever. As a result, she was now an Atlantic vessel, plying much the same routes as Brunel's other ships.

The natural problem was that the Great Eastern was larger, slower, and more expensive - none of which held her in much regard with such a standard transportation route.

The resulting maiden voyage had proven dire - with only thirty five paying customers.

> 'Frankly, William, I'm rather surprised Hargraves hasn't strung you up purely out of rage for the ship's issues.'
> 'The Underground Railway is an endeavour with too much potential, Brereton. Although I do fear that's all which is holding him off.'

Samuel was admiring the bust of Newton sat upon one of Brunel's shelves, which had not been touched or moved, out of respect for our employer. He was listening intently. In what now seems like a rather poetically timed moment, he suddenly dropped a bit of a bombshell.

> 'You did know that Gooch was on board the first American voyage? He's invested heavy amounts of money, by now.'

I choked on my drink. Samuel continued, barely faltering as I wiped my lips with a handkerchief.

> 'He's managed to make himself the director of her new company, William. I expect, in his mind, he's helping to preserve his friend's final project.'

'What, by being part of a failing company?'
'By being on hand at every voyage she takes. How else can he be sure that the vessel is being cared for?'

Brereton was equally surprised, and, true to his usual character, chuckled away to himself.
'So much for him being busy with the Great Western, eh? I should have known. He always did have a way of disappearing whenever the ship was taking movement!'

I felt rather blank - and rife with envy. Why, of all people, would Daniel Gooch take interest in *my* ship? The ship *I* had seen grow from paper to iron?

'Gooch was the man who raised the most ire in Brunel, more than myself and Brereton put together. Why on earth would he be so desperate to preserve Brunel's greatest folly – one he didn't even have a role within?'

Brereton lit his pipe and took a generous draw of it.

'Gooch has always been very fond of Brunel, William. I expect Isambard was fond of him too. They always had immense respect for each other, albeit not lacking friction. Not too unusual for engineers, really – we often attach ourselves to people we feel at odds with. My point is, William, that there is no doubt Gooch has personal reasons rather than financial. A ship of such scale is unlikely to turn a profit on the Atlantic regardless of who owns it. He's smart enough to recognise that.'

Samuel chewed on his cob pipe, still listening intently.

'Perhaps;' he offered, 'He has an idea for an alternative use for the ship? He is quite entrepreneurial. He puts in tenders for many businesses, after all. I'm fairly sure he must have some idea of suiting both means of business and personal attachment.

We likely won't know a thing until one of you confronts him. Get yourself to Swindon and just ask the man. It's not an urgent matter, but it'll probably make you both more comfortable.'

Brereton and I exchanged glances and nodded. As I said; Samuel always proved valuable in any conversation. The stout newspaperman, smoking that little cob, continued gazing around the room at numerous artefacts.

'This very office could be a fine museum to Brunel, really. I do hope the man's legacy continues, regardless of the society's intentions.
Really, it's quite a task you're setting yourself; preserving a legacy. No small feat. We must all consider if we're leaving ourselves behind in exchange. Is that something you'd be happy to do?'

I winced and glanced over at Brereton; his concerns still fairly fresh to me. His worries about his self-preservation and how the world may feel towards him were still etched upon his patched face. He was hesitating.

'I'll leave that amongst yourselves, I suppose.' - Samuel made no eye contact, but clearly understood Brereton's contentions - 'But let it be perfectly clear that you can't save one man's legacy simultaneous to creating your own. That, sadly, isn't how the world works.'

Brereton abruptly changed the subject; and the rest of the evening was spent conversing within the more standard realms of railway construction, newspaper editing and the political stories of the day.

By the latter half of 1860, the Metropolitan Railway had made considerable progress. The line - built to accommodate Brunel's broad gauge as equally as the standard in London - was beginning to cross between Paddington and King's Cross at a fine rate. It did not lack in misfortune or event, of course, but I had taken to regular work site visits to watch those great tunnels take shape - feeling the most immense pride at our enterprise.

My work in Westminster, on a consultancy basis, continued with vigour, too. It was a rare day when I did not have a parliamentary concern on my table. If it was Brunel who had paved the way for these engineers and their masterpieces, I was most certainly the one helping to facilitate them.

However; almost every second form seemed to have Hargraves as a guarantor, a signee or a formative member of the group. His grip was still tight and foreboding, and the society's victories now ascending in pace since the Anthenaeum's intervention had completely ceased. I profited from it, of course; but had no wish to see my trade monopolised.

I thought wistfully of my plans for a resistance, and realised how quickly my plans seemed to continually fail and subside in the interests of my career. The dream of the 'Men of Iron' seemed long dead; only Brereton and I seemed to be in notice of this underground world of bribery and corruption, and only we seemed to be putting any stakes against those majorities.
I considered the presence of Gooch his attempt, by proxy, to involve himself in maintaining the status quo with Brunel's legacy, and guard, protect and maintain all he could - from the great ship, to the railway, to the locomotives.

The eminent engineer was an increasingly towering figure, keeping a watchful eye on the world ahead of him, and trying to ensure that, come what may, it stay in order. He remained independent - uninterested in the affairs of Hargraves - and one of the last major bastions of the enterprising world that the society succeeded in holding with a strangle grip.

Everywhere, there seemed to be his name.

I found myself envying him. Not just so for his honourable position, not just for his freedom from Hargraves; but for his involvement in the Great Eastern - his affection, protection and control of the ship I myself had overseen the construction of.

I felt a twinge of jealousy for the friendship he and Brunel really seemed to have held behind the bluster and arguments. I felt as if, negating the original letter that had this journey forwards, Brunel had never seemed particularly trusting or attached to me, by contrast.

Of course; there had been the model of the Great Eastern, now sat proudly on my mantelpiece, and there had been papers, letters and trinkets - which were still unopened - dedicated to the ship and its construction; items of the immense task that Brunel had favoured me with. But could I really see that as equal to the camaraderie that Brunel and Gooch had shared? Could I really feel we were equals when, by my eyes, I had been a mere student to the world's greatest engineer?

I felt petty; almost like a schoolboy who was envious of his companions' toys. Smiling on the outside but giving a scowl whenever his back was turned. Moreover, I felt ashamed, and surprised by my own lack of emotional conduct.

It was another load of bricks on the wagon in my head; an overloaded little pull-carriage that was beginning to feel like it had truly encountered far too much. Little did I realise just how possessive I actually felt towards the Great Eastern.

That ship made up so much of my career; why shouldn't I be passionate towards it? The fact a locomotive builder could go off to operate *my* ship defied every sense of decency in my mind.

The feelings rattled around me continuously at my work, at home, and at bars or the Duke Street office. With every hundred yards the Underground railway covered; with every brick in the tunnel, I could comfortably say that the route between Paddington and King's

Cross was built from my emotional difficulties, anger and frustrations.

Within time, Fowler was beginning to send me home every second day to ensure my health remained; chiding me for being such a young man with so many troubles. Eliza became concerned, and there was talks of medicating me - something I remained steadfast in refusing. The society had given me fear enough of doctors.

After two more weeks, I was informed that Gooch would be the man providing locomotives for the Underground Railway line, and he invited me to Swindon to see the work going into them, examine their frames and condensing equipment.

It was all too much. My patience had finally been reached; I could no longer allow Daniel Gooch to have so much presence in *my* projects. In things *I* was building.

This latest appearance of Daniel Gooch upon my papers tipped my mind over the edge. This was to be no social meeting, or even one of business. This was an opportunity for a confrontation. I, of course, had nothing to confront him over - not really. But, in my mind at the time, his position was one that wronged me, cheated me, and continuously appeared above me.

I intended to tell him quite how I felt about his status, regardless of what hospitality he offered me - I was, simply speaking, on the warpath.

+ RETURN TO SWINDON +

'William! Oh, it's good to see you. I trust you had a safe journey?'

Gooch slapped my back as he met me at his office in the typically chaotic Swindon Works. It was busier than ever, hammering and thundering with locomotive repairs, manufacture and design.

He shook my hand warmly, with the enthusiasm of an old friend; but must have noticed my own lack of conviction.

'You seem troubled.'
'I'm unsure where I stand with you, Daniel.'
'I don't-'
'You keep interfering with my projects; keep involving yourself in what, rightly, is mine. You keep appearing in my paperwork. You partially own my ship. You were on her maiden voyage. You're building the engines for my railway. What is your prerogative?'

Gooch was taken aback.

> 'I am helping in your cause, William. I am helping preserve the name of Brunel; preserving his work. Going up against Hargraves. Trying to change the cards.'
> 'You are plastering your name upon Brunel's work; and more to the point, my own!'
> 'How?'
> 'How? How indeed! How dare you take stakes upon the Great Eastern! Who on Earth do you think you are, rubbing shoulders with the people putting her on Atlantic trade runs? That company will run the ship into the ground, and you know it!'

I jabbed him firmly in the chest. He remained firm in his stance and scowled.

> 'And then you take stakes in my underground railway! You push money into the pockets of Hargraves, every day, and use *my* toil to push your own name onto the papers! I ask you; again, what is your prerogative?'

Gooch sighed and shook his head, slapping down my hand and turning his back to me.

> 'You're better than this, William. You know better than this.'
> 'Frankly, Daniel, I don't know *what* I know anymore. What I see is a man who keeps plastering himself upon everything Brunel touches.'
> '*Frankly*, William, you couldn't be more incorrect. I care not if my name has any presence with Brunel's legacy. What I care about is preserving what I can, while I can. The Railway and its locomotives are my responsibility, of course, but I also have the capital and business interests to keep the SS Great Eastern, and convert her to an alternative use.'
> 'She's not something to be passed around and tampered with!'
> 'She's been earmarked for scrap by Hargraves, William. Just like

the Hungerford bridge. She has no future if she isn't bought and 'tampered with' by somebody who cares about her.'
'Are you insinuating I don't care about her?'
'Have you seen her since Brunel's death? Travelled upon her?'
'That's of no relevance. I haven't the capitol! Nor the time!'

Gooch quietly, and calmly, poured himself a drink. I found it startling that he would be so willing to turn his back on me after such a confrontation - one supposes he knew me well enough to find me entirely non-threatening.

'Precisely, William. You see, I have the capitol. And the interest. I want to help you protect her, not hog her for my own glory. I'm building the engines for the Metropolitan because Hargraves has contracted me to do so, and I am the only man in the country regularly dealing with broad gauge. Brunel's broad gauge, which I have feverishly protected and advanced. The broad gauge, William, is also under threat. To the politicians, it is an innovation that is none-standard, expensive and embarrassingly efficient. It makes the majority of the country's railways look bad. To Hargraves, that's acting as a traitor.
You see? I'm working on much the same side as you, William. I have only the interest in preserving my dearest friend and colleague's work. He was a damned difficult man, but a man we all had some measure of affection for. Brunel's legacy is my only interest. I'll be frank, I expected you to have better powers of perception. Is this a personal aspect for you? Far be it for me to try and analyse your thinking, but I'd dare say you feel guilty over being so foreign to that great ship.'
'I am not here to be spoken down to, Daniel.'
'As an equal, then.'
'I feel you are trying to fix things your own way, rather than in the way Brunel had hoped. This was not in his plans.'
'That's possible. I have a track record of ignoring Brunel's plans. You must understand, William; I am under no illusions as to my privileged position. I simply take advantage of it to enforce what, I believe, is the greater good. I can understand, perhaps, as a young

engineer who worked closely to him, that a feeling of envy or hostility is natural. I truly do. But you have to be more trusting. You're turning into a paranoid cynic, William. Quite unlike the young engineer Brunel spoke so highly of.'

He offered me a large dram, his strait-laced expression never flinching. I wondered if I was being tested, as my superiors seemed so fond of doing. But the charity of the beverage, and Gooch's character, was enough to disarm most men.

I sipped from the squat glass - engraved with the GWR crest, I noted. It was a harsh, burning sort of Scotch that Gooch favoured; a stark contrast to his rather mild mannered personality.

I considered what had been said; and found myself calming somewhat - a surprising feat considering the hammering, clanging and general commotion in the construction sheds next door.

'You say he wished to scrap the Great Eastern?'
'Oh, yes. He has since the explosion off of Hastings. Hargraves has a grudge against her, I fear, from the controversy the ship flaunted. Her bankruptcies, her overdue construction, her continuous delays and issues - the ship has been a thorn in the society's side since Brunel embarked on her. What Brunel had on his side was his media circus. Make no mistake of it; he was a master of the country's journalists. He knew the importance of public image. By the time the Great Eastern was proving a financial disaster, she had already been published in practically every newspaper in the country. Who could ignore it?'

Gooch drank from his own glass with gusto. He was clearly very well acquainted with his liquor. One figured it was another symptom of any man in the railway trade.

'Hargraves could hardly scrap the world's greatest ship from the world's most reputed engineer. It would be a disaster. That's only

part of the quandary, too. How does one make a profit from instantly scrapping a brand new vessel? He had to at least to try and regain some of his investment.' Gooch grinned. 'My idea, William, is to purchase the Great Eastern for charters. Hire her out, keep her maintained, and keep her under operation. And I have the perfect, I believe, opportunity for her.'
'I'm listening.'
'As a charter, I plan to convert the Great Eastern to lay a new telegraph cable across the Atlantic, and offer her to the telegraph company's gentlemen. To fit her out for the task and create a truly permanent link across the ocean.'

At this time, the failure of the first telegraph cable underneath the Atlantic Ocean was still a recent event, and was still considered, by some, to have been an elaborate ruse - a technological marvel that, to the ordinary man, had no proof of success. As with the Great Eastern, a monolithic attempt against the elements had seemingly ended with disastrous results.

'After the failure of the original cable, Daniel, you believe there's any potential in such an endeavour? Let along with the Great Eastern?'
'I believe so. She can carry the lengths of cable required where no other ship is large enough. She's manoeuvrable and she's powerful. Without a doubt, she is the vessel for the job. I have contacted many mutual parties, including those behind the first. Brunel often considered such an idea; the idea of a connection between the two nations. A physical bridge or tunnel, I do not believe to be possible - but a cable? I have complete faith in it.'
'Is it financially feasible? To hire out the world's biggest ship to such a utilitarian task?'
'Bound to a government subsidy. Not to mention the financiers from the telegraph company. I believe the job would pay for much of her purchase. Besides; she isn't paying as a passenger vessel.'
'And say you're wrong; say Hargraves decides to keep the Great Eastern and repurpose her, himself?'
'Then he shall use it as a warship. And then, God help us all. It's

harrowing to consider what role such an enormous ship could play in the realm of conflict. Hargraves is fully dedicated to his dreams of a conquest of Europe. He is a born dictator; without a doubt. He sees himself as a veritable politician.
I have a theory that this is what he originally wanted her for. I understand he even intends to attempt chartering her for troop transportation in the news year.'

The idea seemed remarkably familiar.

'I do recall, Daniel, that troop figures were bandied about on her launch. Even embossed on souvenirs. I'd estimate myself she could carry a few thousand soldiers.'
'A few thousand. And a few thousand firearms. That's a scary prospect for even the most conservative man, William.'
'My thoughts never really went towards the ship being used so nefariously.'
'Quite. But a little bit of thought goes a long way. Let's not forget that she has a double hull. Perfect for smuggling, William - practically ideal for it.'

It was quite a potential prospect. The Great Eastern's innovations, to Brunel's own ingenuity, included a double walled hull; a giant, bridge like structure of girders and chambers created to increase the vessel's strength, durability and resistance to damage, without substantially increasing her weight.

The Great Eastern, as a result, was a several hundred foot ship, with a wide, comfortable hollow between her hull's plates and lining. These hollows were large enough, by design, for child riveters to crawl between. Oh yes, Daniel had quite a point - there was plenty of hidden storage in the SS Great Eastern's fabric. Plenty of potential, in fact, for illegal profit and business - beyond that of ticket sales, travel fares and on-board dining.

'Does he have no conscience?' was all I could ask.

Gooch sighed and took another hefty swig of his dram.

> 'You have to remember, William. Hargraves is a businessman. In theory, no different to every businessman in the country. He simply believes there is no such thing as bad business – unless it serves no benefit to him. He sees no room for law and morality in industry. He believes in free enterprise to the extreme, provided, of course, that it is *his* enterprise.
>
> He'll use any resource he can until it's exhausted. That includes Brunel's work, your work, and the work of his society. He churns it up, uses what he can and discards of it. Is that evil? No, I do not believe so. No more than how we use people in our trade. It's industry. It's business. And unfortunately for those of us with sentimental sides, it's utterly horrific – and unstoppable.'
>
> 'I suppose in that sense, Daniel, we're a dying race.'
>
> 'You've no idea how right you are, William. The future of business looks bleak; the future of engineering more so. Things will get worse before they get better. Just be assured; I try where I can to keep the balance. That, I promise you.'
>
> 'I feel like a fool for thinking otherwise.'
>
> 'Yes. You were a fool to think I'd defer to Hargraves after my defence of Brunel. I would never. I promised I would remain at his side, and I did. And I shall.
>
> I warn you, with utmost sincerity, that without us, the Great Eastern shall become the world's biggest warship. Imagine it; a three-thousand-strong troupe. All mercenaries, in the world's most famous passenger liner. Practically unsinkable; claiming to be a passenger voyage and allowed to dock. When, inside her inspection hatches, there's munitions and weaponry.'

The tone darkened noticeably as I considered the matter. It was a horrible thought. Where would Hargraves target? Europe? China? America? Who would be liable to stop him? How much resistance could be offered against a sudden influx of 4,000 troops?

Gooch had obviously considered it in some depth. He looked similarly fearful of such an idea.

'Frankly, I believe with enough money – which I'm sure Hargraves has at his disposal – you could convince anybody to join such an army. The Great Eastern is, I'm afraid, a damned good prospect for Hargraves' grand plans for the world. And her creator isn't here to stop him. Sadly, that means she must rely on those willing to sacrifice time to her.'

Gooch took a sharp exhale and sat heavily in his chair.

'I am part of your cause, William. I have been since you first requested me to be so. I simply have to approach pensively. The ship needs you as much as it needs me – you can count upon me for your purposes. Can I count on you for hers?'

I'm sure I needn't tell you how I responded. Before we went to the locomotive manufacturing shed, hands were shook and an agreement was struck.

The locomotives at Swindon were, in retrospect, not Gooch's finest work – though I partially suspect that this was a purposeful decision out of challenge to the society's profiteering on the contract.

The apparatus that made them appear so ungainly was for purposes of condensing steam, to feed back into the boiler and thus reduce the exhaust produced by the locomotive.

Gooch had diagrams and explanations towards this system, of his own design, which he explained were being followed by two other workshops in the United Kingdom, both in the North. His belief was that through such a simple circuit of pipes, the locomotives could not only become more efficient, but cleaner and easier to maintain for the subterranean environment they would operate in.

It was a fine idea – indeed, as of the time of writing, many locomotives running alongside bridleways and in sheltered environments have been fitted with it. But this was technology in its infancy; the shaky, pioneering first steps.

Brunel would have been proud – but Gooch made it clear he didn't want to benefit the society's heads.

> 'Your name, William – will it be attached to the railway's running?'
> 'No. The society has ensured that.'
> 'Then, perhaps, it's for the benefit of us both that these engines shan't perform to Hargraves' expectations. His specification was worse than useless. It was his second in command who sent it to me.'
> 'The Vizier? I might have known. I understand he's desperate to see Hargraves' failure.'

I had to briefly take a detour – it turned out, in fact, Gooch had never considered Hargraves' second in command as a plotting vizier.

> 'He spoke to you about Hargraves in such a way? That's very curious. I've never met the man. I always presumed he was a humble servant; not a jealous rival.'
> 'I'm not sure if it could be said he's a rival. More like a chess piece. Another one of us who seems to think he can topple the society's empire. But damned if I think, for a moment, that he's any more trustworthy.'
> 'Have you informed him of any of your plans?'
> 'No. I don't intend to. I do not believe he's fighting for any side but his own. It's greed, not moral that drives him.'
> 'You said he handed you something. To the pocket of which jacket?'

The coin dropped, and I eagerly fumbled into the lining of my tailcoat, in the hope of finding the note card. It had been steamed a few times, but remained more or less complete; the fine Indian ink held quite firmly against the paper. It had been folded over once, held with a slick of paste.

There was still a soft, yellow finger stain upon the interior of the card - the mark of a generous tobacco habit - and shaky handwriting that felt remarkably familiar.

Gooch looked at the card over my shoulder and audibly gasped. The note was signed, dated and marked - quite clearly - by Isambard Kingdom Brunel.

```
            Dearest William;
    The solution to the mystery, and your
 grandest weapon, is kept within her walls;
    but the gap may be smaller than you
    expect. Seek tin rather than iron.
```

Brunel.

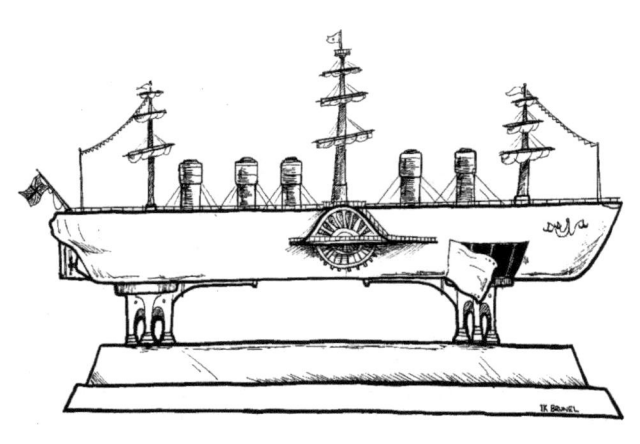

+ SECRET OF THE EASTERN +

Brunel was a genius; but no master of subtlety. I wonder, to this day, if the hint had been intended as a cryptic, puzzling clue - or a patronisingly easy hint to ensure his assistant would follow it to the letter.

What I found especially intriguing was this note card being in the hands of Hargraves' own assistant. I had written the man off as a plotting, untrustworthy rogue - so the idea of Brunel collaborating with him was somewhat unsettling.

'Perhaps he simply saw the lesser of two evils.' I offered.
'You and I both know that Isambard was too stubborn to see anything other than those worth his time, and those who were not. If this - ahm- vizier is as bad as you believe him to be, I highly doubt Brunel would have felt differently. I expect that letter has been stolen. Perhaps to gain your favour.'

Daniel had ceased with his drams and was now drinking a stiff coffee as we pored over the battered note card.

'You say you have worked out the clue already?'
'I believe the card is pointing me towards the miniature version of the ship currently on my mantelpiece.'
'What makes you believe such a thing?'
'The ship itself is double lined. I imagine the model would be too, and nobody would be any wiser.'
'Brereton was the man who presented it, correct? I know myself he's no dedicated piece of the society's machine. We've discussed it many-a-time during the Great Western's public works. Perhaps you should talk to him when you return to London.'
'And for the cause with the Great Eastern?'
'I shall call on you. The process of taking control of such an enormous asset is a complex one. Simply be there for her when I write to you. And don't be a stranger – it's nice to have the odd visitor in our neck of the woods, you know.'

The final details of the locomotive project were laid – and I apologised sincerely for my behaviour and paranoia. Gooch and his effect on others seemed to be perpetually calming. His sense of authority, his lack of need to rush and his insistence of slow, steady progress – with complete practicality and dedication – made him an impressive ally and antithesis to many of our engineering peers.

The train to London was one of reflection. It seemed rather therapeutic to know that Gooch was in our camp of defence, and so willing to work actively – if distantly – in our fight for liberty against the forces of Hargraves and his odious blueprints for the future.

It was clear that Brereton was trying equally in his damnedest to keep the tables clear. The act of providing us with the model that held such a secret felt clear to me that, not only did Brunel explain the matter, but had done so in collaboration with Brereton himself. It felt quite obvious – the plans and methods had been laid quite some time ago.

The train from Swindon roamed Brunel's immense cuttings,

viaducts and tunnels amiably - the gentle rumble of wheels upon rail and the happy pittering of the locomotive helped calm me, and for a moment I was sure I fell into a gentle sleep.

It wouldn't last.

Within a short time, we arrived into Reading. And I cringed. Against the dim station lamps and the fog of the evening, not to mention steam and smoke, the unmistakable silhouette of slim men in round-top hats approached the train.

If the society's plans were the apocalypse, these strange men seemed like the heralds; the crooked horsemen that brought fear and calamity.

The Dealers had arrived, and, in their typical manner, filled up the compartment with their briefcases, bowler hats and strange, round little heads.

> 'Mister Jacomb. So good to see you again.'
> 'The feeling, gentlemen, is not mutual.'
> 'Yes. Well, we have a small matter to discuss regarding the Draughtsman's volume presented to the society.'
> 'You have Brunel's drawings. I have no further involvement.'
> 'You have much involvement. We do not believe the contents of Brunel's Draughtsman's book have been designed to succeed.'
> 'More's to the point, we believe Brunel has sought to bring us into disrepute.'
> 'Further, we wonder if you are, in fact, privvy to this, Mister... ahum... Jacomb. We believe you colluded with Brunel to make a mockery of us.'
> 'We don't appreciate that sort of activity, Mister Jacomb.'
> 'There has already been one railway accident. Let's not have another.'

I gripped my hand subconsciously, and glared at the Dealer ahead of me, straight into his large, round eyes. His brow lowered in contempt.

> 'Gentlemen; I guarantee to you that I had no part in anything to do with the documents. I had no idea they even existed before Brunel was deceased.'

I was more than sincere enough; but their suspicions, I fear, were unquenched.

> 'A likely story.'
> 'We fear you are not trustworthy. We fear you push your nose in and act far too indignant.'
> 'We fear that you are an inconvenience. A troublesome horse, refusing to be broken in. Put simply, we are suspicious of you.'

I continued with my attempts to allay their concerns.

> 'I have no intentions against the society, gentlemen. I simply wish to get back to work on the metropolitan railway; which I shall upon my return to work tomorrow morning.'
> 'We shall be watching you, William. That's your official warning.'
> 'Then I hope, gentlemen, Hargraves is accepting of you wasting his resources. My movements will remain quite uneventful throughout, I'm afraid. I barely have time to visit the butcher's shop, let alone take time from my schedule for this ridiculous, conspiratorial nonsense.'

A pause echoed as the train roared into a tunnel; the clattering of wheels and rattling locomotive rods almost reminded me of that horrible noise before the accident in Tottenham. I briefly wondered if these men were on a mission of self destruction.

When we exited, I swallowed my fears and remained steadfast.

> 'No matter to your claims, the society's interest has been peaked on your activities. We shall be endeavouring to see you make no

approach on the Great Eastern or any other asset affiliated with Brunel.'

'If you do,' one of the others piped in, 'We shall be behind you.'

'I'd be surprised to see any of you on a work site. I look forward to it.'

The train slowed on its approach to Maidenhead – and the curious men stood, in quick succession. They left the compartment as soon as the door had been unlocked – with nary a word.

My disbelief was marked more by the knowing smirk I simply couldn't control. The clue, for its simplicity, had worked. I would find the answer to it all upon my mantelpiece rather than inside the bosom of the Great Babe. I had no reason to leave my premises – and no reason to raise any further suspicion.

All the same, I reasoned, it would be well worth keeping my wits about me at home, too.

I returned to our home in Wimbledon relatively late in the day via carriage, with a plain black one almost constantly tailing us, with familiar, round headed silhouettes. This black carriage reminded me irrevocably of a hearse, as it stood perfectly motionless across from the square that our home led out to.

I made a point of barely moving through the rooms of the home, with curtains wide open and lights fully lit. I reasoned that, eventually, the motionless cart would move along. To my surprise, it did not – quite the opposite. It stood motionless, stubborn and disciplined.

Every so often, in the corner of my eye, it was possible to see the silhouette inside shifting, a head peaking up over the window frame of the cart, or bodies changing position in the tight, claustrophobic space.

It was a bizarre thing to think of – the idea that men would so loyally remain inside a cramped wooden box for so many hours on end. Perhaps my notion of hearses was, in hindsight, closer than I had imagined...!

'Darling, must you pretend to read that book all evening?'
'I *am* reading it.'
'You've been on the same page for hours, William. I know you're being watched; but do try and act naturally, dear. They aren't that foolish.'
'I didn't tell you I was being-'
'I'm not that foolish either, dear...!' sang the response from the kitchen. I rolled my eyes and smirked - but found my glance moving to the window once again to keep an eye on that foreboding, sinister wagon.

It took hours before the wagon's dim lantern faded from view, and I slipped into action - presuming the men were either asleep or attempting to relight it.
I almost grabbed the model of the Great Eastern in my hurry - but paused myself before I risked damaging her. I sat back down and examined the model closely.

A beautiful piece she was; and at first glance, one with no weakness in her frames or lining - bar a slim, hairline join ahead of her paddle wheel's housing, covered by the observation deck on the port side.

I grabbed my magnifying glass from the table and took a closer look - not an easy task - but with the aid of a hat pin hastily taken from Eliza's haberdashery drawer, I managed to ease out one of the iron plates from the model ship's hull, trying, by candlelight, to clearly examine her bowels.

Tucked between the miniature girder ribs was a slip of paper. Narrow, thin, silk like paper that captured the light. It seemed so fragile and delicate that I feared trying to remove it - but with a gentle scrape of the hat pin, the slip freed itself.

It featured the engraving of a key. No more, no less than a delicate, beautifully drawn diagram displaying a Mortice key, with long, sweeping curves and brass foliage on its handle.

To say I was confused was an understatement. Was I supposed to get another key cut? Was the key originally intended to be attached to the paper? I looked inside the model ship for the item itself, to no avail.

I scratched my head and popped the miniature notelet down, close to the candle. To my surprise, a stamp began to appear, heated into view by the melting candle wax. Rather typical of Brunel to work in a secret somewhere.

Anthenaeums Club, Pall Mall.

The Anthenaeums? I hadn't spoken to members of the gentlemen's club at Pall Mall since we had argued the society's morals. The idea of returning to them seemed less than palatable. I was certain I'd be far from welcome in the Pall Mall clubhouse.

I didn't feel a grudge towards them, mind - I felt quite sure, however, that they would towards me. Who could blame them after my behaviour against my superiors? Who could blame them after my display of such hubris and arrogance?

I could practically see the scowling face of that grisly old bulldog in my mind's eye, glaring from behind his dominoes. It would be a less than pleasant meeting - that much I knew.

I still had my membership with them - I was not much in the habit of cancelling such things - and reasoned that a visit and sincere apologies were in order.

There was nothing for it. Whether it was another clue or a definitive end to the newly emerged puzzle; the club was my next stop. It had to be. I would pass the clubhouse almost daily on my business, and could never quite steal myself to enter. I foolishly wondered if that old bulldog's liver-spotted fist would meet my nose upon first entrance.

My attendance with them was a month later. My nerves, it seems, found the idea more frightful than I imagined.

It had been a difficult slog with the latest stages of the Metropolitan line, and my schedule was making these back and forths increasingly difficult. It almost seemed as if my workload was being inflated, with the intention to stall my plans.

I made sure to attend early – in the hopes of beating the members to the drawing room and steeling myself.

You can imagine my surprise to find the cantankerous bulldog sitting there, dominoes rattling, as the fireplace crackled. He barely looked up to acknowledge me; simply continued laying those battered wooden game pieces upon the table in seemingly spontaneous sequence.

Tack. Tack. Tack.

> 'It took you a while, William. I have been waiting.'
> 'Am I to suppose you are the solution to this?'
> 'You would be supposing correctly. Brunel was my friend, William. I tried to guide you where I could. But to be so easily blinded by the society? I must confess my feelings were hurt. I was ashamed for you.'

Tack. Tack. Tack.

> 'And now? You're here; tail between your legs. Here to apologise and ask for the help Brunel told me to give you before he passed away. That was far too long ago.'

I opened my mouth to speak. He held up his hand and shook his head.

'I carved this key myself, William. It took weeks. It's a perfect forgery. Brunel's original plan was to do all of this himself. Naturally. We dissuaded him; he said his new assistant was the most promising character he knew. We agreed. And here he is; the prodigal son. Ashamed. Brought down via arrogance. I pity you.'
'I can only apologise. It was ignorance. Not arrogance.'
'Hrm.'
'Brunel would no doubt agree.'

Tack. Tack. Tack.

The bulldog unslipped a chain from under his collar, and brought out a finely carved, intricate key. Every line was perfectly hand captured. Every fine, sweeping curve and ornament was smooth, and perfectly shaped. The polished shape of it was nearly mirror perfect. The testament of craftsmanship.

'Here.'
'What is this?'
'This, William, is the key to the society's chamber. The location of the Eternal Tome, and, moreover, your target. We want to see the thing stolen.'
'And taken where?'
'To oblivion, Jacomb. And, eventually, across the Atlantic. Brunel intended for the Tome's destruction aboard the Great Eastern. That is to be the book's final resting place. The vessel that the society itself has interfered with. Most methods of destruction, I'm fairly sure, that book could survive. A trip through paddle wheels to the bottom of the ocean... no. That's how it must be done.'

Suitably poetic, I thought - but rather a surplus of dramatic flair. I'd have preferred to burn the thing, or bury it, rather than take the trouble of setting off on a voyage. Typical of Brunel, in retrospect - to take ownership of a relatively simple task and turn it into an act of ridiculous poetry.

> 'Quite simple, I'd say. Drop her off of the viewing platform next to the paddle housing, let the paddles do their job and the ocean do its own. There shan't be as hope in hell for the Tome to survive.'
> 'And you believe this shall be as simple as that? A few jolly, optimistic sentences and the ship will redeem her intervention and interference?'
> 'Frankly, Jacomb, I have no care for the ship. The book? Now... that book has, in my mind, been a thorn in the civilised world's side for its remarkably uncivilised life. It has to be destroyed to see countries on even stakes again. To put back in place the natural laws of industry, and moreover, the globe.'
> 'You know Hargraves will resist us.'
> 'Of course. It'll be a dangerous little mission for you. That much is certain.'
> 'And I presume I shall be acting alone?'
> 'Well, preferably.'
> 'Am I so disposable?'
> 'You aren't disposable. That's rather the point. You're a sprightly young man with bright ideas - if anybody can get the book to the Atlantic, I'd rather reckon you can.'

I rolled my eyes, sat in a chair and sighed.

> 'Bloody marvellous.'
> 'Think about it, William. With a single drop, Hargraves will lose his empire. You'll be saving us from war. You'll be preserving your master's legacy.'

I wish, reader, that I could tell you such extravagant wording was all I required to agree to this final task from Brunel - and the old Bulldog. I refused with all energy I had - it wasn't until the agreement that the 'drop' should take place on a charter voyage with Gooch and Brereton nearby, and a financial reward was offered, that I agreed.

The Bulldog remarked that I would have been a damned good salesman. I dare say Brunel himself would have been surprised at my resistance. Hold my ground I did – and it feels today like a rather proud moment.

>'Do you know how to use a gun?'
>'Good grief, no.'
>'Then I'd advise you to learn. It'll likely prove useful against the man. And you feel you know the ship inside and out?'
>'Of course.'
>'Then, if I were you, I'd use her as a labyrinth and lose Hargraves inside her. Try and get him caught somewhere.'
>'So long as that is all I am expected to do, fine.'

The expression on the Bulldog's face made clear that this wouldn't suffice.

>'We shall see, William.'

I paused. Was it being insinuated that I was to kill Hargraves? That I, a young civil engineer from Wimbledon, would have to commit murder?

I had seen lives taken in front of me – whether by incompetence and poor regime at work sites, or taken by illness and poor lifestyle. But to take a life at my own hands?

No. I couldn't do such a thing. And my refusal was steadfast.

>'Then don't kill him, William. But he shall kill you. I dare say the only reasonable way to rid the country of his brand of despotism is to rid the country of him. Just tell me, honestly, my lad. If push came to shove – would you see to a killer's demise? It's the honourable thing to do.'
>'Honour and morale seems to be a buzzword against this group. And nothing much else. Are you going to profit from Hargraves' death?'

> 'My boy, my life will be made intensely more awkward from the loss of the society. I profit from its existence as much as Brunel and Stephenson did. But I have seen many a great man fall, and many a great idea squandered. The future is not supposed to be monopolised - and I refuse to allow Hargraves to do such a thing.'

By now, the rest of the club's familiar faces were stood in the room, listening eagerly.

> 'So;' the Bulldog held his lapels, grandly. His authority and belief in the cause was obvious. 'What say you, my boy. Are you willing to save the industrial empire?'
> 'I shall do what can be reasonably expected.'
> 'That's good enough for me.'

A vigorous handshake occurred to the respectful applause of the other members. For better or worse, I was the toast of The Anthenaeums for the future.

But, my dear reader, work continued to call - and it wasn't until a dark evening, early next year, that I had managed to group the integral figures together at Brunel's home.

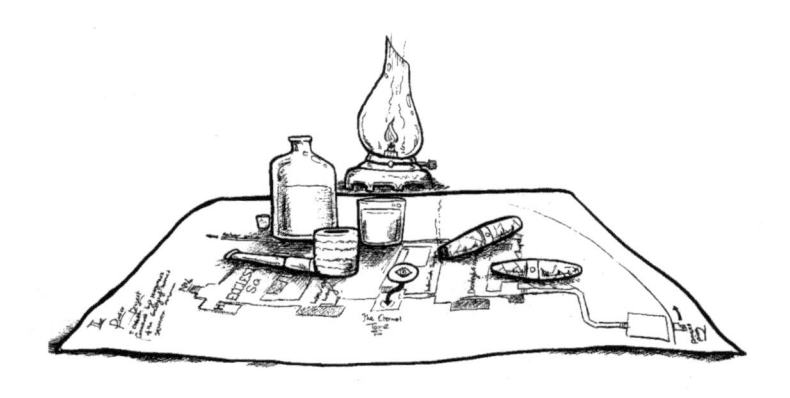

+ THE PLAN +

'**M**y goodness! The man himself, finally hauled down from Swindon! My dear Daniel, how are you?'

Brereton's welcome as Gooch walked into the Duke Street premises was, as typical for him, warm and attentive. Gooch smiled weakly at the joke and sat down at the specially prepared table, with myself, Brereton and Samuel Lucas gathered round it - with a detailed map of Eccleston Square laid across it.

'It's a pleasure, gentlemen. I'm glad to finally take part.'

Gooch sat down and unloaded his own paperwork to assist in our planning. He gave a brief questioning look to Mr. Lucas, but was quickly disarmed when the journalist gave a wry smile and brought out a bottle of brandy.

For the first time since Brunel's death, the Duke Street premises seemed like a hub of activity – a buzzing hive of gentlemen planning a world changing project.

Brereton puffed on a cigar, carrying a surprising resemblance to Brunel, while Mr. Lucas blew clouds of thin smoke from his pipe. The office of Isambard Brunel resembled itself far more when enveloped in tobacco smoke.

Everybody knew of the plan. Everybody knew what had to be done – the difficulty was in working out how this was meant to properly take place. *How* an ancient book of otherworldly original was going to become our possession. The conversation was hesitant by nature, and within time, stalled when we came to the subject of the society's mysterious headquarters.

Brereton and myself had been there – but the other gentlemen had faint knowledge; little more than recited discourse.

> 'Of course, gentlemen, we cannot proceed if you do not know the location of our great heist.'

Brereton gave a wry smile and unwrapped his next map; this one of Eccleston Square's internal workings. Samuel and Gooch both looked up at him in surprise.
He grinned in response – clearly proud of his own contribution.

> 'I am a senior civil and structural engineer. Of course, I get to see plans when maintenance is required.'

He pinned the map down against the table, revealing the labyrinthine depths of the society's cellars, running from Eccleston Square's underground tunnels and archways, leading through the Royal Army's Uniform Store. This bizarre network reached a length of nearly a mile, all buried underneath the surface of the nation's capital.

Brereton explained the somewhat unusual layout.

> 'Hargraves uses the military store for weaponry. Nobody would ever question why they were delivering weaponry to a building owned by the war office. It also means there's a direct tunnel from here to the cellar, bypassing the house at the square.'
>
> 'Good grief. Does the war office know about Hargraves having access?'
>
> 'I'm afraid Hargraves' money does indeed go a long way. The factory was paid for with it. He had enough control over blueprints for him to connect his little empire up to the Thames without question.'
>
> 'I would have never thought...'
>
> 'You need to understand William; while the concept of the British Authorities being so pure, well established and sophisticated is a very nice selling point for the common man, it's as fictional as Hargraves' table manners. You bribe an officer, you have complete freedom.'

He pointed to the Pimlico pier. This humble little wooden structure was often used by Thames Steamers, pleasure craft and even the odd luxury yacht. The river had grown so filthy and stinking that few ever set their feet on the tumbledown jetty – save light goods barges and the odd utility vessel.

> 'Hargraves – as you likely know, William – is a paranoid sort. The idea was that through the pier and the uniform premises, he'd have a quick getaway with the book should anything go awry; not to mention a prime location to unload his arsenal for the Great Eastern. He has a little pleasure steamer to take him back and forth should he ever need to. Clapped out little thing, it is, but I'm sure it serves. He's not exactly a man to move quickly.
>
> The most obvious way to enter – and, of course, escape – with the Tome is via the military tunnel. I'll go in with you, of course – I can claim it's for structural inspections. We're both civil engineers; we can both make a convincing claim for entrance.'
>
> 'And how do we do this without him noticing?'

'Fairly simple, William. He'll be asleep on the Great Eastern after being wined and dined by Mr. Gooch.' Brereton smiled and patted Gooch's shoulder firmly.

Samuel looked up in confusion. My own expression must have betrayed similar feelings – as Brereton continued his explanation.

'This mission is set to take place on the voyage to lay the new transatlantic cable.'
'Quite.' Gooch smiled. 'I understand the ship is due for auction if she doesn't turn a profit; and I guarantee she won't. I and some associates are planning to purchase her, to lay the cable to America.'
'Who? Who has the financing to purchase a gigantic, iron white elephant?'

Gooch smiled. 'Thomas Brassey and John Pender, no less. The ideal men to help us connect up two great empires. Beyond this project being of great importance in of itself, it gives us an opportunity to bring Hargraves on board. My associates and I are, it must be said, fairly distinguished in the realm of engineering. Add that to a good meal and an offer for him to take shares in the cable company… it's a wonderful lure for a greedy, predatory brute. We'll simply pretend we're in financial straits, in requirement of help, turning to the society at last with tails between our legs…
And, of course, offering to give the ship back to him for his Army plot.'

Samuel puffed on his pipe, as usual. His interest had been peaked.

'So, the new cable's actually going ahead? Fascinating. I apologise for breaking focus – but I'm surprised you are all taking this figurehead book more seriously than such an enormous piece of infrastructure. Surely that is a greater achievement than the theft of a dusty old book?'

Gooch smiled. 'I agree. The new cable will be a monumental achievement. And I agree the result will be incredibly important. But this dusty old book means far more to the society than you give it credit for, Mr. Lucas.'

A small debate broke out between the men – peaceful, of course – regarding the Eternal Tome and its contents. Mr. Lucas argued for reason as an outsider as the two other gentlemen tried to point out the contrary.

I sat at the table, listening quietly, and staring at the maps and diagrams festooning the table. What on Earth had led me to this point? A few years ago I was little more than a young engineer working as an apprentice at Paddington Station. Now, I was suddenly going on espionage missions to preserve peace, and prevent my biggest project turning into a gigantic gun locker.

I was still conflicted, and the idea from the club that murder was the solution continued to rattle around in my thoughts. The very concept still felt terrifying – an affront to my own principles from which they could never recover.

Yet, part of me wondered if the others even knew...

'Of course, Lucas, with Hargraves-'
'They asked me to kill him.'

Silence. All eyes fell in my direction, eyebrows raised.

'The Anthenaeums. They believe the only solution to this event is to see Hargraves off of the Earth. They want me to murder him.'

The office's atmosphere changed entirely as the others exchanged glances. Each tried to formulate a reply – but Brereton was the first to do so successfully.

He coughed into his hand and stepped closer, patting my shoulder firmly.

'Well, William... I can't deny it would be an easy solution...'

Lucas chewed on the stem of his pipe; typically calm, unphased and relaxed. He laid back against his chair and smiled.

'You're no murderer, William. I know you better than most and know the kind of man it takes to steal a life. You are not of the character or motivation. To pot with what the Anthenaeums say.'
'Saying that;' Gooch murmured, 'How else do we ensure our own business's safety? We'll all be connected with this little plan. The society will hear - and, book or no book, is powerful enough to see the end of us all. Perhaps, more importantly, the end of our prospects. The Great Western Railway would be doomed. Along with your underground railway, Brereton's infrastructure, Lucas's campaigns...'

The table hesitated; but it had to agree.

'I hate to admit it; but to clear up the dregs of the society's grip on the empire, Hargraves cannot return from the voyage. Even if he's brought home in handcuffs, he will find a way to continue business. He's too powerful and has too much corruption under his thumbs to remain in prison.'

The table was now silent, save the puffing of Samuel's cob pipe as he relaxed in the chair, thinking away like some kind of eternal philosopher. I wondered if he ever stopped thinking to himself and gave attention to what was at hand.

'The question is, gentlemen,' He spoke up, 'how do we see the end of Hargraves without getting blood on our hands? Murder is entirely against our principles.'
'I suppose we'll find out when the event comes to pass.' I offered.

But we all knew such an improvisation was poor planning at best - and catastrophically unwise at worst.

The tone of the meeting had declined into a somewhat scared group of men discussing what was beginning to seem like a foul deed. What justice could be proclaimed in removing a man from the mortal coil?

> 'I don't need to point out;' Brereton mumbled, 'that he has the power to take many more lives. And if his invasion plans go ahead, he no doubt will. He's an international despot waiting to happen.'
> 'I dare say;' Lucas remarked, 'A powder keg.'
> Gooch poured another large glass of brandy. 'If, perchance, there was a chase through the lower levels of the ship - and he, by some calamity, was caught in the engines...'
> Brereton spluttered on his drink and slammed it on the table. 'Daniel, please!'
> 'It was only a suggestion. We can hardly make death seem like a positive happenstance, can we? I'm thinking purely of a set up for it to happen. A set up wherein we can't, moreover, be held responsible.'
> 'But such a situation, Daniel...'
> 'I understand.'
> 'Such an awful happenstance. So grisly. I shudder to think-'
> 'Gentlemen, we're getting nowhere with this speculation. We know how to destroy the Tome and that is that. We'll just have to... wait and see what happens.'
> 'One thing is for sure; once the Eternal Tome has been destroyed, the world will never quite be the same way again. I bloody well hope so, at least.'

The night rattled on; time ticking by with impressive vigour.

As we pored over those plans of Eccleston square, we slowly mapped out the optimal route between the Eternal Tome's chamber and the war office supply house.

The plan required getting, of course, into the chamber itself, which formed a pillar for the uppermost structure of the Square's gardens. The room's doors were impossible to open quickly - nor without notice - and as a result, we reasoned, access through the house's staircase would have to be blocked.

We continued going over such fine details without a further thought to the perturbing finale at hand: The grim realisation that somehow, through some method, Hargraves himself would have to meet a similar fate.

Over cigars, alcohol, and anecdotes of a career with Brunel, we soon lost ourselves into camaraderie. From then on, we were at peace, save our uproarious laughter.

What we had, I fear, failed to consider was that more than one man had voiced his disapproval with Hargraves.

More than one man had pledged his intent to destroy the society's status quo.

And I had completely underestimated him.

The vizier; Hargraves' second in command. That horrible, portly man with the crooked grin - who had given me that first clue, from Brunel's own hands.

He had heard nothing from me; had no idea if his clue had progressed within means. I had only the belief that the little notelet had been stolen from Brunel's own pocket to arm myself with, and little more awareness of his intent.

It all seemed like water under the bridge, that the vizier's role was simply a passing help that had, by some circumstances unforeseen, led to the loss of his own ally. I had, by all purposes, forgotten his part in the great caper.

And, after the meeting, as our lives continued with a strict silence on our activities, things on the society's side fell silent, too. Was it suspicion?

It transpired that, in fact, Brunel's book of false draughts was being processed and experimented with, and the results were, without fail, dreadful. The experiments ongoing at Eccleston square were disastrous, a constant operational failure for the society's teams of engineers and workers. Brunel's book was, for the intentions it had been designed, an incredible success.

It had bought us time, and caused them an influx of embarrassment - neither of which, I fear, put us in the positive view of Hargraves and his vizier.

+ A MAN SCORNED +

It was a particularly wet April in 1861, and work was proving awkward on the Metropolitan line. Fowler had spent most of his time hunched over his desk and swearing, while I had spent much of it wading through the treacle like mud that was collecting in our tunnels, trying to motivate workers to keep us on schedule.

We had not been without calamity. Boiler explosions were still a somewhat regular occasion in these early days of railway technology, and at least one contractor's locomotive, to memory, had succumbed to this. I also remember a train overshooting at King's Cross and flying into the site. Gooch was convinced, when he heard, that this was the society's doing - but it was impossible to tell.
Hargraves' money, in end, paid for these accidents. It hardly seemed like good economy.

There had been substantial progress made towards Euston Station, and another railway line had already been authorised. I had wasted no time commenting on such hubris, which, it seems, had largely gone disregarded, and a secondary sort of railway boom seemed to be taking place inside London's city boundaries, as companies began applying to construct their own subterranean rails underneath the city's streets and buildings.

Activity had been rumbling across the city, indeed – the Hungerford Bridge, still condemned, was being kept open to allow for foot traffic, as the construction of the South East railway's own footbridge was proving a rather ill planned affair. Rumours had it that some of Brunel's false blueprints were being used in the planning process, and had, naturally, failed terribly during conception.

The Charing Cross station – which we believed was being constructed with the society's convenience equally in mind to London's population, for it was expected to create international links, as well as a glorious route into London's 'centre' – was still in progress, and yet to show much of meaningful construction. Rumours, again, abounded that Brunel's plans were being used – and proving unwieldy.

As the railway crossed over such heavily populated parts of London, the costs were astronomical and construction awkward, exacerbated by the unhelpful drafts and cramped area.

What was planned as a two mile-long railway link was moving at less than half a mile per year, sticking into the city like an outsized needle, scraping some of London's most famous areas.

Gooch and Brereton dismissed it as a vapid display of power from the society, and felt sure that the railway company involved were in heavy collusion with Hargraves, and his desire to monopolise – and out price – the world's economy.
The bridges striping through London were heavily criticised as

hideous and blighting, and many saw the railway itself as a colossal carbuncle that nobody, in essence, required.

However, so close to Westminster and the Palace – it would be a perfect way for Hargraves to capitalise on the public press. To make himself a figure rubbing shoulders with ministers and royalty.

It was all a touch too convenient and, it must be mentioned, somewhat close for comfort to the Metropolitan's own target of Farringdon Road.

Our Metropolitan railway steadily moved forward – I'm pleased to say, at least, that we progressed at a far better pace considering the difficult construction methods – and was being visited daily by curious bystanders, eager to see the futuristic underground system.

The tunnels were a marvellous spectacle, when finished, but caused great disarray to the traffic and general public above – to mention nothing of those who feared their homes were at risk.

Everything had been engineered with certainty. There was, I felt, no scope for calamity for those above our infrastructure – but I had little planned for the event of the vizier's arrival that May.

> 'Ah! Jacomb!' came an echoing bellow from the street above, as he strutted – as much as such a gentleman's frame can 'strut' – confidently down the workings and climbed the ladders.

I pretended not to hear him.

> 'Jacomb, my dear fellow, don't you ignore me now! I've come as a friend! You recall, I'm sure, how good I have been to you! Come my lad, shake my hand!'

The workmen stopped with their shovels and picks and watched with surprise as the slithering, grinning gargoyle stepped straight in front of my eyeline.

'It's been a long time, William.'

He snatched my hand, making me drop my plans into the thick mud, and shook it vigorously.

'How have you been? Hard at work, or hardly working, eh?' He laughed. Loudly. I dare say people passing a street away could hear him.
'I've been well, Sir. How are you?' I spoke through gritted teeth as I collected my papers.
'I've been superb. Of course, it's always nice to catch up with friends after so damned long. I've barely heard a thing from you since our last chat...'

He slipped a hand into my jacket's pocket, with nary a word of warning, and grinned.

'So you did receive the card, eh? I am glad.'
'Yes. I did. A lot of nonsense wasn't it? I didn't see a thing inside the Great Eastern. I'm not convinced it was even written by Brunel.'

I walked away from him – and heard heavy, angry footsteps squelching behind me as he followed me through indignation.

'It was written by the man himself! I know as I was given it by Brunel, hand to hand!'
'If that's so, Sir, why exactly was this never referenced by him in his letter to me?'

I kept walking. The man, momentarily, stood, dumbfounded.

'What are you insinuating, William?'
'I am insinuating that you are a thief. A lazy, opportunistic cad, who's trying to drag me into your plans, so you may tip the

society's coffers into your own hands.'

I turned to face him, and found myself raising my voice.

> 'You have no interest in justice for your empire, Sir. You wish only to further your own nameless, cackhanded career! You stole that notelet, and damned if I don't believe it was from his own jacket whilst bedridden!'

Thwack! - his meaty fist connected rather heavily with my face, sending me into the mud of the cutting. Two workmen dropped their tools and lifted me back up, with the rest of the group trying to restrain the vizier, who was quite ready to continue with fisticuffs.

> 'I'm the thief? *I'm the thief,* William? I may have taken advantage of my situation, but I do not turn men away from what is rightfully theirs! You are a braggart! A filthy, two faced braggart! I shall see to it that you hang for your troubles!'

The man who had seemed so well composed and conscious of his movements was now little more than a raging buffoon, spitting and screaming expletives and anger indiscriminately.

The police were soon called upon. It took several of them to properly cuff the man and lead him away, leaving me bruised and the men on the site shaken.

> 'I promise you, Jacomb! You're as good as done for! Your career will be on crutches, and you'll join it! Oh, believe me, you will rue the day you crossed my path!'

We opted to stop work for that day, and regroup on the next when the shock had passed.

The next morning, as I left for the work site - kissing Eliza at the door of our growing home - I had quite forgotten the incident, despite an obvious black eye that turned heads as I walked down the street.

My head was swimming with ideas of the worksite and improving our efficiency, increasing our mileage as well as we could, taking on the developments elsewhere in the city with vigour, and capitalising on this secondary Railway Boom in the name of the country's progress.

My carriage arrived at the Euston work site, where my encounter with the Vizier's foul language had taken place. The area was a remarkably difficult one for the Metropolitan railway. It encountered difficult earth, a complex of roads and - in at least a few instances - businesses, homeowners and landowners who outright opposed the idea.

I felt quite sure that, instead, they found the horrific congestion beneficial to business - driving foot traffic into their cocoa houses, their pubs, their restaurants - but for the people on the roads themselves, the prospect was horrific.

It was, in all, the biggest weakness - that area wherein Stephenson's Station sat included our strongest detractors.

You can imagine, then, my yell of horror as I alighted from the carriage to find a scene of destruction.

The wooden struts and brickwork that supported the earth had fallen, allowing much of the surrounding square at our Melton Street approach to collapse inward. The result was piles of rubble, buildings leaning at a perilous angle, and our own tunnels blocked with the resulting sediment.

It was raining; and the mouth of our beautiful Euston tunnel, every bit perfectly planned and meticulously put together, was now left shattered.

The workmen stood around it, silent and bewildered.

The night watchman was soon found unconscious, and we huddled around him inside his little hut to discuss what he'd seen.

He was an elderly man, but a hardy one. His whiskers twitched as he spoke, and as he clutched his tea can and warmed himself by his stove, he told us everything he had witnessed. To many, it would have appeared impossible. To myself, it seemed all too obvious.

> 'Th' must've been twenty of 'em, sir.'
> 'Twenty?'
> 'Aye, all in matchin' outfits, wi'lamps. Muscular lads, th'were, wi'sledge'ammers. This big bloke, he weren't muscular but big, if y'get m'picture -he were directing them, see - these weren't yobs, no sir, I can deal wi' yobs. Th'were coordinated.'

The old man was covered in bruises. It was a brutally savage way to treat a lowly watchman.

He lifted off his flat cap and scratched his head. Inside it was a little note of paper that the old timer plucked out with confusion.

> 'Must be fer you, sir. 'As yer name on it, Sir.'

His hands were shaking as he held up the note for me in his filthy hands, covered with fingerless gloves. I found myself appalled by the very idea that anybody could attack an innocent old gentleman in such a way.

He smiled weakly as I took the note, and sipped at his tea can quietly as I unfolded it.

The message was sharp, short and less than pleasant.

> *Dear Jacomb;*
> *Such a shame. I hope your tunnel shan't be too difficult to fix. I shall get that book long before you do. And I shall not forget your slights. My brother has had his filthy hands on that book for long enough.*

'Brother? Brother?! For pity's sake, there are *two* of them now?'
'Two of whom, sir?'

I looked up to the railway's work crew and the battered watchman with all eyes on me, awaiting instruction - and surprised by my outburst. Not a single man was unshaken by the events overnight - they were perhaps concerned their superintendent was feeling unstable himself.

'Oh. Never mind, gentlemen - I shall take this note to the constabulary and see to it that the perpetrator is properly dealt with.'

The message was clear. A sibling rivalry, no less, had formed - and my own business was the target of both.

It was a perilous situation. And had already cost us weeks of work, let alone, I had no doubt, a swathe of negative press.

Work began to try and re-stabilise the damaged arches and broken struts that had fallen inwards, and the tunnels had to be partially uncovered so we could ensure their integrity. It was embarrassing - and nobody - if anybody - was to know the society's part in it all.

Samuel warned me, that evening, that the journalists would not hold back from an industrial mishap regardless of the society's role, and to prepare for a barrage.

Right enough, the next day, the headlines were rife.

GREAT FOLLY AT LONDON EUSTON

THE UNDERGROUND CALAMITY

INDEPENDENT TRADERS IN RUIN

THE MENACE BENEATH OUR STREETS

To say the papers were distracting would be an understatement. The news stands at Paddington, King's Cross and Euston were all proudly announcing the above in a constant line of overly bombastic headlines.

'I'm sorry to say that a few subscriptions have already made their way. But I've a good chunk of them.'

Samuel met me later that day, sat on one of the benches in the Paddington station concourse with a pile of what he could purchase, attempting to stem the circulation. A good hearted attempt, to be sure, but one I felt somewhat futile in the circumstances.

'I can't believe, of all people, Hargraves' own flesh and blood is trying to usurp him.'
'I can. Power struggles always start in the family. The close ties are sure to breed jealousy - Flesh and blood can be very explosive, you know. It starts with the son against the father, then the brother against brother...'
'I believe the two Hargraves boys are both intent on bloodshed, and certainly not just each other's. We need to be vigilant against them, Samuel.'

Samuel nodded and lit up his cob pipe; I had grown used to this being his expression of thoughtfulness - and he had developed a habit of motioning with it wildly when speaking.

'Is this –ahem – vizier brother a lesser of two evils?'
'Frankly, Samuel, I doubt it.'
'Hm. I often find the smaller animals to be the happiest to attack, out of fear, paranoia and defence. If I were you, William, I would bait him into barking at your next society meeting. The two may be powerful, but they're arrogant. It shouldn't be too much work for an engineer to outsmart a would-be politician.'

He puffed on his familiar cob pipe. I wondered if he ever replaced it, if he had - or if he simply smoked the same cob until it fell apart. I had known him for two years, and still the pipe seemed to leak smoke in the same areas - thin, silvery wisps leaking from the bowl.

Samuel was no man short on money; quite why he opted to stick with pauper's pipes, I was unsure.

'Of course, William... I expect a full report. I would so like to hear of it. What I'd give to be a fly on the wall at that meeting.'
'I wouldn't mind having company.'
'Will you not have Brereton?'
'I rather meant company that doesn't have to give fake allegiance.'
'Sorry, William. You know as well as I do that Hargraves would take a dim view on a journalist being in his presence.'

I couldn't honestly claim otherwise. A journalist in Eccleston square would be suicide. But, I must admit, I felt nervous - with no real knowledge besides a note as to the relationship via the Hargraves brothers, the situation was incendiary and unpredictable.

+ BROTHERS IN ARMS +

The environment in Eccleston square felt tense and uneasy as the Vizier glared at me, viciously. Hargraves sat at the head of the table. He had been halfway through a generously sized cigar that now hung from his lip, his mouth agape.

'Repeat yourself. Now.'

The investors were silent. Staring at me with what seemed like, above all else, horror. The powder keg had been lit.

I adjusted my cravat before I continued, pointing to my paperwork for the incident.

'My concern, gentlemen, is that Euston Road fell after his visit. I know you all have heavy investment in the Underground Railway, and feel it's only worth telling you where my suspicions lay. My night watchman was attacked but saw, with his own eyes, a group of men led by one. That one suits your br-... our friend's description.'

Eyes went back to the vizier, who was now breathing heavily. His hands were clenched into fists, and beads of sweat were developing on his brow.

Hargraves put down his cigar, slowly, and glared at his sibling. One of the older men spoke up, his hands resting on his stomach as he spoke in a thick, Yorkshire accent with a droning, grizzled tone.

> 'If this is true, Hargraves, I'm sure I don't need to say we expect some kind of ramification. I have money in that railway's completion and I do not like to see it squandered. This society is meant to be a force for development and profit, not some sort of sabotage.'
> 'Hear, hear!' echoed the table.
> 'I gave up my wife's inheritance for that network!' spat another.
> 'I had twelve shares in that business, Hargraves. You sold them to me.'
> 'It's the Great Eastern all over again – but this time it's being wrecked by some suspicious buffoon who sits at the table and does nothing but reap our rewards!'

Uproar began; the men began standing and arguing their point with the two brothers – until, at last, Hargraves bellowed out to silence them and slammed his sizeable fist on the table. A glass of water spilt as a result.

> 'I understand! Shut up! The lot of you! If this is true-'
> 'It is.' I remarked, calmly.
> 'If it *is* true...then the repercussions upon our documenting officer will be serious.'

A rumble of discontent echoed around the board table once again. It seemed somewhat as if nobody realised there was such a position in the society - and that Hargraves was woefully ill prepared for this sort of uproar. It was one thing for people to dislike him - it was another for his funding to be threatened.

All eyes fell again upon the accused. He was still snarling and breathing heavily.

> 'Are you going to believe this... this little shed builder's word against me? The words of a half blind night watchman who was knocked unconscious against a senior documenting officer? I did no such bloody thing!'
> 'Frankly,' I began, remaining steadfast, 'I have no idea why he would sabotage our infrastructure. One would think I had slighted him, when as you all know I am an upstanding member of the society.'

Hargraves kept his poker face. His brother did not – he snorted, loudly and spat on the table.

> 'You know why I would sabotage your piffling little tunnels! You're a two faced bastard! You deserve every little mishap coming to you! If I had my way I'd have buried you in the rubble!'

Hargraves wrapped an arm around his neck in an effort to silence him – but it was too late. A gasp of scandalised horror came from every investor's lips.

I tried to hide my smug smile. I've no idea how effective this was, but even now, as I sit here, I still feel that self-contentment. I can only thus presume it was about as subtle as a brick to the chin.

> 'This meeting is adjourned until tomorrow!' Spat Hargraves. 'I and our Documenting Officer are going to have a little conversation.'
> 'Get your hands off of me, Hargraves! If you know what is good for you, you shall let me keep watch on that little tunnel-burrowing rat!'

Hargraves hauled his livid, foaming brother down the stairs that led to the Eccleston Labyrinth. The sound of a slamming door echoed from beneath.

Silence erupted in a spectacular fashion as the other men exchanged glances.

'A brave thing you did there, William.' Spoke one.
'We'll not see him again.'

Each of the wealthy, greying individuals nodded solemnly. While they were businessmen with poor moral fibre, they were men all the same. Each was all too willing to voice opinion - at least, when Hargraves himself was not in the room.

'I'll be glad to see the back of him;' The Yorkshireman piped up. 'I never understood his purpose here. Documenting officer. Pah! If you ask me, he was an elephant in the room.'
One of the other gentlemen burst out laughing. 'I'd say Hargraves is closer to an elephant between them!'

The laughter continued for an uncomfortably long period. I had more than one concern from what had just been said, mind.

'Hang on.' What do you mean we shan't see him again?'

The - seemingly oldest - gentleman at the foot of the table lifted off his monocle and polished it. I would have probably assumed he was the wealthiest, too - his clothes were remarkably fine, in colourful checks, and the monocle perfectly fitted to his eye socket. His face was slender - but seemed to be permanently contorted into a wry smile.

'Hargraves will likely be looking to either fire him or - ahem - put him away, so to speak. Put simply, Jacomb, Hargraves has a marvellous tendency to make troublesome individuals disappear. His father disappeared in much the same way, if I recall.'
'And you're all... in agreement with this?'
'Any delay to these projects can cost hundreds of thousands of pounds, William. You should be glad to see an obstruction in your business removed.'

> 'We're not talking about dirt. We're talking about a living soul.'
> 'But he was an insufferable living soul. He shan't be missed. He's as immoral as Hargraves himself. Perhaps the pair of them are completely amoral.'
> 'You're not sounding particularly moral yourselves.'
> 'We aren't interested in morals, William. We're businessmen. Now, what say we retire to an inn, gentlemen?'

I stared, dumbfounded, as the senior gentlemen at the table agreed - and, with nary the slightest hesitation, walked out of the room. The entire building now seemed vacant.

Brereton sat there, silently. I had almost forgotten his presence in the Eccleston square lounge - he had observed every word, every moment and every argument carefully.

He looked ashamed of his fellows. And highly concerned for what we had just seen take place. He rested his head in his palm; a defeated, tired and worn look upon his face.

> 'I told you, William. They're insufferable.'
> 'I had no idea there were more so uncaring towards their fellow man.'
> 'Hargraves isn't as rare a breed as he may seem. But I am fearful they're right - the younger Hargraves may never be seen again.'
> 'I suppose in some way, we should be thankful.'
> 'It does make our intentions far, far easier to see through.'
> 'Does that cheapen our own resolution? To see the death of another man as a positive?'

The eyepatched engineer rubbed his chin thoughtfully. He glanced at the whisky decanter and hesitated - though for only a moment, then began pouring himself a generous glass.

> 'I suppose the perspective we should take is sacrificing the few to save thousands, William. I would certainly rather there be no

bloodshed, but if that's what it takes...'

He took a hefty gulp of the liquor and sat back in his chair, studying the glass and its etching of the society's emblem.

> 'In the end, we're trying to prevent bloodshed at Hargraves' hands on a far grander scale. A few lives to save thousands, eh?'
> 'I suppose. And you feel so sure Hargraves would do such a thing to his own flesh and blood?'
> 'As the gentlemen explained - we believe his father met the same end.'
> 'Barbarians.'
> 'No. Businessmen. And budding politicians. I reckon a fair amount of parliament's finest would happily see a rival drown with their foot on his head.'

My disdain and sheer hatred for this world I had stepped into must have betrayed itself, as Brereton pushed an equally generous glass into my hands.

> 'I completely understand your feelings, William. Is it any surprise I myself am so willing to see the end of it? It's a generous payroll, but the lengths and sights we have to witness in order to receive it... I may well jump off the Great Eastern myself if it has to continue like this.'

He looked at the contract that flowed from the company's ledger. That signature of every great man - and every unscrupulous horror - that had joined Hargraves' society. That private social club of individuals who were moving towards a private army of mercenaries.

I swore I could see tears in his eyes as he glanced upon Brunel's own penmanship.

> 'I believe both he and Stephenson were dispatched, William. I know that doctor well. He has more experience in poisons, I fear,

than any medication.'

'Stephenson assured me otherwise, Brereton.'

'And he died himself, only a few days later. I don't believe that's convenience. I think the society is only growing more ruthless and grim. I believe that since Hargraves' master plan was put into motion, they are planning to dispatch all in their way. What better way than with a medical man? Many great men have died over the past few years, William. Many were society members. Many were friends. All of them were threats to Hargraves' cause in one way or another. People with a sense of justice. I would dare-'

I interrupted him quickly and motioned for silence. We could both hear something. Shouting, yelling and arguments echoed from the staircase that led into the society's secretive labyrinth underneath Eccleston Square gardens.

Thump.
Thump.
Thump.

The thumping came closer and closer, with the sound of panting, grunting and growling.

A hand slapped against the wall as a large silhouette appeared.

To the horror of both of us, the younger Hargraves brother stepped into view, blood pouring down his face. He had been beaten black and blue, and angrily spat one of his own teeth onto the fine, Persian carpet beneath our feet before taking his next shaky, rough step towards us.

He limped forward, his right arm hanging loose at his side, blood trickling down his bruised, swollen face with one of his eyes seriously blackened.

We backed away from the portly, limping vizier as he came ever closer. He reached for my throat, panting with fury, and grabbed my windpipe viciously - squeezing me between his fingers. For a man so seriously injured, he maintained a surprisingly firm grip. I tried to fight him off, but, with his weight against me, I slammed against the wall, his hand pressing harder and harder against my throat.

It was all too familiar to Hargraves' own tactics. I grunted and began to choke, desperately trying to protest - but he only spat at me - his saliva stained red from his own injuries.

His speech was slow, slurred and punctuated by his heavy, desperately furious breathing.

> 'You sealed my death, Jacomb.' he spat. 'I shall seal yours. And do so with pleasure. I shall be all too glad to know my death led to your-'

Thwack!

He fell to the floor with a hefty thump.

Brereton stood behind him, holding a brass candlestick in his hand. He was spattered in a lurid red. Breathing heavily, trembling, and staring in disbelief at his actions.

We both waited. But the Vizier was motionless. Silent.

The first blood had been spilled.

Without a word, we tossed the candlestick into labyrinth, allowing it to tumble down the stairs - and left the building. Brereton trembled for the next few days. We never spoke again of this incident. It was, we felt, the loss of our innocence for the first time. Our conquest was no longer bloodless.

There was much calamity that could erupt from what, put plainly, was murder. The uncertainty we felt was stronger than ever. The fear was evident in Brereton's eyes, his posture, and his shaking hands.

I probably owed my life to the man; but even I had been shaken by his swift dispatch of the Vizier.

Brothers had now become one. The Hargraves clan had lost another member. And we, in some capacity, had become responsible for the death of the society's most senior officer.

+ THE WAIT +

T he men of iron - I had decided to resurrect the title, now I had my small group of allies - eagerly awaited for the plan to finally be feasible, and for the failing Great Eastern to be put up for sale. However - Hargraves stubbornly held onto his largest asset with vigour. The ship's journeys became quieter and more accident prone, but continued to operate - at substantial loss.

Independent of the Great Babe, however, I remained hard at work. Save for a burst sewer on Fleet Street, my underground railway met completion swiftly, and we had - to much public interest - operated test services with alumni such as William Gladstone himself, and some members of the Athenaeum club besides, that spring, while work continued.

I am pleased to say that, with these influential gentlemen enjoying their journeys, and the sight of trains operating - albeit with standard Great Western Classes - the controversy regarding our failures had fallen quite to the wayside.

Those three continuous lengths of shining, steel rail on each side of our grand tunnels were a welcoming, wonderful sight to me. I almost felt drawn to tears.
What had once been cynicism and fear had given way to celebration and a greatly impressed public. The similarities to the Great Eastern were not going unnoticed.

At last, with a celebratory driving of the final tooth into the rail sleepers and chairs, we cheered. November 1862 had come with completion.

The Metropolitan Railway finally reached its destination in a bitter 1862 winter - and passed inspections with flying colours, save a few switch and signal changes.

The second most momentous project of my career was completed. Another marvel, with my name attached - uniting the city's railway termini into a grand, subterranean link that no other city in the world could lay claim to.

Gooch delivered the first batch of the unwieldy locomotives at Hargraves' expense only a few days before. The top heavy engines waddling through the metropolitan's tunnels made a thrilling sight, though they did indeed prove expensive, ungainly runners, but, in the eyes of the now sole brother and the despot of the society's operations, they were ideal. He did, after all, provide the plans - and was quite certain the engines were masterpieces.

The ceremony was an incredible one, with a grand banquet, and the Great Northern had to provide extra engines and carriages to help keep with passenger demand. The railway was practically as much of a pleasure trip as it was a formal link of business.

Samuel Lucas, Brereton, Gooch and myself all sat in a

compartmentalised carriage and enthusiastically discussed the momentous occasion, as the engine clattered along in front.

'Quite an achievement. I could do no better with my own hands.'

Brereton smiled. He knew well railway tunnels, and seemed remarkably impressed. I dare say that meant as much to me as compliments would from Brunel himself.

Samuel feverishly wrote up his glowing report; and was quite certain the world's press would do the same. As a man with no engineering experience, he felt the entire situation was quite miraculous. How I envied him! The pleasure of being amazed by progress had been quite jaded to my eyes.

I wondered if this was how the fatigued Brereton felt when we met at Duke Street. I sat back, comfortable but utterly exhausted.

Occasionally, Brereton and I exchanged glances. The scenes at Eccleston square were still fresh in our mind. I could only presume Gooch had taken notice, as he gave my back a friendly slap.

'The engines of progress move forward, eh!'
'They do indeed, Daniel. At last, the caper is over.'
'And onto the next one, I expect.'
'How does our plan progress?'

Gooch rubbed his chin and smiled in a false thoughtfulness.

'Steadily, William, steadily. But we've some time of leisure, yet - provided Hargraves doesn't make the first move. I doubt he will.'
'What's stopping him?'
'Rumour has it the ship's expenses are. I hear she hasn't once exceeded a hundred passengers. If he's going to be doing anything, it shan't be a large investment. The ship will be veritably bleeding him dry, and Hargraves shall be trying to find a market for her, so he has reason to keep her for his grand invasion plans. If he

doesn't find one, he'll be pressured into an auction. Then it's as good as ours.
You see, gentlemen, the society mostly puts money into investments. It is a valuable, profitable one, of course - but most of the money goes to Hargraves, his director's wages, and his grand plan. The capitol of the entire thing is never fully secured as cash. Only in property, firearms and people.'

The locomotive ahead of us let out a ghostly whistle as it rattled into King's Cross Station - it was late, and the engine inspectors were writing a rather scathing report.

Gooch gave a devilish grin, leant out of the window and made sure the inspectors could hear him.

'Good grief, these engines are terrible, aren't they? If only Hargraves had taken my advice... Such wide, outside cylinder engines are no good for balanced running.'

The inspectors bore a rather uncanny resemblance to the dealers. I raised an eyebrow as the round headed, pencil moustached gentlemen strode over to the carriage.

'You believe you have the remedy, Mr. Gooch? It would be a trifle unfortunate if we discovered you had tried to sabotage the project.'
'I did no such thing. I followed his drawings.'
'Then perhaps you were expected to use your own expertise.'
'Then, gentlemen, he should have paid for them.'

The engine hooted, hissed, and - without the inspectors aboard, pulled away. They shouted for it to stop - but the rattling and cylinder beats of the waddling locomotive muffled them as it picked up speed.

Gooch laughed and closed the window.

'It's the little things in life, gentlemen. One does need these small pleasures.'
'Are you not concerned, Daniel? These locomotives will raise the society's ire.'
'Are you not concerned by the low quality motive power on the railway you oversaw the construction of, Jacomb?'
'Of course not. I worked to build it; once it's done, my obligations are dealt with.'

I leant back in the first class, parlour seat and held my arms behind my bed with more than a touch of self-satisfaction. Daniel chuckled, holding a cigar in his lips.

'Then I'm not concerned about the society's arguments. I'm concerned about when I can retract our rolling stock. Our contract is only in place for six months.'
'You plan to take your engines?'
'I plan to take those engines, and Hargraves' money. Both will be put into my own railway, and properly reallocated besides. Then we'll see where the capitol for his little plot will go.'
'You fiend!' Brereton laughed.
'Nonsense!' Daniel gave a wry smile as he countered. 'It's business...'

Unlike many of the men I had met in the past few years, Gooch was a man of his word. Traffic on the Metropolitan had developed quite substantially, and Hargraves had celebrated with vigour as he began increasing ticket prices. Trains were soon running every twenty minutes, and twice as frequent for worker's trains.

That was a problem – the broad gauge engines were far from smokeless, with steam condensers unable to tackle the larger issue of soot and smoke from their inefficient, constantly hungering fireboxes. The Metropolitan had been designed with smokeless engines in mind; but the technology Hargraves and Fowler had attempted was a miserable failure.

The result was some 22 steam locomotives from the GWR - supplemented with further engines from the Great Northern - belching thick clouds of smoke and layers of soot into the tunnel.

Hargraves, never one to back down from business opportunity, colluded with a certain weasely doctor to produce what was called *The Met' Mixture*; an expensive medication intended to cure tunnel sickness.

As a hot summer rolled on, the smoke only seemed to develop in density. It was not my problem, I had claimed to Gooch - but the sight of my tunnels caked in soot and locomotive clag made me feel frightfully insulted. The railway's lack of ventilation was becoming a severe issue for passengers, crews and staff.

The typical lack of support and care towards the common man from Hargraves' hands was obvious. The society's ticket money continued flowing in regardless of the suffering in what was beginning to resemble an enormous network of mine shafts.

Finally, it happened. July hit, and when Hargraves insisted on more locomotives, Gooch was the first to protest.

We were, sadly, not privy to the letters between the two. But a small celebration was had by all to see the GWR locomotives depart on a hot summer evening in August- in their unusual, waddling gait - for the last time, resulting in Hargraves' business venture quickly slipping into the red.

The Met was in turmoil, and the Great Northern had to supply any spare standard gauge locomotives they could to supplement the struggling railway.
Hargraves was furious, but his investors were in far worse temperament. It was the society's head who took the brunt of the blame.

We sat in Eccleston square to a tense, difficult scene. August was hardly the most fitting weather for meetings - but Hargraves, desperately fanning his round, dripping face, suffered worst of all. The searing anger from his investors and directors only seemed to fluster him further.

> 'This is a pathetic move to intimidate us.' He panted. 'We cannot bow to suffer at the hands of the Great Western-'
> 'Do not make this any other's issue than your own, Hargraves. We invested in this railway with the belief we would equally invest in locomotives and carriages.'
> 'We did attempt, gentlemen-'
> 'And you failed. Instead, well, we ask you - to let a broad gauge tin pot railway run on our infrastructure?'
> 'Gentlemen, please. This was, to my eyes, the best opportunity to-'
> 'And where did the money for the locomotives go? If it went to your damned gambling clubs, Hargraves, we shall see to it that the board of trade-'

Hargraves hit his fist on the table in a manner that now seemed all too familiar. The investors had hit a nerve with him - I felt I knew his unspoken languages all far too well.

'Gentlemen, enough. I can assure you I know not of any gambling clubs, and will place an order for locomotives before the end of the year.'
'You had better. Twenty locomotives of our own, I should hope!'
Hargraves tapped the side of his nose. 'Forty. I shall give you forty locomotives, gentlemen. If not, then more. I promise you the most efficient, profitable railway in London!'

But the slight crack in his voice was clear. The heat of the room and the awkward situation had made Hargraves clumsy and awkward in his composure. He wiped his forehead on his sleeve and exhaled, deeply.

The gentlemen were silenced, and shook hands on the arrangement.

The investors would not relinquish their funding, provided rolling stock was supposed to the fledging underground railway.

Brereton and I exchanged glances of satisfaction. It would be interesting to see forty locomotives spring out of nowhere. If Hargraves was hoping to purchase any kind of arsenal or mercenary services, he certainly couldn't until he had his engines.

Gooch had successfully bought us some time – and, as Hargraves grappled with locomotive manufacturers for rush orders, the society's meetings were put on hold.

Promises slowly began to decrease, until, at last, 18 locomotives were placed on order. Queer, boxy, albeit attractive machines with side tanks, enormous cylinders and gradiated smokeboxes, with a network of condensing pipes. Fowler had offered specifications for wheel spacing and sizes, while Beyer Peacock – an engine builder of Manchester - assembled and delivered them, with contracts for five more locomotives each year.

The bill was far from comfortable for Hargraves. Just shy of £50,000 was spent on the first batch of locomotives, an amount close to the cost of the SS Great Eastern's paddles and boilers. This was quite a sum of money to any company, and would be far from insubstantial at the time of writing – especially when this was only eighteen locomotives of the forty Hargraves hoped to receive.

The purse strings were being tightened across the society's activities – and Hargraves had to begin looking for ways to make a quick burst of financial return.

The clock was ticking for our big moment, and Daniel Gooch, with his friends and own likeminded investors, were eagerly awaiting the first glimpse of opportunity.

+ THE AUCTION +

Just before the new year was to begin, a notice was released in several trade magazines and newspapers. I had been eating a simple breakfast with Eliza when I came across it - and nearly shouted in elation.

THE MUCH CELEBRATED
SS GREAT EASTERN

TWIN PADDLE & SCREW DRIVEN STEAMSHIP

WILL BE AUCTIONED IN THE LIVERPOOL EXCHANGE ON THE 11TH OF JANUARY 1864. SALE PRICE TO BEGIN AT FIFTY THOUSAND POUNDS.
PLEASE CONTACT THIS ADDRESS FOR A FULL INTENARY.

The society, feeling the pinch of the locomotive order and Hargraves' other investments, saw no other option than selling off its biggest loss making asset.

The SS Great Eastern, one of the most important aspects to Hargraves' grand plan, was pressured by his financial backers into the auction house.

This was far from a small situation to the country's industrial minds and businessmen – this was a potentially gigantic prospect. Interest was expected to be high. The window of time available to us was pitifully short – and, the very next morning, I made a point of visiting Duke Street.

The chief assistant, though he looked as typically exhausted as I had come to expect, was waiting for me with a bag packed and a travelling book in his hand.

We made our way to Swindon, as swiftly as we could, and arrived late that afternoon, with the intention of discussing our bid.

The news had travelled quickly, and Daniel had already prepared cigars, drinks and a quiet place of discussion for us.

The meeting took place in the relative secrecy of Daniel's private locomotive museum, with he himself perched upon the footplate of Hurricane, quite relaxed with a smile on his face.

We had rather frantically started the discussion. Gooch remained calm and leisurely, smoking a cigar quite happily as he listened.

'We aren't placing a bid.'

We both went silent.

'Daniel, excuse me – but is it not within your business interests to purchase her?'

'Yes, William. But consider this; you have the world's largest ship, an enormous, floating white elephant with no other financial prospects or relevant passenger demand. Who will spend £50,000 on her?'

'She's worth at least double that in materials.'

'Not if you consider the cost of breaking her up.'

It still felt saddening to consider that my master's greatest achievement – and my own – was now diminished to such a pitifully low price. She was unwanted by all except Daniel Gooch and his friends in the United States.

'Simply speaking, gentlemen, I do not intend to bid until her reserve is low enough to further sabotage Hargraves' hope of refinancing. The Hungerford bridge is already being sold off for thruppence; why should we pay so much for the biggest thorn in his side?'

He puffed on his cigar in a manner not unlike Brunel himself.

'We shall see it go down in price; you see if we don't.'

Brereton was all too swift to agree – but I felt cautious. I greatly feared the potential of Hargraves' plan being achievable in any proportion. It would take only a single, wealthy sympathiser to scupper our own plans for the ship, and send her into a battle she could never escape from.

It was quite a gamble.

I remained nervous until the very day she was to be sold, but did the sensible thing. I took a trip, personally, to the Liverpool Exchange to watch the auction.

There, in the exchange's cotton rooms, the mahogany panels and intricate brickwork did nothing to loosen the purse strings of the men present.

Many people gathered to watch the spectacle, but not a single bid was placed. More seemed there out of curiosity, or to report on the ship's final value, than they were to put their own finances on the table.

I could see Hargraves in the audience, biting his nails in a rare show of weakness. It was little wonder. His wrapping down of certain assets – many of them by Brunel's hands – was doing little to allay the cost of locomotive construction.

As a matter of fact, many familiar faces were present. The chairman of the company who so desperately tried to wring profit from her, and even Mr. John Scott Russell, who's yard had built her. He noticed my presence, and, from then on, remained as hidden from view as he could. He had garnered much celebration from the great ship – and I knew better than anyone, I felt, how ill-gotten any positive terms to his name were.

The auctioneer was a prim gentleman. I dare say he had never stepped foot on a ship in his life.

His pince-nez glasses perched on top of a sharp nose, with a twirled, well-kept moustache underneath. His yellow and brown checked jacket would make the most flamboyant gentleman blush.

He was visibly flustered; as he saw his generous auctioneer's fees disappear before his eyes.

> 'Gentlemen, am I not bid a single hundred pounds over our starting bid for this vessel? The world's most famous ship? Over 692 feet of luxury passenger carriage-'
> 'Pull the other one!' came one voice from the rear. The more official gentlemen in the audience blanched.

'Eh-hmm. Well, as the world's most famous passenger vessel, the most prestigious ship in the world, is unable to achieve a mere fifty thousand pounds...'

Silence.

'No?'

Hargraves' deep, frustrated breathing could be heard from across the room as the hammer fell, and the next lot's auction began.

The colossal ship, just as Gooch estimated, went unsold, and would have to go to auction again. Hargraves remained in financial peril.

And the Great Babe sat, forlornly, awaiting her fate. A great beast with no place in the world; a giant before her time.

The room slowly emptied at the end of the auction, the gentlemen in the audience scattering with their booklets and purchase ledgers; none, sadly, for Brunel's masterpiece.

I lingered in the doorway as the room's hundred men became two; one snorting in frustration.
Hargraves held his substantial head in his hands and sighed as the auctioneer trotted, in his somewhat stiff and overly starched manner, to him.

'You may do well to offer her without a reserve, Sir. Fifty thousand pounds is a trifle high for a ship with so many demands.'

He yelped as the society's head grabbed his yellow lapels and lifted him off of his feet.

'I need that money, you prim little prick. Mark my words; if that ship doesn't get at least forty thousand pounds, it'll be your waxed face under the hammer!'
'I-I guarantee it! It's a common auction trick to drive interest, I'm

sure it will make all of the difference!'

Hargraves growled.

> 'I got you this position in trust. I can send you right back to a back-end Opium parlour and leave you to rot.'

He physically threw the perfectly groomed young man to the floor and lumbered towards the door. I made a quick exit, and decided a return to Swindon was necessary.

The Liverpool Exchange had never seemed so foreboding, and the mark of corruption and poor business practise seemed to continue following the society wherever it may step.

My reports to the other men of iron were more of concern than the celebration of the others.

Gooch lay on his entire liquor cupboard with glee as he began writing his letters. He planned to send an assistant to the Exchange at the next auction, with firm instruction.

Not a penny over £37,700 – a tenth of John Scott Russell's infamously inaccurate quote for the ship's tender. For Gooch, it was a frightfully amusing caper.

I must confess, I found far less to celebrate. The Great Eastern remained my greatest achievement; still the most momentous project in my career. To see her barely garner her scrap metal value felt enormously depressing.

She was intended to be a momentous, luxury vessel with the power and strength to travel the world. She was now barely able to pay for her own journeys to America.

I had witnessed the Great Babe grow from a fresh idea from the brain of the country's most esteemed engineer – to an enormous iron structure boasting the finest in shipbuilding technology and dogged, human determination.

To see the world's largest man made, moving object reduced to such a mere trifle? It felt like a terrible statement on the world in which we lived. No matter how great the idea, the bankroll was king, and the investors had their final world.

As to whether that was a better fate than being used for Hargraves' terrible invasion plans, there was no question. But, in my mind, it felt like the ship was akin to a lump of clay without the potter's hand to form her.

I felt downtrodden for the next few days, considering my role in the world and the ship's miserable failure.

Three weeks later, the second auction was held. Daniel contacted his friends to garner their backing.

Mister Yates was the name of the man who attended for the Great Ship Company. He had assisted Brunel greatly in the ship's construction, and often acted as a beleaguered, long suffering middleman to the shipyard conflicts between Isambard and Scott Russell. He was, I am pleased to say, every bit as dedicated and just to the cause as any man amongst us – and took his instructions very seriously.

Daniel's friends, and contacts in the United States, were sure of their chances. The two men joining Gooch in business were very forward thinking gentlemen, both of whom had immediately recognised the Great Babe's potential.

John Pender was an expert in submarine cables, and Thomas Brassey a civil engineer and contractor – indeed, the latter was the man who had built over a third of the country's railway lines, and one of Brunel's most fervent investors and supports.

All were emotionally attached to the vessel – and all eager to go against the monopolistic, sinister goals of Hargraves, the society and his grand plans of invasion and violence.

They, and one Mister Cyrus Field of the Atlantic Telegraph Company, were in essence breaking the very ideology of Hargraves. Rather than tearing the world apart for the empire's gain, they wished to bring it closer together for mutual benefit.

I was no expert in the ideas of cables and underwater construction, and Gooch himself was acting more as a superintendent for ship, as opposed to a chief member of the party – but the plans had been drawn for the Great Eastern with impeccable detail, and had been extent for some time.

Clearly a great deal of forward thinking had been necessary.

I made a point of attending the Liverpool exchange on the wet February morning that she was due for auction. This time, the young auctioneer had been replaced by Joseph Cunard himself – who spoke far more authoritatively, the intention being to garner the interest of the audience with sharp barks and expertise.

Hargraves was there – clearly exhausted. A man at the end of his tether – and with good reason, too. The first locomotives had arrived on schedule, and had required immediate payment upon receipt. The Metropolitan's finances were worsening.

There was no sign of Scott Russell, and no sign of the investors I had noticed previously. The SS Great Eastern had garnered a pathetic audience for her second turn in the cotton rooms of the Liverpool Exchange, and we were confident that our day had finally come. The final judgement had only taken a few minutes.

   'Am I really to receive no further bids, gentlemen?'

There were none. The world's most advanced vessel, and the empire's very own biblical ark, had managed to raise less than a quarter of her material value.

The documents were signed and the ship signed over.

Yates leaned back in his chair and smiled. He had won the day; well below the budgets afford to him.

Hargraves only stared, his jaw slack and his eyes wide.

We strode out of the auction hall, and, as the doors closed behind us, we heard that familiar voice erupt into expletive laden ranting.

We had, at least, won the vessel. But the great Telegraph caper had only just begun, and there was much work to do.

I was cordially invited by the Telegraph Company - and Daniel himself - to watch over the conversion work on her, preparing her for the next great adventure for the world's most miraculous paddle steamer.

+ THE CONVERSION +

With John Scott Russell no longer trusted, and practically bankrupted, the works to convert the SS Great Eastern were kept strictly within the new company set up by Daniel.

The Great Eastern Steamship Company, as they had dubbed this new undertaking, had rapidly made the headlines with its intentions, and people were already lauding the idea of a telegraph cable being trailed in one, continuous journey.

The cost of the ship's hire was £50,000 worth of shares in the telegraph cable company - far beyond the ship's purchase value, and, even taking into account the costs, Gooch had successfully turned quite a profit from his newest asset.

The works to convert her were enormous, and started very rapidly. The ship had barely been inspected before the engineers began measuring up the changes required to allow her to carry over two thousand miles of submarine cable.

I watched over the coming weeks as her silhouette began to change. A funnel – and its two enormous, rectangular boilers, were disassembled and sold, which provided even greater financial benefit to the company's operation.

The next stage, and for I, the most painful, was seeing some of those beautiful interiors ripped free from their comfortable housing. Mahogany and ceramic tile were indiscriminately torn out and sold, lush furnishings, chandeliers and floors delivered into warehouses for resale. The process was brutal and harsh. There were times wherein I felt ready to beg for mercy to Brunel's designs, but there was no room for argument or emotion. The ship's future depended on these changes.

By the time this was completed, her corridors and saloons had become colossal open topped tanks, filled with enormous cable coils and riveted in iron for stability.

What had once been inviting and luxurious now felt dark and foreboding. An open topped, enormous series of holds, filled with over two thousand miles of coiled cables.

The Great Eastern was now the world's largest cable laying vessel; no longer was she something designed for comfort and convenience.

I felt almost as hollow as her decks.

Daniel smiled to me, and sympathetically patted my shoulder.

> 'I understand, Jacomb. But trust me – this will avenge her name; and, I dare say, Isambard's reputation.'
> 'I shall never be happy to see her in any other form than that in which she was designed, Daniel. I understand – but I shan't be happy.'
> 'And, let us not forget the main attraction, eh? Have you made a decision on what we are to do with Hargraves?'
> 'I have not. I fear he shall likely make the decision for us.'

'You might well be right. And for our own preservation...well, so be it, Jacomb. We cannot give him the benefit of a potentially winning final move.'

'Do you not fear the significance such an event could have on your project?'

'My dear Jacomb - how many major engineering projects don't encounter some kind of misfortune? It's part of our work. It's part of the Great Eastern's fabric. I am willing to make sacrifices to see our country a better place.'

Daniel rubbed his chin as the cable machinery was worked onto her. It was a bizarre thing; a disorientating series of winches, wheels and rocking levers. I inspected it with great interest, while Gooch and Pender explained the purpose of this great network of rods, cogs and gears that, in theory, had such a simple purpose - dropping wires into the ocean.

I was under no such illusion. The very idea and scale of it all seemed impossible in my mind, and Gooch was showing an obvious result of the challenges. It was clear he hadn't shaved in a few days; the work was proving to be a very tiring project for the engine builder. A single cable seemed to be giving more stress and difficulty than the entirety of the Great Western Railway, its locomotives and rolling stock.

But to see the somewhat stout gentleman, his hands on his hips with a confident, enthusiastic smile on his face - it was rather startling to contrast him with the expression of anxiety and frustration that had acclimated Brunel to the Great Eastern's decks.

I was beginning to believe, by proxy, and through these men's confidence, that this truly was the best option for her.

The Anthenaeums contributed thousands to the project - most likely from my contact with the old bulldog - and had regularly visited the workshops with great interest, one shared by the gentlemen who had worked with Daniel so enthusiastically.

I was quite taken with Mr. Pender and Brassey. They were both very agreeable; completely innocent, it seemed, from the grasp of corruption and anger that had fuelled the last few years of our lives - and, unlike many of the men I had dealt with - they treated me as an equal, and a valuable source of information towards the Great Babe's fabrication.

Mr. Pender was a particularly honest, jovial - and unusually liberal - businessman, and had placed everything to his name into this business prospect.

He was a stout, deceptively short gentleman, with flashes of silver in his hair, a rounded face, and eyes that could see right through to the bottom of any man who crossed his path. He had become a very dear friend to all of us; and one who truly recognised the benefits of the Great Eastern's size and abilities.

His Scottish accent was unmistakable, and gave him a naturally authoritative voice - aided with a deep, booming tone and a sharp posture.

He patted my back firmly as he admired the enormous pistons and cylinders inside the Great Eastern's bowels.

> 'With paddle, sail and propeller, you could lay a cable using this ship in any weather. She's an incredible thing, William.'

The cable was being fed in short intervals by two Naval sailing ships - that the Great Eastern made more likely resemble stray, floating pieces of driftwood, thanks to her own impossible size.

The old matchstick boats, as our crew called them, fed the thick woven cable onto the Great Eastern at a speed of two miles of cable per hour, constantly swapping shifts to ensure a convenient supply - and as much continuous length as plausible.

We stood together, Pender and I, and watched the task with great interest.

> 'I've been an admirer of Mr. Brunel for a long time, William. But I do feel he overestimated the Great Eastern's requirements. What he has built is an enormously stable, accurate vessel which is flawlessly designed to sail in a straight line. She'll have a substantial career in submarine cables, I wager.'
> 'I do hope you're right, Sir. I fear any mishap on her decks at this point.'
> Pender gave a smile. 'There shan't be. We shall run her tightly and flawlessly.'

If only he knew. I felt enormously guilty to be using Pender's business for our disposal of the society – I expect all of us did. The ship's preparation, for many of us, was like a clock counting down to a grim event we'd rather avoid. It was difficult to share the passion, enthusiasm and joviality of the telegraph cable project when the thought of murder had been brought up.
It felt like we were deceiving every step of the way – and I felt ashamed.

Samuel Lucas arrived on the Thursday, still smoking his characteristic cob pipe as he strode along, admiring the decks and machinery. It was his first time on the Great Eastern, and every sight to him was as it was to me when I first saw the plans.

> 'I'm glad I could finally see her in person, William. Really, she's quite a marvel.' He gave a harsh cough onto his handkerchief, which soon erupted into a fit of them. 'A minor throat complaint.'
> – So he put it.

I exchanged a worried glance with Daniel as we continued touring him across the vessel. The journalist was still a relatively young man, but to see him coughing so harshly was more than a slight concerning. He was not a man so regularly involved in industrial work sites - the coalman's cough, as many of us labelled it, was not likely to afflict a gentleman of the press.

'It doesn't sound all that minor to me, Samuel.'
'Nonsense - I have been prescribed medication. It will clear in a month or so; I'm quite sure. Now come, on with the tour, eh? This is fascinating.'

We did so; but he had to take regular breaks as he became short of breath. He had very little stamina to his person - something that seemed quite foreign to him.

Gooch tried to convince the journalist to visit the on-site doctor, but Samuel, being the optimistic character he was, refused - and continued, regardless, smoking his cob pipe and cheap tobacco that he so favoured.

March went by with incredible progress, and, with a comfortable deadline still ahead of her, the Great Eastern already resembled Gooch and Pender's plans of the perfect cable layer.

She looked considerably more utilitarian - little wonder, of course, considering the changes to her internals - but, as boiler work and test steaming began, the plumes of smoke from her funnels ensured that she looked and sounded every bit of the ship I had come to know so well.

I watched the crews stoke up and inspect the number one boiler with pride, and found myself somewhat settled by the familiar hissing and whisping that made up her comfortable, simmering innards as she warmed.

A test of the ship's whistle cemented it clearly. The Great Babe lived once again; eager to command a new adventure.

We watched - the men of iron, Brassey and Pender - as the vessel made her first move in over a year; a slight manoeuvre to ensure all was well - and she did so, flawlessly, with a smooth chug of her paddles, egged on by cheers, waves and applause from us upon the ground.

We retired to the inn that evening to celebrate; and solidify our partnership for the telegraph laying over a stout drink and a jovial chat.

I felt exhilarated. Beyond overjoyed, and still had a broad smile on my face when I arrived home a week later. We had saved the Great Eastern with Gooch's determination for the future.

We communicated with letters over the next few days - in a code that Brunel himself had taught me and used when he was young - and laid down our plans for the project's operation. Perhaps more accurately, we laid down our own plans for the Eternal Tome's destruction.

The ship would make her move to Valentia harbour from the Thames on July the 15th, with shareholders, Hargraves and Daniel on board. We would then catch up, eternal tome in hand, with the vessel - and make our move when the cable was in progress.

It was after this that things remained a stubborn mystery - and a constant source of anxiety.

Meanwhile, Samuel Lucas enthusiastically discussed the project with us whenever he could - but with declining health. The journalist's so-called minor throat complaint did not clear. It worsened. As time went on, Samuel became less and less fit for his regular visits, and by the end of February, was no longer able to attend meetings or discussions in person.

Every time, from then on, that we gathered to play cards and discuss the ship's progress, there sat an empty chair at the table.

Letters from him became less common, and when they were, they seemed short or uncomfortable, stained with stray ink - a far cry from his usual penmanship. Sometimes his wife even wrote them from his dictation.

After a final letter dated April the 8th, they stopped. There were no more letters from the enthusiastic journalist.

The silence continued for some time on his end, and soon the subject of excitement, planning and progress on the world's largest ship was being replaced with anxieties and concerns for our friend.

The next week, we made a point of visiting Samuel's home to ensure all was well. I'm sorry to say it was no happy trip.

We rapped on the door of his home. It was early morning when we had agreed to meet before work, and it was still very cold, shrouded in a fine drizzle. We must have cut a motley looking visage of gentlemen, in retrospect. It was rather odd to see three gentlemen of varied ages, dressed in identical rain jackets with worker's bunnets. This fact must only have been accented with Brereton's eye patch and our solemn expressions.

Mrs. Lucas ushered us into the parlour and asked for us to wait, while she checked if Samuel could give us his attention.

Samuel's London Townhouse was fairly standard, and, as one may expect, loaded with piles of books and correspondence from his campaigning.

While our plans kept him busy, his passion was always set firmly in human rights, peace and the abolition of slavery. He had prided himself on taking the 'right side' - the Union of the United States were whom he swore to, a fact he often reaffirmed to us.

Gooch flicked through the odd paper on Samuel's writing desk as we waited.

Finally, the doctor came down, his leather bag in hand. He was a stout gentlemen, with a square face and naturally quizzical eyebrows – as white and dense as the outsized sideburns that crossed his face. He cut quite an authoritative image.

'Here to see Mr. Lucas, eh?'
'We are, Sir. We're close friends.'
'Indeed, he seems very enthusiastic to see you. He is medicated, however. Please do be patient with him.'
'How is he? What's the matter?' Daniel piped up.
'A severe bronchial illness. I'm sorry to say he is not a well man. The medicine should help. Please, feel free to go up.'

Brereton and I walked up to see him, while Daniel stayed behind to speak to the doctor.

Samuel was sat quite upright, through ashen faced, and hoarse, with a swollen throat. His parlour was simple and clad in wood, with even more bookshelves across the perimeter, broken by the occasional wardrobe or table.

'My dear fellows; how are you?'
'We were rather hoping to ask you the same.' Brereton put, sitting himself on the chair alongside.
'Oh, I'm quite well. The doctor has given me the latest medication; brand new, he says. He thinks it'll have me right as rain.'

I raised an eyebrow at the little brown bottle by his bedside. It smelt very chemical in nature.

'Doesn't taste very pleasant, mind.' he chuckled – before erupting into coughing fits.

I had my fair share of distrust for the medical profession after my encounters with the society's own doctor; but the gentleman who served Lucas seemed quite different to the weasel-faced, eccentric man who had facilitated Brunel and Stephenson's untimely death.

We spent a few hours explaining our situation to the journalist, with Daniel soon joining us to give his own news of engineering.

Lucas listened intently with a smile on his face - occasionally glancing with great longing for his favoured corn-cob pipe, which was now forbidding from him - sat just out of reach, emptied of tobacco, on his bedside table.

His wife was naturally maternal; and very strict with the ill man. She brought up drams of whiskey for us, with an insistence that his was diluted for his throat.

She was a charming, tall and remarkably dignified woman with a broad smile; One who would later find her own great prominence in political campaigns. We all marvelled at her capability to run the household, with two children, while still maintaining Samuel's health and his campaigns.

There was no doubt that Samuel's life had proven kind and simple for him; a Quaker's lifestyle of home comforts and confidence in his maker.

His son, a deaf mute, was clearly a favourite of Samuel's. He was, he maintained, a 'most brilliant young man', and quite an artist - while his daughter was a splitting image of her mother.

We both felt relieved.

If nothing else, Samuel was being kept happy and comfortable with a family that shared his want for the world.

+ THE FIRST STEPS +

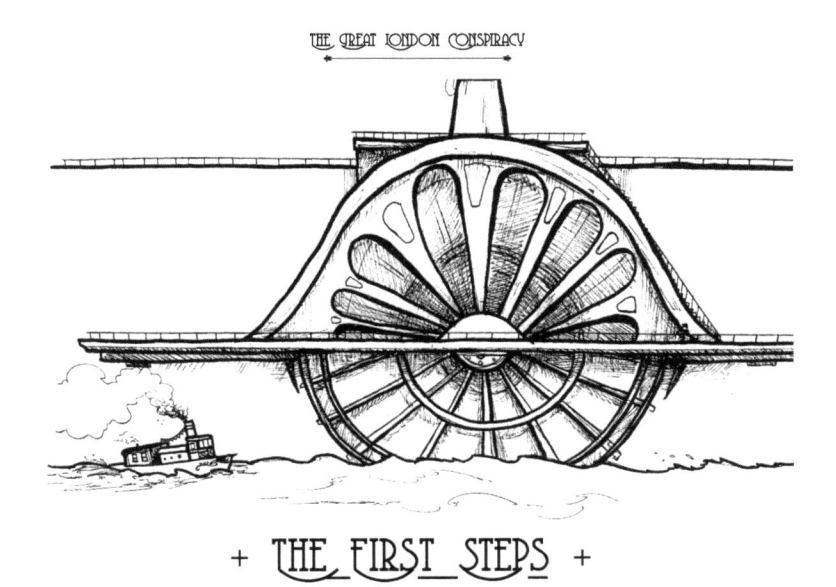

Samuel Lucas died on April the 16th - shortly after hearing the result of The Battle of Richmond - and thus, the end of slavery in the United States.

We took comfort that he passed with the knowledge that much of his life's work rang true. But this was small mercy for his family and friends; and we were crippled by our own disarray and mourning from the loss of an ally - and friend.

It was but a week later when Gooch stormed into the telegraphy office, seething with anger. We followed him to his desk, where he slammed down a familiar brown glass bottle.

'The brute has done it again.'
'Eh?'
'Hargraves. The medicine Samuel was given? It was supplied by the society. It's bloody poisonous!'
'You mean-'

> 'That abhorrent bastard had poisoned by his own doctor. It's a poison. He killed Samuel with medication, and I bloody well guarantee he's done it before.'

Gooch had grown chiselled and dark from the kindly gentlemen he was when we had first met. He was now a rightfully furious, red faced figure who swore like a sailor, and felt quite unfamiliar to us. He paced the office, then slammed his hands down on his desk. The little brown bottle jumped and rattled.

> 'Brunel. Stephenson. I guarantee it! Murdered! Poisoned! Knocked off like second rate livestock by a first rate villainous ghoul. That unwashed cockroach shan't come back from the telegraph voyage. To hell with keeping a straight profile, he deserves seawater in his lungs more than anyone on this Earth.'
> 'What reason does he have to kill Samuel? Why would he even bother with an independent journalist?'
> 'Revenge against us for buying the ship. As I've said before, Jacomb – he's amoral. There's no concept of good, bad, or overreaction for Hargraves. Everyone and everything is just a bloody asset. It's not barbarism. It's business. To him those are one and the same.'

The anger and sorrow we all felt was testament to the success of Hargraves' plan. Samuel had not joined as part of the engineering field, nor part of Brunel's own group. He was an innocent bystander, seeking the truth. He wanted nothing more than his fellow man to be on an even keel.

Samuel's doctor was devastated. The more brutal aspect of medicinal supply meant that a poisoned batch of throat medication had gone to more than just Samuel. Twelve. Twelve patients had been killed at the hand of Hargraves' intent for revenge.

We received news that the Doctor had jumped in front of a train two weeks thereafter, once Daniel told him the reality of his latest miracle drug – such was his grief at being indirectly responsible for the death of innocent people, who trusted and relied upon him.

It was another tragedy. It felt as if, by now, the rap sheet of one Mr. Hargraves was endless. A line as long as the society's own contracts - mapping out a motley selection of murders, espionage, and his villainous intent for the S.S. Great Eastern.

Despite the loss of our friend, the telegraph company continued its activities. Mr Pender offered his sympathies and even offered us a few weeks from the worksite, but Gooch, hardened by his anger, resolutely refused, as did we. Brereton and I were now steadfast - Hargraves could not be permitted to return. He was too dangerous. Such a man barely deserved the gift of life.
Moreover, the telegraph had to succeed. The two great countries deserved to be linked in harmony. After all, we reasoned, what could disgust Hargraves more than two empires living in peace?

July the 14th arrived swiftly - and Eliza woke me, promptly, at 04:00AM - with freshly baked bread and quince.

> 'You must get on your way, my love. After all, it's rather a big day is it not?' She smiled as she prepared my razor.
> 'My darling, you have no idea.'
> 'I'm sure that I don't. But no doubt I shall hear some day. For now, I'm only proud to have you as my husband. I'm sure you're doing the right thing, whatever secretive plans you have in that mind of yours.'

We spent a precious hour together. At 5AM I was forced to leave my happy home - and boarded a train towards London, to meet Brereton's chartered boat.

There was thin smog in the air, as ever there seemed to be in London, and through the haze I had only the dim, glowing lights of Westminster Bridge as my target.

Brereton stood there in the fog, a lantern in one hand and a cigar in the other.

'Good to see you, William.'
'Likewise to you, Robert. What's the plan?'

He walked me down the narrow steps to a tiny little pleasure boat, with a wood clad boiler, copper funnel and unusually low profile. The name *Victoria* was painted delicately onto her bow.

'This is our little steed, William. She isn't much, but she's got a decent pace to her. Brunel's own design, in fact...'
'I must confess, Robert, I am no fan of sailing.'
'Then I hope you get your sea legs quickly.'
'She's frightfully small.'
'We're only two people, Jacomb. What, did you expect me to get a paddle steamer?'

The little boat tweeted her whistle and gleefully set off on its way, with a thick bearded boatsman at the helm. I realised this was the fisherman Samuel had pointed out to me at the inn every time we visited.

'She's a luvverly little boat, Mister. I don't know where Brereton got 'er, but she 'andles like a dream.'

The little ship sailed through the thick, filth ridden current with surprising ease, and merrily chugged on through smog and hints of emerging daylight towards Pimlico pier.

Brereton stepped onto the pier and instructed the boatsman to wait as he boldly walked towards the Military Stores, some fake plans in one hand and his lantern in the other. I followed him with his paperwork satchel - which, by our calculations, would be just big enough to facilitate the Tome's enormous size.

'Halt. What can we help you with?'

Brereton held up the lantern to his face, showing his eyepatch clearly to the nightwatchman.

'Ah, Mr. Brereton. Inspection work, is it?'
'Quite. And Mr. Jacomb too.'
'Jacomb is not permitted inside the works. Hargraves' orders.'
'Where is Hargraves?'
'Ireland. Business matters, he said.'
'I shall keep Jacomb on a tight leash.'
'...I'm not sure if my instructions are so flexible, sir.'
'Would a bit of cash help your instructions free up?'
'It wouldn't hurt.'

The transaction was prompt - though I'm unsure of the exact financial benefit of the guardsman - and we walked through the silent workshops, to a small, bricked up arch at the far end of the enormous room. The chief assistant stepped ahead of me, and inserted a key into a concealed keyhole that sat deep into the wall. The entire thing opened up like some sort of bizarre, textured doorway with mortar and clay cladding.

'Quite a trick, Brereton.'
'Quite; A shame I got into railways, Jacomb - I think I'd have made quite the conjurer.'

He chuckled as the dim, glowing lights strung across the granite tunnel led us deep underneath the bowls of Pimlico; all with the exquisite detail that made Cubitt such a legendary architect.

Every few hundred feet, there stood barred iron gates, which Brereton had to unlock. The security of the arrangement was even more significant than I expected - or rather, more tedious. Was the concept that an intruder would give up after the third or fourth barrier?

The atmosphere so deep underground felt murky and amphibious; the drip of water deep inside the caverns and a scarce amount of light ensured a most imposing environment.

Signposts hinted at our location, taking inspiration from the street names above - occasionally peppering the tunnel walls above heavy iron doors that led into areas most secretive and important - Hargraves' most essential projects.

We emerged inside the main chamber, underneath Eccleston square. It was silent. The scientists, doctors and workmen who made up a hive of activity were either inside their individual workshops, or yet to begin their shift.

Brereton hushed me, regardless, as I inserted the ornate key into the holding chamber's lock, and turned the screw valve that operated it.

The door clicked once, then again, and slowly, that enormous iron door creaked open - releasing a familiar scarlet glow, and the breathing of the book's preservation apparatus.

The ornate glass chamber that held the tattered tome wheezed and huffed that gentle clay scattering, with a slow, laboured breath that felt similar to Hargraves' own.

We glanced at each other and approached the puffing, queer structure.

We couldn't help but take notice of the pages the book was opened upon - spanning a collection of drawings and blueprints for firearms and weaponry. The occasional diagram was labelled with 'complete' or 'failed' in Hargrave's ornate penmanship.

Brereton slipped off the case, and I took hold of the sacred tome - preparing for a great weight. To my surprise, it was light and fragile, despite the hefty materials and gilding that made it such a sight to behold. Rather than hammered bark and leather, the great tome felt more akin to a wafer.

> 'No need to be careful with the thing, William. It'll be at the bottom of an ocean soon enough.'

'I feel like we could quite as easily destroy the thing here, Brereton. It feels far lighter than any book I've known.'
'We have our orders, William.'

I stuffed it into my satchel. Brereton replaced the case, locked up the chamber... and we made our leave, as casually as we could.

Speed was not of the essence - but leaving as light a trail as we could? That was imperative.

We locked every door, replaced every gate and locked the hidden brick doorway. We left, quite comfortably, just as the uniform factory's hooter sounded to mark the beginning of the work day. I expect that our so called get-away spanned a greater time than our secretive entrance, such was our approach to not being caught.

The little boat tweeted in a shrill celebration, as we made our way to the Nore - the sandbank at the Thames estuary - with the intent of meeting the Great Eastern before she departed.

She glided on her merry way, her little steam engine puffing quite happily along as Brereton fed her with coal.

It all felt remarkably simple.

Brereton was unsurprised. While the paranoia of Hargraves was legendary, his faith in the society's system was unshakable. The authoritarianism of The Society of Exceptional Engineers was a convincing blueprint for obedience.

> 'It's rather like the collapse of the Roman empire. The smallest weakness can topple a giant. A sort of David and Goliath, I dare say. The society doesn't plan for internal weakness. It is a traditional dictatorship - it believes loyalty can be instilled to people through fear, success and finance. I certainly don't think they'd bet on weak old man Brereton stealing their precious bible.'

The little boat weaved in and out of the larger steamers, cutting an impressive pace across the Thames as she made her way through the city of London – past Millwall, where the Great Eastern was constructed – and weaving between the cluttering of boats at the numerous import docks, shipyards and harbours, its tweeting little whistle feeling every bit as teasing and joyous as the toothless old man steering her, who seemed to be having the time of his life.

The journey was far faster than we had prepared for. Within seven hours – each one feeling quicker than the last – the great silhouette of the Great Eastern, thin wisps of smoke pouring from her funnels and steam from her valves, appeared on the horizon – coming ever closer. Her shape upon the horizon was unmistakable. A giant iron heel, with four imposing funnels.

The old man silenced the little boat – and she pittered obediently as she glided up alongside the enormous telegraph vessel.

Our necks craned upwards to catch sight of Daniel, who stood on the paddle-house walkway, and lowered a ladder down to us, with shouts of pleasantries that were drowned out by the smothered hissing of the Great Eastern's bowels inside her iron frame, and the gentle whispering of our own steamboat's boiler.

I felt quite ill. The steamboat, for all of her pleasantries, had done little for my constitution – and the idea of climbing up the side of the world's largest ship on a teetering rope ladder was far from a happy one to me.

'Is there no better way to board her?'
Brereton chuckled and slapped my back. 'We were sailor enough to get here; we have to be sailor enough to board the ship.'
'I'd be fine if it was a ten foot sailboat, but this–'
'The world's largest steamship. You built her, you should climb her. Enough of the dockyard staff had to.'

I sighed, relented, and took grasp of the first wooden rung. We began a slow, nervous ascent to the Great Babe's walkways, where our allies awaited us.

The sea spray was more than a little distracting, and I felt very liable to fall. In one slip, our entire adventure could be over – the entire plan destroyed, along with my life, career and voice.

I grunted as I hauled myself up, desperately holding on through the bitter spray sand cold wind of the ocean's currents from the North Sea beyond. The great ship's gentle motion now felt more like a colossal, terrifying swing to my eyes. A single inch now felt like a foot.

Finally, I reached the railing, and clumsily scrambled aboard, backing against the vessel's iron platework – as far from the gilded railings as I could reach.

Daniel found it very amusing.

> 'You made it, I see.'
> 'If I ever see another rope ladder in my life, it will be too soon.'

The locomotive builder laughed heartily as Brereton joined us, waving to the sailor as the little steamboat tweeted a final good luck greeting, and puffed away back to London.

> 'So, Brereton, how much did the sailor's fees amount to?'
> 'I just gave him the boat.' Brereton smiled. 'He's going to become a charter steam captain as opposed to a fisherman. We may as well improve other's lives too, eh?'

We all waved farewell to the old, grizzled sailor, and entered the vessel's main chambers to inspect the final preparation work –not to mention, of course, the ship's kitchen.

> 'Hargraves will be boarding tomorrow. We've got a feast planned

for him, plenty of alcohol... I expect that within just over a week we'll have him where we want him.'

The other investors were due to visit too, with John Pender, Thomas Brassey and Daniel Gooch hosting them with pride, discussing the doubtless impeccable progress the ship would make on her mission. The Great Eastern was once again raising the interest of the industrial elite.

The next morning, we woke to the ship's almighty fireboxes being stoked and woken. The Great Babe's enormous boilers were ready; she had steam in her stride, ready and waiting.

The men worked hard to feed her monstrous appetite, and the steam pressure rose quickly. Before we had even to leave, the eager Great Eastern's valves lifted to vent off excess steam.

There were tourists and sightseers on the coast, admiring the leviathan as she hissed in anticipation.

Hargraves boarded at 10AM that morning, and was given a tour of the vessel. He lumbered along the ship's decks, sneering and growling with every piece of equipment, every chamber and every room ahead of him. He seemed quite intent on making a nuisance of himself - and, despite Brereton and I being hidden from view - did so loudly enough for all, including ourselves, to hear.

At noon, after taking on supplies and undergoing an inspection - the Great Eastern hooted loudly and began to steam way from the Nore, making its headway towards Ireland, where the first cable's end was already being laid.

We had little idea of what awaited us as the world's largest ship - and first dedicated cable layer - left the Thames estuary behind.

+ CABLE LAYER +

Gooch was firm in his instructions. Brereton and I stayed out of Hargraves' sight, and the sight of the senior staff, including an American team headed by Cyrus Field. While hidden, we were assisting in the engineering challenges synonymous with such a monumental task.

Staying hidden from our adversary was not difficult - such was the size of the vessel - but with a trip expected to span well over a fortnight, my own sickness and the inevitable boredom, it's of little wonder that waiting in Valentia Harbour was tedious.

We were continuously waiting for any form of excitement - and at Berehaven, on July the 23rd, we finally saw action, as the laid cable from Ireland was grappled aboard.

Caroline, the shore end cable layer, was a rather fanciful little steamship with a low profile and single funnel, that looked positively antiquated compared to the Great Eastern's enormous bulk.

She whistled up to the Great Babe's decks, and the grapple was dropped to her – hooking the thick, dark, serpentine cable from her and hauled it aboard the decks – like a group of eel fishermen collecting a prize catch.

The shore end cable was fused to the Great Eastern's own with hot irons, until a solid connection was created – and the ship hooted; as if to tell *Caroline* she could return home and leave the rest to us.

At 4:30PM, the spliced cable was dropped – and the Great Eastern set off on her way, slowly stringing the telegraph behind her. She had departed right on schedule, and Gooch stood on the rear of her deck with a pocket watch in hand, his chest puffed up with pride.

The great transatlantic project had officially begun.

The concept was simple enough – Brunel's giant ship would move across the Atlantic slowly, with her two smaller partner vessels alongside, laying the cable across the ocean floor as she sailed on her way to the Americas. In the process, she would send test signals to ensure the cable's integrity. Her size and stability made her as close to perfect for the job as any other vessel on Earth.

It's rather humorous, in hindsight, to think that the height of this pioneering telegraph technology was as simple as stringing along a giant length of metal wire across the ocean floor. But the unique environmental hazards and the sensitivity of the operation is where the complications lay.

The complications were entirely in scale – and, as Gooch often reminded us, a single cable was a sensitive thing to string along for so many miles. Compared to the God-given forces surrounding this serpentine iron wire, it was as durable as a silk spider's thread in gale force winds.

Gooch spent most of his time in the telegraph cabin that lay in one of the ship's saloons – tapping out signals through the cable with every foot laid, to ensure there was no fault at hand; with an eye on a queer device he called a Galvanometer. I figured it was much out of his depth as it was ours, but he was a rapid learner and spoke as if he was an expert within only a few hours.

The result was an almost constant ticking as the ship crawled along, the cable slipping out of her like a thread through the eye of a needle.

Brereton and I explored the bowels of the great vessel, my satchel never leaving my sight, examining the ship's operation and evaluating her performance. It's likely unsurprising for most if I were to say she performed admirably, and Gooch would give consistent compliments as to her capabilities for the project.

Hargraves, unsurprisingly, saw nothing as better than his original ideas for the Great Eastern. He would make regular jabs at the potential for failure, and would constantly pick fault.

As our voyage went on, he gathered plenty of ammunition, too.

On July the 24th, as the weather on the horizon seemed to grow ever more sinister, the ship was forced to a halt. The Galvanometer's light disappeared and the warning bell was rung – a sure fire sign that all was not well.

It was 3:15AM.

Hargraves stood in the telegraph room with his typically vulgar tongue wagging. I'm sorry to say the sight of Hargraves in bedclothes is an image that may never escape my memory.

> 'Your 'perfect cable' is a bollock-up, Daniel. I've never known such a farcical operation.'

'It is standard for there to be faults.' Spat Gooch in return.
'The fault here is you buying my company's ship for such a bloody faulty enterprise!'
'Now you listen here-'

Mister Field was not so acclimated to the savage arguments so typical in British industry, and tried to break them up in a typically pacifist manner. He dove between the two before fisticuffs began.

'Gentlemen, please! We'll turn around, find the cable and repair it. Mister Hargraves, please allow Gooch to go up deck and start up the donkey engines.'
'The only donkeys here are you lot of unfettered idiots trying to lay a bloody piece of string with my ship! If it was my choice every jackass aboard would be in the knacker's yard!'
'Mister Hargraves, you are invited aboard this ship as a guest! Please, allow us to do our jobs!'

Hargraves lumbered away, grumbling about 'damned yanks' and 'stupid projects'.

Three hours were allowed before the retrieval operation began - necessary, of course, for extra natural light. As the ship was spun into reverse upon daybreak, we gathered at the little donkey engines connected to the winches and gears of the ship's grappling equipment.

The engine warmed, and began to operate with a juddering, high pitched chug - before immediately silencing.

Thudda thudda thudda thudda - clunk.

Gooch looked at Brereton. Brereton looked at me. I looked at the stokers. A single cloud of thick, black clag erupted from the donkey engine's funnel, with barely a move of the flywheel that was meant to uproot the telegraph.

'It's knackered.' One of the stokers replied.
Gooch's hands clenched into fists and his voice raised. 'It's what? How? Did nobody inspect these boilers before we left?'
'They worked then. Might be the sea air.'
'Sea air?! *Sea air?!* Don't try and tell *me* about steam engines in sea air, I built enough of them to know when a boiler should and shouldn't-'

I recommended we make use of the ship's own boilers, which the desperately impatient Gooch agreed to. He already seemed close to tearing out his hair. Hargraves had riled him more than enough to do so.

It was decided upon, and with the ship's own supply of steam, the donkey engines began slipping up the cable, with every inch hand inspected, while the ship retraced its trail at a snail's pace.

Nautical mile after nautical mile followed – until, ten miles along, at 9AM on the next day, a single fault was seen. A single piece of armouring wire, no more than a few centimetres, was piercing the insulation.

Hargraves was on hand to see the damage and found it most amusing.

'Good God. I've seen mere trifles, but this?'
'It's the nature of a sensitive cable project, Mister Hargraves.'
'Shut up, Cyrus. I know more about sensitive technology than you give me credit for. The fact you've spent an entire day looking for this? *This!?* I could use that wire as a toothpick!'
'I don't like your tone, sir.'
'My tone isn't all you get if you try arguing with me. Fix it. I want to be in America *before* the 1900s!'

Cyrus rolled his eyes as Hargraves lumbered away. The gentlemen began grafting a repair into the cable's sensitive wiring, talking about how much of an annoyance the society's head really was.

Brereton and I stayed out of sight, listening in. It had taken a not insubstantial amount of effort to resist taking stakes against him.

The ship began moving again - then, half a mile later, the bell rang. The weather beyond was looking even worse, and the waters growing choppy - but the warning bell was our greatest fear.

Gooch laid his face in his hands as the blank Galvanometer sat ahead of him, and the ship once again restarted its procedure, taking the painstaking operation to reverse and collect up its payload.

Only half an hour later, the light returned. The cable was tested - and proved to be in fine working order. The ship had barely even managed to turn her engines into reverse at this point, and a further delay had to be permitted for the ship to correct herself.

The exhausted crew reversed the picking procedure and turned back towards America; bitter, impatient and desperately hoping this would be the end of the difficult 37 hours now passed.

Gooch confided in us that, thus far, through no fault of the ship, he felt like the voyage was an impossibly frustrating one. He had not slept throughout the entire interference.

Cyrus remained confident, in a typically blaze manner. He was a man who seemed insistent on patting our backs, brushing his shoulder and moving on past the hurdle - a vast difference to our typically defeatist natures.

The weather worsened, and the great ship began to slow as the ship rocked and swayed in a hardening ocean, but the crew insisted on persevering. There could be no further delay - and every man from the stokers to the investors agreed that it would do us no good to await better weather. Should any vessel be capable of taking these conditions, it was the Great Eastern.

One of our side ships, *Sphinx*, was not so dedicated – and flagged behind, until soon she had disappeared from sight, a thick fog, the spray of rain and the darkening night clouding her from view.

We tried to communicate with lights, but to no avail.

The decision was made to hold and wait for her to reappear.

She had been the vessel with sounding gear, used to investigate the ocean floor for any unforeseen obstructions and approximate depths of each mile of the vast unknown beneath us – a most essential piece of kit for any voyage such as ours. It was practically impossible to think of going blind. We all hoped she had simply slowed and would eventually catch up.

We waited. And waited – but *Sphinx* remained invisible to the eye. The helmsman flashed his torch, and talk began of sending the other spotter vessel out to seek her – but, as a sudden gust of wind hit, these thoughts were soon put to close. We couldn't risk such a thing, should that vessel disappear too.

Hargraves sneered when he overheard – in his usual way.

> 'You've fucked this up, haven't you?'
> 'We've done nothing of the sort. We have ocean charts, we have maps and we have route knowledge.' Cyrus replied.
> 'You have no eyes. You're as good as useless. You try to go on and you'll break your cable on every trench and rock underneath you.'

Pender and Brassey exchanged worried glances. Hargraves had a point, not only from the sharp tongue he so loved to make use of.

We gathered to make a decision – trying to work out the next steps of our enterprise – in the board room the next day. Hargraves, naturally, was not invited.

Every gentleman in the room had an opinion.

It was exceptionally unwise to lay the cable 'blind', the more conservative argument constantly reaffirmed – but markedly more so, many of us retorted, to return after so many days into our expedition, which was already behind schedule.

Cyrus Field was committal – the cable continues, sound or no sound. Gooch, as reluctant as he was, agreed. The Great Eastern hooted, and once again jolted herself forwards as those mighty paddles began to spin.

The weather continued to act against us, but our crew powered on – the ship standing like a great iron windbreaker against the furious ocean currents as she slowly ran her course.

The next two days were uneventful – and, for the moment, we felt like the calamity was over. We even considered if, with hardship, our best practises had been established. While we had lost much of our precision with *Sphinx*'s departure, we had lost none of our attitude.

Mile after mile laid – fatigued frowns became broad smiles.
We were winning, albeit not for long.

On the following Saturday, the dreaded bell sounded once again, echoed by a howl of anguish from every team aboard the gigantic ship. A dense fog had set in, and the Great Babe, chugging at just under five knots, ground to a halt. She had to open her valves to release her boiler's frustration as the waves rocked her.

The signal on the Galvanometer had disappeared, once again, and the painstaking, frustrating process of grappling began for the third time.

The fog was so severe that we could quite happily walk along the decks without risking Hargraves seeing us, and we were lucky enough - if one could count hard work as 'lucky' - to assist the men in scouring the ocean bed for the faulty cable.

We felt more than happy in rolling up our sleeves and doing our bit, and took gusto in trying to find the issue.

It took hours. Mile after mile of cable was uprooted from its roost, before the dust had time to settle around it. Our initial enthusiasm soon gave way to impatience, until finally, by lamplight, at ten to midnight, a shout echoed from the inspector. We had trouble working out where to actually turn; the fog was now so thick that our own hands were capable of disappearing before us.

'I've found it! The armouring's gone again!'

We rolled our eyes. Gooch could be heard cursing.

Under the cover of fog, Brereton and I assisted in the splicing to remove the faulty cable.

Cyrus stood there, in a leather raincoat, overseeing the splice work.

'Let's start laying again, gentlemen.'
'Not a chance, Cyrus.' Gooch stepped into the lamplight. 'It'd be foolish in this weather. We should anchor up and regroup.'
'It's only a bit of fog!'
'It's a bit of fog with only one vessel to tell us our location, and rain getting into our machinery. We'll restart in the morning.'
'That Hargraves will be having plenty of laughs at our expense, Daniel.'
'Perhaps. But I refuse to allow our crews to work in these conditions when we barely have sight of the ocean we're paying out into.'
'Hear hear!' Pender shouted. I looked around to try and get a vague idea of his location, to limited avail. 'Everybody back to their cabins. Carefully now; we can't have anybody walking off of the

decks!'

He was joking – but I have never felt so insecure in my position. It was a good twenty minutes until I felt I had my bearings. I really was not a sailor – and longed for my tunnels rather than this foggy, aquatic landscape.

It wasn't until 10AM on a Sunday, after many of the gentlemen had finished their prayers, that the laying recommenced – but the pace was so poor in the face of the terrible weather that the entire evaluation team in the telegraph room made the decision to strike the day's work off of the record.

By now, many of us were feeling restless, anxious and constantly instilled with dread. The Great Eastern was doing her job admirably – but the cable's quality and staff integrity was being called into question.

Some considered sabotage – to which our suspicions fell entirely on Hargraves – while some considered that the cable would go quite the same way as Mr. Field's previous attempt – an unsuitable piece of equipment which could not bear the elements.

The cable was unequivocally fragile; the armouring that seemed to be the thorn in our sides had given out more trouble than any of us could expect. But the faith in the men aboard with us had started to falter, too.

Extra foremen were provided for each cable tank to inspect the cable and prevent any sabotage. Staff were now all hands on deck; a new sense of determination prevailed.

The laying methods were improved – and, for the next day, we achieved an average of seven knots. This continued for the next, with Tuesday almost setting a new record.

We were resolute. We were even rather desperate for success. Gooch,

Brereton and I all kept eager, hopeful eyes upon the cable as she slowly fed into the lapping waves.

However – the eternal tome remained over my shoulder, inside my leather satchel. And with Hargraves proving more and more of an irritation, my peers were making it very obvious that we were overdue 'the drop'. The idea had almost slipped my mind completely.

It was time to consider the reason we were really aboard the decks in the middle of the Atlantic. The book's time was nigh – as was that of our adversary.

+ CONFRONTATION +

I spent the Wednesday morning inspecting the Great Eastern's steam chests, ensuring that they were suitably tightened and the engines themselves properly lubricated.

The walkway underneath me creaked.

'I suppose you thought I wouldn't notice you on board my ship, Jacomb.'

Hargraves snarled as he stepped up behind me. It was somewhat surprising to see the foul creature awake so early.

'I wasn't under the impression this was your ship anymore, Hargraves. As a matter of fact, I don't believe you own a single share in her. We know all about your plans.'
'Oh, I did work that out, William. That's why I had to see to it that your little reporter friend didn't make it through to report about it...'

I bristled, and stood upright, my back still to the odious man as he spoke.

> 'Have I angered you, office boy? Please. What will you do? Throw your pencils at me?'
> 'I would advise you to shut up while you're ahead, Hargraves.'

His brow furrowed, and he stepped closer, his hand taking grasp of my cravat. His breath felt like a flame on my face.

> 'I would advise you to get out of my way, before I force you out of it. This ship was mine. I dedicated myself entirely to ensure it would fall into my hands. The world could have belonged to our empire.'

He spat on my face and shoved me back against the walkway's barrier.

> 'Believe me, office boy. If we don't get our ship back, the world won't have you back.'
> 'You speak as big as your measurements, sir, but we have far more than your ship in our possession!'

Brereton and Gooch grabbed Hargraves' arms in an attempt to restrain him – rather like one would a man insane or a wild animal.

I wiped my cheek of his foul smelling phlegm and pulled out the Eternal Tome.
His face dropped, and, for a moment, his head tried to calculate the situation. The penny soon dropped.

> 'You- you- Brereton, I know this is your doing! I'll take more than your remaining bloody eyeball! You insidious, over washed little cretin!'

He threw Gooch and Brereton off of him. For the first time in his life, it seemed, Hargraves attempted to reason with me, his efforts to contain his temper and his genuine, mortal fear for his sacred tome did not go unnoticed.

> 'Jacomb, you do not understand! You need to keep that book covered. It's fragile. Please, put it back in your satchel and we can discuss the matter-'
> 'We're done with deals and contracts, Hargraves. This isn't an industrial theft. This is the end of your career. This is the end of this ancient book and the end of the society.'

Hargraves hesitated, then roared - and lunged at me. It was a slow, clumsy movement, giving me ample time to replace the book into my satchel, and, without a second thought, began my escape from the ship's innards, with Brereton and Gooch doing the same.

I would hesitate to call what ensued a 'chase' - but with us trapped aboard one ship, no matter her size, there was not great opportune for escape the increasingly frenzied Hargraves.

By the time he had cornered us on the paddle housing, he was even more filthy, short of breath and untidy than usual, his hair streaked in lines of sweat and grease that dripped down his face.

He snarled, panting, with little care - not that it was a surprise to us - for his unkempt, shabby appearance.

Gooch and Brereton stood with me, every bit as stubborn and steadfast as I myself.

> 'It's finished, Hargraves.' Gooch shouted, over the noise of the paddles clattering alongside us. 'You've lost. We've pulled the cloth out from under you.'
> 'I shan't rest until the lot of you are dead. I shan't rest until the name of Brunel is as forgotten as that of Robert bloody Brereton!'
> Brereton stepped forward. 'My achievement will be in seeing you fail. My legacy will be my knowledge of doing what we could to

stop you. My life will end happily knowing that you are unable to rule us.'

'Without that book, none of you will have careers. None of you will have a future. There shall be nothing! Don't you understand? You shall be damaged by the loss of the society more than anyone on earth. There shall be no grants, there shall be none of my money in your pockets!'

'Then;' I countered, 'I shall take pride in working from the backs of my own abilities.'

'Abilities? Abilities? You're an office boy! You'll always be an office boy!'

'...With more of a future than your knobstick society.'

His eyes widened as I reached into my satchel, and brought the society's precious bible into the open sea air.

The sea spray, the wind of the harsh ocean between us, and the drizzling rain was about as close to the opposite of the book's home environment of dry clay, airtight glass and velvet as one could get.

The effect was almost instantaneous. Hargraves shouted and screamed in protest, but the elements were too much for that fragile, sacred tome. No amount of information held within its pages could protect it.

Pages began to flake and slip free, the binding came loose – that wafer light book that once seemed so stately, grand, all-encompassing and powerful was pulled apart, piece by piece, as the elements pushed against them.

The dried, mummified remains of over an entire humanity's worth of history were desiccated into the ocean in only a few moments.

Before long, I held onto a bare leather cover.

The world had put rest to the greatest tool – and the greatest weapon

- the British Empire had ever held. I unceremoniously dropped the remaining cover in front of Hargraves, who fell to his knees. His face was chalk, his hands shaking. We could almost make out the mumblings of 'no...no...no...' from his jowls as he panted and hyperventilated.

Our adversary, for all of his assets, businesses and interests, broke down as frightfully as the book he worshipped. His last semblance of power, scattered across the turbulent Atlantic. One of the world's most powerful businessmen, a giant of industry - a silent, shadowy king of the deck.

His ace had gone. And could no longer be recovered. The society - all he had worked for, and, more to the point, all he had killed for - it had been destroyed in nothing more than a gust of wind.

I remembered how much he revered it. How much he adored it. I remembered his quiet, respectful tones when walking around its casing.

Hargraves had lost everything he lived for.

I am unable to realistically ascertain, dear reader, what happened next, or went through Hargraves' mind.

Brereton suggested that he had come to the realisation of all he had sacrificed, having seen through the end of his own family, his peers and partners - thousands upon thousands of pounds, lost to the high winds in only a few moments. That with the loss of the book, he had lost the last scraps of that which added value to his life.

Gooch believed that it was a final act of piggish selfishness - a way of proving his unrepentant nature and going unpunished for his crimes. A refusal to have those whom he saw as beneath him take charge.

In any sense, Hargraves stood, and spat onto my face with his putrid, rotten phlegm.

'I'll see you in hell, Jacomb.'

Without another word, or eye contact, the beast threw himself off of the paddle housing, plummeting towards the lapping waves and the pounding wake of the Great Eastern. He impacted with the ship's paddle wheel, which unceremoniously continued in its travels. His back and his skull both shattered against it, with a sickening crunch and a splash of red spray - a sight I fear shall never leave me.

Brereton felt incredibly ill and had to shield himself from our view before he vomited; while Hargraves' enormous, motionless body sunk into the dark, grey waters threw up around the ship he intended to commandeer.
We fell silent.

'Gentlemen; we must keep quiet regarding this.' Gooch mumbled.

We nodded. Awestruck - and with a deep seated feeling of nausea across all our stomachs. The short silence felt like an hour. We were, for the first time in our caper, completely clueless. Dumbfounded.

'Oi! There goes a piece of wire!' came a shout from the tank alongside us.

We snapped back to reality as another of the Transatlantic Cable's calamities began. The foreman tried to halt it, but a faulty cable slipped free of the paying out equipment and into the ocean. The ship ground to a halt as fast as she could.

'Sweet Mary.' Gooch mumbled, his eyes fixed to the water. We could soon see why.

A large, rounded bulk seemed to tangle into the cable, muddied in view from the waves and sea foam beneath us. A red trail swirled behind the gigantic shape as it slowly fell beneath the waves.

There was a jolt – and the cable snapped from its cradle, falling into the ocean.
Hargraves, in death, had succeeded in sabotaging us. His body tangled up amongst the cable's bulk, and began pulling it downwards as he sank like a stone. Our hearts did quite the same - the weight was enough to break the cable like a piece of twine. If he was only alive, I would say he had gotten the last laugh.

The cable broke free, and fell into the current below - disrupted by the ship's propeller.

The crew were unaware of what taken place at the ship's wheelhouse, and completely oblivious to the enormous, pig headed man now on his way to his final resting place. They only focused on trying to fish out and splice the fractured telegraph cable. It was one thing to hunt for faults when the cable was still attached to the ship, but a broken cable was practically impossible.

   'it'll be waggling around like an eel down there." Gooch sighed.
   "fitting, really.'

We were speechless. I wiped the fetid smelling phlegm from my face and stared out at the paddle slat that was now washed clean by the waves below.

There was now little evidence Hargraves was even aboard the vessel, save his slovenly, unkempt cabin below deck.

We returned to the decks to a great period of disarray and frustration.

   Cyrus was riled. 'I cannot take any further delays.'
   'You shan't get any further delays.' Gooch replied.
   'You'll have to cancel and return to Valentia. There's not a chance of finding that cable length down there. It must be 2,500 fathoms.'

Moriarty, the navigator, was equally concerned. 'I fear we shall not have much interest in knowing how far we are from Cape Race. We're over one thousand miles out. We'd only need another seven hundred to reach our destination.'

Cyrus looked back to Captain Canning. The plucky American was desperate. I have never seen a man so terrified of failure - and utterly unaware of the terror that had taken place under his nose.

Captain Canning looked at Daniel, then Moriarty... then sighed and ordered the men to set about hunting the cable down.

The men hastily put together a wire rope, fastening and lengthening it with iron shackles so it may reach the sea bed, then grafting up an iron grapnel to the end. It was a rather rag and bone operation, and would have made most investors horrified. But this was the open sea - we had no time to be picky.

The ship sailed a few miles further, and was set to drift, with the grapnel fixed onto the picking up equipment and donkey engines.

The men threw the grapnel overboard, and waited. And waited. And waited! It took over an hour - and two thousand fathoms - until it reached the bottom of the ocean. The ship was set to drift, and we had no other choice but to wait and see what happened.

Pender was the first to notice the odd behaviour carried by myself, Brereton and Gooch.

> 'You chaps look like you've seen a ghost. Are you well?'
> 'We're fine, Sir. It has been quite a turbulent operation.'
> 'Mm. I expect we'll be sailing home soon enough. My optimism can only stretch so far. I do empathise with Cyrus, mind. Especially with that awful Hargraves fellow. I expected him to come out for his usual rant.'
> 'We haven't seen him.' Gooch put in before we could respond.

Pender chuckled. 'Maybe he got sick of the delays and charted a boat!'
'Ah, well - you joke, sir,' Brereton stuttered. 'But he could well have been our saboteur, and made a quick getaway.'

Pender's brow raised. But did fit his own thoughts of the foul man who had raised so much temper in the preceding days. He agreed with us wholeheartedly.

Several attempts and ten days passed until Cyrus Field and the other telegraph company gentlemen admitted defeat. The time had been sufficient for the rumour to pass - Hargraves was the saboteur, and, following his villainous act of sabotage, had left the ship in the dead of night. How else could he have escaped the Great Eastern? Perhaps he was planning a rival cable. Perhaps he was a spy.

The ship gave a mournful hoot of submission, and the deflated crew and gentlemen made their way back to Crookhaven, with only 1,100 miles of loose, broken cable to call for their troubles - which had now amounted to over a month.

However - the Eternal Tome had been destroyed, as had its owner. Gooch, Brereton and I maintained silence on the matter - still unsure of how we felt about our final encounter. Not a soul could know.

Hargraves would go on to be publicly disgraced - and nobody seemed to consider the fact he had not returned to London. Many presumed he was lost at sea.

The reality? That would remain with us for a life time. There was no pride to be had in seeing the death of a man, no matter how odious. But life in London would surely never be the same again.

+ COMPLETION +

Our story, in truth, ended upon the death of Hargraves and the loss of the Eternal tome. Both were never recovered, in any form, from the Atlantic, and the society would slowly fracture much as the tome's binding had.

The memories we had gathered from the telegraph voyage would never leave us. The image of Hargraves spattering to the winds from the Great Eastern's paddle wheel still seems to appear before my eyes whenever I close them.

The knowledge of what we have seen, and what we have done.

The continued horror and confusion that the society placed upon us will never quite be satiated or calmed.

My return to the United Kingdom would see the end of the Men of Iron, although our small group remained close friends. I would soon find myself working as a Junior Partner to my cousin, Mr. Jacomb-Hood, at the Brighton Railway company.

It was a far quieter, more peaceful life – and my role in the destruction of the society behind so much of our culture was heavily celebrated by the men whom knew me.

In 1871, the South Western Railway invited me to become their resident engineer, a position I now hold with great pride, to this day.

However, regardless of comfort, and our incredible achievements against a conspiracy that could well have toppled the world, it would be wrong of me to proclaim it a frictionless transition. And I would still see those mysterious, round headed figures at every walk of life; and develop a great unease for the world around me. Eliza often told me it was nary more than rampant paranoia.

Let it be remembered, dear reader - the society had many members, many engineers and many scientists – not to mention, of course, the great financial investment placed within.

Many companies that relied upon Hargraves for financing met great disarray upon the realisation that he would not return. Many believed he had embezzled money and disappeared, and what little positive reputation he had as a financier was soon destroyed.

He is all but erased from history – but the men whom worked with him, planned with him and developed the Eternal tome's concepts would have no lack in ire or anger.

For many years since, I have often seen those mysterious dealers, or recognised members of the elders from the society's boardroom. I have received death threats, and many have argued that the tome is still in my possession - used to garner great progress for my employers.

I still see those queer, round headed men, scowling at me on trains and in the road. Though I believed them to be now without an employer, I do so wonder if – in fact – they simply now lack a purpose, one they desperately wish to recapture. Perhaps they hold a vain hope that the criminal activity of Hargraves may begin once again, and has simply hidden from prying eyes.

Eccleston square, Pimlico and Cubitt's vision is completed, but the catacombs are now empty and silent; bricked up and erased in the same way as much of the history I now record in these pages. The chambers, rooms and labyrinthine areas that characterised the society's infrastructure are now more often mistaken for sewers in the grand water systems that have cleaned up so much of the country's capital.

Industrial progress for our empire continues, but now does so independently, reliant on great minds once more to see our society and the globe improve at an organic, realistic pace. The natural order – so much as this can be used, at least, for heavy industry – has largely been restored.

No longer is there an arsenal in planning, or a grand invasion forecast for our rivals in the world market. There is now only the hope that our technology and progress may help maintain world relations.

The Great Eastern, now celebrated as a cable ship, had a long, illustrious career and helped to bring the world closer together – something Brunel had shared a vision within, despite the change in tact for the world's largest ship.

However, progress continued for cable laying, and, as techniques and technology improved, the great ship soon became out dated – and reached the end of her career.

In 1874, after completion of another Atlantic cable, she was left at Milford Haven, eagerly awaiting her next duty. Sadly, now faster, more agile ships could do the job better than her – and a new job never came.

In 1880, Daniel Gooch - or, should I say, *Sir* Daniel Gooch, retired from the Great Eastern Steamship Company - and parted with the ship he had spent much of his career protecting. It was a difficult decision, one which we discussed for many months - but we both felt she had, at least, proven herself under his stewardship, and she would be secure until the end of our own days.

Henry Brassey, the son of Gooch's co-investor and close friend, took over the steamship company - but was left with a worn out, oversized ship that no longer had the demand to continue working at telegraphs.

She was sold in 1881 - but we had no real business prospectus for taking her back under purchase. There could be an entire book populated with the tales of attempting to sell her - but the ship was soon laid up on exhibition in Liverpool, a floating advertisement hoarding for the Lewis department store.

Her cable tanks were now music halls, her Grand Saloon a rough and difficult bar, and the ladies' saloon a dining room. Her decks are a market and fairground, with some 500,000 people visiting her to marvel at the world's largest ship - and raising the highest profit of the vessel's lifetime.

A dignified end, it was not - but I sought solace in the love she received from much of the public.

Her future is now uncertain, following a poor attempt to replicate this practise in Dublin, and I fear that despite my many attempts to secure her, she is now all but doomed.

I have taken many times to rally in the press, and many have gotten behind me - perhaps, through a miracle, The Great Babe will continue living beyond me.

There are, however, many questions, in my mind, that continue rattling around my head. Questions that I fear may never be answered. Are we to ever discover the truth behind the eternal tome, and the world that has created it? Of what origin could mankind's accomplishments be catalogued?

I am sorry to say that, despite my efforts, I have no answers.

Any answers that may have existed were destroyed with the book to the winds of the Atlantic. There is no solution to the puzzle – there are no conclusions. I know only that there are greater forces at work. What these greater forces could be, I am afraid, goes beyond my understanding of this world and its laws of logic.

Many still accuse me of keeping the tome; that it may be somewhere upon my person, or within my desk.

This could not be further from the truth – in fact, I only wish I could claim to have profited from the great conspiracy caper that occupied nearly ten years following Brunel's death.

I have, in fact, nothing to show for the book's existence. I have nothing within my grasp or evidence to prove, in fact, that any of this is truth. I only require and beg for your trust.

The society, I fear, is still in existence – merely lurking in another location, underground, with the hopes of reassembling its power; with or without the vile musings of Hargraves and his mysterious volume. It is these people, I fear, that are most likely to begrudge us, and work to threaten that which we have toiled for. I have no proof of their existence, likewise to that of the Eternal Tome. My paranoia has so often proven accurate – and my more morbid persuasion wonders if, perhaps, there is more value in a martyr for raising awareness of injustice.

I would advise any men without our field to be wary; maintain an eye behind your shoulder, and, should men in bowler hats with pencil moustaches approach you, politely refuse and go back on your way.

There can come no good of monopolising, restricting or controlling the flow of creativity and intelligence that has led to such progress for our kind. There can come no good of fascism or forced authority. We must allow ourselves to organically learn, and construct based upon necessity and requirement.

I have grown to heavily fear the large companies and clubs that try to control so much. I believe with sincerity, that corruption comes with facelessness.

Hargraves was, in my mind, the face of corruption. And I do not believe his kind is anywhere near extinct.

Robert Brereton continues enthusiastically building railways, solemn in the belief that his own legacy is surely secured. I have no doubt that he will be as well remembered as Daniel Gooch. The two gentlemen are some of the finest I feel I shall ever regard - and friends for life, as was - and is the name Samuel Lucas - a man who will remain a most positive influence upon me for the years to come.

Together, we have witnessed great change in all of our endeavours, and illustrious careers - but none of us shall forget our great caper and our work to topple such a malevolent force that risked the sanctity of our trades.

The world is constantly growing and changing, now, of its own accord - and we feel comfortable that this is the correct pace and influence of life.

We shall never forget the work, ethics or pride of Stephenson and Brunel, and their own efforts upon death to see the end of Hargraves' torturous impact upon society.

We are always indebted. And we are secure that we will not be forgotten for the work we have done.

As I sit here, at my desk, I am constantly astounded by my memories of the events captured upon paper here. The air is cool, a soft May breeze agitating the atmosphere into one of peace and tranquillity.

The sound of shunting trains – the wisping of steam. It feels peaceful; it feels correct. It feels, in fact, that I have changed the world – and that much of the peace and happiness the engineering trade has experienced since is of my own hand.

It is perhaps unsurprising to many; but I speak with sincerity when I say that I have never felt so happy or content.

This has been a story spanning far further than my own career, or that of Brunel's. This is a story of our kind's desperation for foreknowledge – the want to achieve best practise at first try – to remove the essential aspect of creation; the most natural process of humanity – one of failure, and humility.

Even a man so vile as Hargraves cannot, in earnest, be looked down upon for capitalising on one of the most simple of man's desires; despite his evil, he offered many a solution. And it would be wrong to fault those who fell for his plans. And what of his brother? Are we not all guilty of hideous things through jealousy and insecurity?

Justice was done. And while I sit here, in my twilight years, I feel comfortable for my role within. I only hope the future will continue to be one of fairness – and that any of those murky undercurrents of the society fail in their hope of re-emerging or realisation.

Of course, there lies a more sinister aspect to the tale in that I have just imparted to you. Where did the Eternal Tome, in truth, come from? From what origins did the sum of human knowledge approach us?

This is something I and my fellows have often wondered. And it remains a fearful thing to consider. Could there have been another iteration of humanity before us? An otherworldly presence in our civilisation's past, present and future?

The book may have been destroyed - but the questions remain very much in situ, and very much relevant. I begin to wonder if our world is different to that which we understand.

I begin to wonder if more of these books exist; if more Eternal tomes remain in place across the world. I fear that, through some means, the monopolisation of technology and the great minds of our world will continue. That, through some circumstance, a great power will continue puppeteering us into wars and conflicts.

The time of the society may be over; but the reign of fear, silence, and paranoia may well continue. If my hunch is correct - and I solemnly believe it is - we may be yet to see many iterations of this story repeat themselves. I fear that this tale shall not become one so unusual and esoteric. I fear that, instead, my story will become the norm.

I continue seeing those round headed men, with their sneers and their bowler hats. I continue receiving increasingly sharp threats and sinister letters. I continue feeling the eyes of the world placed squarely upon my shoulders. I feel them reading from behind my back. I sense them watching from across the platform.

I understand the danger in me writing this. But I refused to be silenced any longer. I refuse to allow myself to be overcome by fear. I refuse to go without telling my tale, to you, dear reader. I hope that your future remains secure. And thank you, once again, for taking the time to educate yourself. Whether you believe my tale or otherwise.

Please; approach this strange, sinister world with caution. And should you see an enormous bulk of a figure, lumbering towards your door... you may well wish to ensure it remains locked.

Beware of those boasting forbidden knowledge.
Yours truly;
William Jacomb
Chief Engineer of the South Western Railway
Waterloo Terminus
May 25th, 1887.

This manuscript was found underneath the body of William Jacomb on May the 26th, 1887. He died suddenly at his desk at Waterloo station. The official cause of death was apoplexy.

The reader may come to their own conclusions.

THE END

This work is a work of fiction.

We say this categorically, after reading over the documents found with this manuscript, and interviewing any surviving individuals discovered. There is no evidence of a society such as that described, nor proof the existence of one 'Hargraves' within its management.

While it can be ascertained that most of the events held within this manuscript are historically accurate, and that William Jacomb, Brereton, Lucas et al being real people, we do not see evidence of William Jacomb on passenger lists for the Atlantic Telegraph Voyages, nor do we find proof of him being involved in the Tottenham train crash.

Brunel's Duke Street home is long demolished, Samuel Lucas is but a footnote in history, and William Jacomb's life is poorly documented. The existence of Brereton's accomplishments is only marked with a memorial plaque in his home church.

With this in mind, we would prefer for readers to treat the events they have read about as fictional. There was no eternal tome, a Hargraves, or a society behind his control.

Cornelius Graves;

Head of the Society of Exceptional London Historians & Individuals.

Scientia Est Imperium.
Ignorantia Est Fragilitas.
Fortitudo Est In Silentio.

THE GREAT LONDON CONSPIRACY

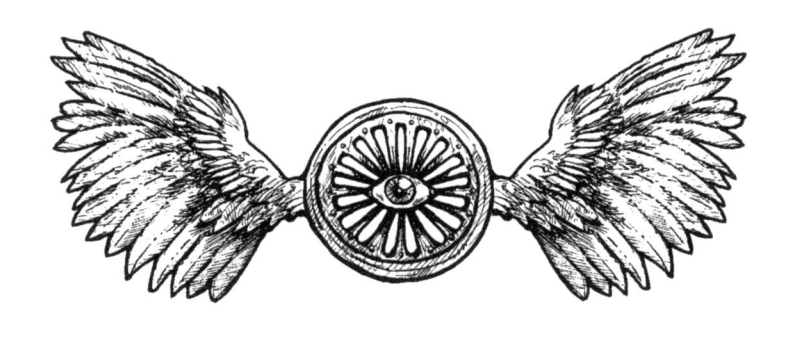

THE GREAT LONDON CONSPIRACY

SCIENTIA EST IMPERIUM.
IGNORANTIA EST FRAGILITAS.
FORTITUDO EST IN SILENTIO.

For more information on the world of the Great London Conspiracy, the people featured in the story and the events that inspired it, visit

WWW.THEGREATCONSPIRACY.CO.UK

Lightning Source UK Ltd.
Milton Keynes UK
UKHW020640291221
396330UK00011B/740

9 780464 243359